A GARLAND
FOR GIRLS

LOUISA MAY ALCOTT

1st WORLD
LIBRARY
Literary Society

A Garland for Girls

Louisa May Alcott

© 1st World Library – Literary Society, 2004
PO Box 2211
Fairfield, IA 52556
www.1stworldlibrary.org
First Edition

LCCN: 2005906527

Softcover ISBN: 1-4218-1583-4
Hardcover ISBN: 1-4218-1483-8
eBook ISBN: 1-4218-1683-0

Purchase *"A Garland for Girls"*
as a traditional bound book at:
www.1stWorldLibrary.org/purchase.asp?ISBN=1-4218-1583-4

1st World Library Literary Society is a nonprofit
organization dedicated to promoting literacy by:

- Creating a free internet library accessible from any
  computer worldwide.
- Hosting writing competitions and offering book
  publishing scholarships.

A Garland for Girls
contributed by Tim, Ed & Rodney
in support of
1st World Library Literary Society

CONTENTS

PREFACE

These stories were written for my own amusement during a period of enforced seclusion. The flowers which were my solace and pleasure suggested titles for the tales and gave an interest to the work.

If my girls find a little beauty or sunshine in these common blossoms, their old friend will not have made her Garland in vain.

L.M. ALCOTT.

SEPTEMBER, 1887.

MAY FLOWERS

Being Boston girls, of course they got up a club for mental improvement, and, as they were all descendants of the Pilgrim Fathers, they called it the Mayflower Club. A very good name, and the six young girls who were members of it made a very pretty posy when they met together, once a week, to sew, and read well-chosen books. At the first meeting of the season, after being separated all summer, there was a good deal of gossip to be attended to before the question, "What shall we read?" came up for serious discussion.

Anna Winslow, as president, began by proposing "Happy Dodd;" but a chorus of "I've read it!" made her turn to her list for another title.

"'Prisoners of Poverty' is all about workingwomen, very true and very sad; but Mamma said it might do us good to know something of the hard times other girls have," said Anna, soberly; for she was a thoughtful creature, very anxious to do her duty in all ways.

"I'd rather not know about sad things, since I can't help to make them any better," answered Ella Carver, softly patting the apple blossoms she was embroidering on a bit of blue satin.

"But we might help if we really tried, I suppose; you know how much Happy Dodd did when she once began, and she was only a poor little girl without half the means of doing good which we have," said Anna, glad to discuss the matter, for she had a little plan in her head and wanted to prepare a way for proposing it.

"Yes, I'm always saying that I have more than my share of fun and comfort and pretty things, and that I ought and will share them with some one. But I don't do it; and now and then, when I hear about real poverty, or dreadful sickness, I feel so wicked it quite upsets me. If I knew HOW to begin, I really would. But dirty little children don't come in my way, nor tipsy women to be reformed, nor nice lame girls to sing and pray with, as it all happens in books," cried Marion Warren, with such a remorseful expression on her merry round face that her mates laughed with one accord.

"I know something that I COULD do if I only had the courage to begin it. But Papa would shake his head unbelievingly, and Mamma worry about its being proper, and it would interfere with my music, and everything nice that I especially wanted to go to would be sure to come on whatever day I set for my good work, and I should get discouraged or ashamed, and not half do it, so I don't begin, but I know I ought." And Elizabeth Alden rolled her large eyes from one friend to another, as if appealing to them to goad her to this duty by counsel and encouragement of some sort.

"Well, I suppose it's right, but I do perfectly hate to go poking round among poor folks, smelling bad smells, seeing dreadful sights, hearing woful tales, and running the risk of catching fever, and diphtheria, and horrid things. I don't pretend to like charity, but say right out I'm a silly, selfish wretch, and want to enjoy every minute, and not worry about other people. Isn't it shameful?"

Maggie Bradford looked such a sweet little sinner as she boldly made this sad confession, that no one could scold her, though Ida Standish, her bosom friend, shook her head, and Anna said, with a sigh: "I'm afraid we all feel very much as Maggie does, though we don't own it so honestly. Last spring, when I was ill and thought I might die, I was so ashamed of my idle, frivolous winter, that I felt as if I'd give all I had to be able to live it over and do better. Much is not expected of a girl of eighteen, I know; but oh! there were heaps of kind little things I MIGHT have done if I hadn't thought only of myself. I resolved if I lived I'd try at least to be less selfish, and make some one happier for my being in the world. I tell you, girls, it's rather solemn when you lie expecting to die, and your sins come up before you, even though they are very small ones. I never shall forget it, and after my lovely summer I mean to be a better girl, and lead a better life if I can."

Anna was so much in earnest that her words, straight out of a very innocent and contrite heart, touched her hearers deeply, and put them into the right mood to embrace her proposition. No one spoke for a moment, then Maggie said quietly, -

"I know what it is. I felt very much so when the horses ran away, and for fifteen minutes I sat clinging to Mamma, expecting to be killed. Every unkind, undutiful word I'd ever said to her came back to me, and was worse to bear than the fear of sudden death. It scared a great deal of naughtiness out of me, and dear Mamma and I have been more to each other ever since."

"Let us begin with 'The Prisoners of Poverty,' and perhaps it will show us something to do," said Lizzie. "But I must say I never felt as if shop-girls needed much help; they generally seem so contented with themselves, and so pert or patronizing to us, that I don't pity them a bit, though it must be a hard life."

"I think we can't do MUCH in that direction, except set an example of good manners when we go shopping. I wanted to propose that we each choose some small charity for this winter, and do it faithfully. That will teach us how to do more by and by, and we can help one another with our experiences, perhaps, or amuse with our failures. What do you say?" asked Anna, surveying her five friends with a persuasive smile.

"What COULD we do?"

"People will call us goody-goody."

"I haven't the least idea how to go to work"

"Don't believe Mamma will let me."

"We'd better change our names from May Flowers to sisters of charity, and wear meek black bonnets and flapping cloaks."

Anna received these replies with great composure, and waited for the meeting to come to order, well knowing that the girls would have their fun and outcry first, and then set to work in good earnest.

"I think it's a lovely idea, and I'll carry out my plan. But I won't tell what it is yet; you'd all shout, and say I couldn't do it, but if you were trying also, that would keep me up to the mark," said Lizzie, with a decided snap of her scissors, as she trimmed the edges of a plush case for her beloved music.

"Suppose we all keep our attempts secret, and not let our right hand know what the left hand does? It's such fun to mystify people, and then no one can laugh at us. If we fail, we can say nothing; if we succeed, we can tell of it and get our reward. I'd like that way, and will look round at once for some especially horrid boot-black, ungrateful old woman, or ugly child, and devote myself to him, her, or it with the patience of a saint," cried Maggie, caught by the idea of doing good in secret and being found out by accident.

The other girls agreed, after some discussion, and then Anna took the floor again.
"I propose that we each work in our own way till next May, then, at our last meeting, report what we have done, truly and honestly, and plan something better for next year. Is it a vote?"

It evidently was a unanimous vote, for five gold thimbles went up, and five blooming faces smiled as the five girlish voices cried, "Aye!"

"Very well, now let us decide what to read, and begin at once. I think the 'Prisoners' a good book, and we shall doubtless get some hints from it."

So they began, and for an hour one pleasant voice after the other read aloud those sad, true stories of workingwomen and their hard lives, showing these gay young creatures what their pretty clothes cost the real makers of them, and how much injustice, suffering, and wasted strength went into them. It was very sober reading, but most absorbing; for the crochet needles went slower and slower, the lace-work lay idle, and a great tear shone like a drop of dew on the apple blossoms as Ella listened to "Rose's Story." They skipped the statistics, and dipped here and there as each took her turn; but when the two hours were over, and it was time for the club to adjourn, all the members were deeply interested in that pathetic book, and more in earnest than before; for this glimpse into other lives showed them how much help was needed, and made them anxious to lend a hand,

"We can't do much, being 'only girls,'" said Anna; "but if each does one small chore somewhere it will pave the way for better work; so we will all try, at least, though it seems like so many ants trying to move a mountain."

"Well, ants build nests higher than a man's head in Africa; you remember the picture of them in our old geographies? And we can do as much, I'm sure, if each tugs her pebble or straw faithfully. I shall shoulder mine to-morrow if Mamma is willing," answered Lizzie, shutting up her work-bag as if she had her resolution inside and was afraid it might evaporate before she got home.

"I shall stand on the Common, and proclaim aloud, 'Here's a nice young missionary, in want of a job! Charity for sale cheap! Who'll buy? who'll buy?'" said Maggie, with a resigned expression, and a sanctimonious twang to her voice.

"I shall wait and see what comes to me, since I don't know what I'm fit for;" and Marion gazed out of the window as if expecting to see some interesting pauper waiting for her to appear.

"I shall ask Miss Bliss for advice; she knows all about the poor, and will give me a good start," added prudent Ida, who resolved to do nothing rashly lest she should fail.

"I shall probably have a class of dirty little girls, and teach them how to sew, as I can't do anything else. They won't learn much, but steal, and break, and mess, and be a dreadful trial, and I shall get laughed at and wish I hadn't done it. Still I shall try it, and sacrifice my fancy-work to the cause of virtue," said Ella, carefully putting away her satin glove-case with a fond glance at the delicate flowers she so loved to embroider.

"I have no plans, but want to do so much! I shall have to wait till I discover what is best. After to-day we won't speak of our work, or it won't be a secret any longer. In May we will report. Good luck to all, and good-by till next Saturday."

With these farewell words from their president the girls departed, with great plans and new ideas simmering in their young heads and hearts.

It seemed a vast undertaking; but where there is a will there is always a way, and soon it was evident that each had found "a little chore" to do for sweet charity's sake. Not a word was said at the weekly meetings, but the artless faces betrayed all shades of hope, discouragement, pride, and doubt, as their various attempts seemed likely to succeed or fail. Much curiosity was felt, and a few accidental words, hints, or meetings in queer places, were very exciting, though nothing was discovered.

Marion was often seen in a North End car, and Lizzie in a South End car, with a bag of books and papers. Ella haunted a certain shop where fancy articles were sold, and Ida always brought plain sewing to the club. Maggie seemed very busy at home, and Anna was found writing industriously several times when one of her friends called. All seemed very happy, and rather important when outsiders questioned them about their affairs. But they had their pleasures as usual, and seemed to enjoy them with an added relish, as if they realized as never before how many blessings they possessed, and were grateful for them.

So the winter passed, and slowly something new and pleasant seemed to come into the lives of these young girls. The listless, discontented look some of them used to wear passed away; a sweet earnestness and a cheerful activity made them charming, though they did not know it, and wondered when people said, "That set of girls are growing up beautifully; they will make fine women by and by." The mayflowers were budding under the snow, and as spring came on the fresh perfume began to steal out, the rosy faces to brighten, and the last year's dead leaves to fall away, leaving the young plants green and strong.

On the 15th of May the club met for the last time that season, as some left town early, and all were full of spring work and summer plans. Every member was in her place at an unusually early hour that day, and each wore an air of mingled anxiety, expectation, and satisfaction, pleasant to behold. Anna called them to order with three raps of her thimble and a beaming smile.

"We need not choose a book for our reading to-day, as each of us is to contribute an original history of her winter's work. I know it will be very interesting, and I hope more instructive, than some of the novels we have read. Who shall begin?"

"You! you!" was the unanimous answer; for all loved and respected her very much, and felt that their presiding officer should open the ball.

Anna colored modestly, but surprised her friends by the

composure with which she related her little story, quite as if used to public speaking.

"You know I told you last November that I should have to look about for something that I COULD do. I did look a long time, and was rather in despair, when my task came to me in the most unexpected way. Our winter work was being done, so I had a good deal of shopping on my hands, and found it less a bore than usual, because I liked to watch the shop-girls, and wish I dared ask some of them if I could help them. I went often to get trimmings and buttons at Cotton's, and had a good deal to do with the two girls at that counter. They were very obliging and patient about matching some jet ornaments for Mamma, and I found out that their names were Mary and Maria Porter. I liked them, for they were very neat and plain in their dress, - not like some, who seem to think that if their waists are small, and their hair dressed in the fashion, it is no matter how soiled their collars are, nor how untidy their nails. Well, one day when I went for certain kinds of buttons which were to be made for us, Maria, the younger one, who took the order, was not there. I asked for her, and Mary said she was at home with a lame knee. I was so sorry, and ventured to put a few questions in a friendly way. Mary seemed glad to tell her troubles, and I found that 'Ria,' as she called her sister, had been suffering for a long time, but did not complain for fear of losing her place. No stools are allowed at Cotton's, so the poor girls stand nearly all day, or rest a minute now and then on a half-opened drawer. I'd seen Maria doing it, and wondered why some one did not make a stir about seats in this place, as they have in other stores and got stools for the shop women. I didn't dare to speak to the gentlemen, but I gave Mary the Jack roses I wore in my breast, and asked if I might take some books or flowers to poor Maria. It was lovely to see her sad face light up and hear her thank me when I went to see her, for she was very lonely without her sister, and discouraged about her place. She did not lose it entirely, but had to work at home, for her lame knee will be a long time in getting well. I begged Mamma and Mrs. Ailingham to speak to Mr. Cotton for her; so she got the mending of the jet and bead work to do, and buttons to cover, and things of that sort. Mary takes them to and fro, and Maria feels so happy not to be idle. We also got stools, for all the other girls in that shop. Mrs. Allingham is so rich and kind she can do anything, and now it's such a comfort to see those tired things resting when off duty that I often go in and enjoy the sight."

Anna paused as cries of "Good! good!" interrupted her tale; but she did not add the prettiest part of it, and tell how the faces of the young women behind the counters brightened when she came in, nor how gladly all served the young lady who showed them what a true gentlewoman was.

"I hope that isn't all?" said Maggie, eagerly.

"Only a little more. I know you will laugh when I tell you that I've been reading papers to a class of shop-girls at the Union once a week all winter."

A murmur of awe and admiration greeted this deeply interesting statement; for, true to the traditions of the modern Athens in which they lived, the girls all felt the highest respect for "papers" on any subject, it being the fashion for ladies, old and young, to read and discuss every subject, from pottery to Pantheism, at the various clubs all over the city.

"It came about very naturally," continued Anna, as if anxious to explain her seeming audacity. "I used to go to see Molly and Ria, and heard all about their life and its few pleasures, and learned to like them more and more. They had only each other in the world, lived in two rooms, worked all day, and in the way of amusement or instruction had only what they found at the Union in the evening. I went with them a few times, and saw how useful and pleasant it was, and wanted to help, as other kind girls only a little older than I did. Eva Randal read a letter from a friend in Russia one time, and the girls enjoyed it very much. That reminded me of my brother George's lively journals, written when he was abroad. You remember how we used to laugh over them when he sent them home? Well, when

I was begged to give them an evening, I resolved to try one of those amusing journal-letters, and chose the best, - all about how George and a friend went to the different places Dickens describes in some of his funny books. I wish you could have seen how those dear girls enjoyed it, and laughed till they cried over the dismay of the boys, when they knocked at a door in Kingsgate Street, and asked if Mrs. Gamp lived there. It was actually a barber's shop, and a little man, very like Poll Sweedlepipes, told them 'Mrs. Britton was the nuss as lived there now.' It upset those rascals to come so near the truth, and they ran away because they couldn't keep sober."

The members of the club indulged in a general smile as they recalled the immortal Sairey with "the bottle on the mankle-shelf," the "cowcuber," and the wooden pippins. Then Anna continued, with an air of calm satisfaction, quite sure now of her audience and herself, -

"It was a great success. So I went on, and when the journals were done, I used to read other things, and picked up books for their library, and helped in any way I could, while learning to know them better and give them confidence in me. They are proud and shy, just as we should be but if you REALLY want to be friends and don't mind rebuffs now and then, they come to trust and like you, and there is so much to do for them one never need sit idle any more. I won't give names, as they don't like it, nor tell how I tried to serve them, but it is very sweet and good for me to have found this work, and to know that each year I can do it better and better. So I feel encouraged and am very glad I began, as I hope you all are. Now, who comes next?"

As Anna ended, the needles dropped and ten soft hands gave her a hearty round of applause; for all felt that she had done well, and chosen a task especially fitted to her powers, as she had money, time, tact, and the winning manners that make friends everywhere.

Beaming with pleasure at their approval, but feeling that they made too much of her small success, Anna called the club to order by saying, "Ella looks as if she were anxious to tell her experiences, so perhaps we had better ask her to hold forth next."

"Hear! hear!" cried the girls; and, nothing loath, Ella promptly began, with twinkling eyes and a demure smile, for HER story ended romantically.

"If you are interested in shop-girls, Miss President and ladies, you will like to know that *I* am one, at least a silent partner and co-worker in a small fancy store at the West End."

"No!" exclaimed the amazed club with one voice; and, satisfied with this sensational beginning Ella went on.

"I really am, and you have bought some of my fancy-work. Isn't that a good joke? You needn't stare so, for I actually made that needle-book, Anna, and my partner knit Lizzie's new cloud. This is the way it all happened. I didn't wish to waste any time, but one can't rush into the street and collar shabby little girls, and say, 'Come along and learn to sew,' without a struggle, so I thought I'd go and ask Mrs. Brown how to begin. Her branch of the Associated Charities is in Laurel Street, not far from our house, you know; and the very day after our last meeting I posted off to get my 'chore.' I expected to have to fit work for poor needlewomen, or go to see some dreadful sick creature, or wash dirty little Pats, and was bracing up my mind for whatever might come, as I toiled up the hill in a gale of wind. Suddenly my hat flew off and went gayly skipping away, to the great delight of some black imps, who only grinned and cheered me on as I trotted after it with wild grabs and wrathful dodges. I got it at last out of a puddle, and there I was in a nice mess. The elastic was broken, feather wet, and the poor thing all mud and dirt. I didn't care much, as it was my old one, - dressed for my work, you see. But I couldn't go home bareheaded, and I didn't know a soul in that neighborhood. I turned to step into a grocery store at the corner, to borrow a brush or buy a sheet of paper to wear, for I looked like a lunatic with my battered hat and my hair in a perfect mop. Luckily I spied a woman's fancy shop on the other corner, and rushed in there to hide myself, for the brats hooted and people stared. It was a very small shop, and behind the counter sat a tall, thin, washed-out-looking woman, making a baby's hood. She looked poor and blue and rather sour, but took pity on me; and while she sewed the cord, dried the feather, and brushed off the dirt, I warmed myself and looked about to see what I could buy in return for her trouble.

"A few children's aprons hung in the little window, with some knit lace, balls, and old-fashioned garters, two or three dolls, and a very poor display of small wares. In a show-case, however, on the table that was the counter, I found some really pretty things, made of plush, silk, and ribbon, with a good deal of taste. So I said I'd buy a needle-book, and a gay ball, and a pair of distracting baby's shoes, made to look like little open-work socks with pink ankle-ties, so cunning and dainty, I was glad to get them for Cousin Clara's baby. The woman seemed pleased, though she had a grim way of talking, and never smiled once. I observed that she handled my hat as if used to such work, and evidently liked to do it. I thanked her for repairing damages so quickly and well, and she said, with my hat on her hand, as if she hated to part with it, 'I'm used to millineryin' and never should have give it up, if I didn't have my folks to see to. I took this shop, hopin' to make things go, as such a place was needed round here, but mother broke down, and is a sight of care; so I couldn't leave her, and doctors is expensive, and times hard, and I had to drop my trade, and fall back on pins and needles, and so on.'"

Ella was a capital mimic, and imitated the nasal tones of the Vermont woman to the life, with a doleful pucker of her own blooming face, which gave such a truthful picture of poor Miss Almira Miller that those who had seen her recognized it at once, and laughed gayly.

"Just as I was murmuring a few words of regret at her bad luck," continued Ella, "a sharp voice called out from a back room, 'Almiry! Almiry! come here.' It sounded very like a cross parrot, but it was the old lady, and while I put on my hat I heard her asking who was in the shop, and what we were 'gabbin' about.' Her daughter told her, and the old soul demanded to 'see the gal;' so I went in, being ready for fun as usual. It was a little, dark, dismal place, but as neat as a pin, and in the bed sat a regular Grandma Smallweed smoking a pipe, with a big cap, a snuff-box, and a red cotton hand-kerchief. She was a tiny, dried-up thing, brown as a berry, with eyes like black beads, a nose and chin that nearly met, and hands like birds' claws. But such a fierce, lively, curious, blunt old lady you never saw, and I didn't know what would be the end of me when she began to question, then to scold, and finally to demand that 'folks should come and trade to Almiry's shop after promisin' they would, and she havin' took a lease of the place on account of them lies.' I wanted to laugh, but dared not do it, so just let her croak, for the daughter had to go to her customers. The old lady's tirade informed me that they came from Vermont, had 'been wal on't till father died and the farm was sold.' Then it seems the women came to Boston and got on pretty well till 'a stroke of numb-palsy,' whatever that is, made the mother helpless and kept Almiry at home to care for her. I can't tell you how funny and yet how sad it was to see the poor old soul, so full of energy and yet so helpless, and the daughter so discouraged with her pathetic little shop and no customers to speak of. I did not know what to say till 'Grammer Miller,' as the children call her, happened to say, when she took up her knitting after the lecture, 'If folks who go spendin' money reckless on redic'lus toys for Christmas only knew what nice things, useful and fancy, me and Almiry could make ef we had the goods, they'd jest come round this corner and buy 'em, and keep me out of a Old Woman's Home and that good, hard-workin' gal of mine out of a 'sylum; for go there she will ef she don't get a boost somehow, with rent and firin' and vittles all on her shoulders, and me only able to wag them knittin'-needles.'

"'I will buy things here, and tell all my friends about it, and I have a drawer full of pretty bits of silk and velvet and plush, that I will give Miss Miller for her work, if she will let me.' I added that, for I saw that Almiry was rather proud, and hid her troubles under a grim look.

"That pleased the old lady, and, lowering her voice, she said, with a motherly sort of look in her beady eyes: 'Seein' as you are so friendly, I'll tell you what frets me most, a layin' here, a burden to my darter. She kep' company with Nathan Baxter, a master carpenter up to Westminster where we lived, and ef father hadn't a died suddin' they'd a ben married. They waited a number o' years, workin' to their trades, and we was hopin' all would turn out wal, when troubles come, and here we be. Nathan's got his own folks to see to, and Almiry won't add to HIS load with hern, nor leave me; so she give him back his ring, and jest buckled to all alone. She don't say a word, but it's wearin' her to a shadder, and I can't do a thing to help, but make a few pinballs, knit garters, and kiver holders. Ef she got a start in business it would cheer her up a sight, and give her a kind of a hopeful prospeck, for old folks can't live forever, and Nathan is a waitin', faithful and true.'

"That just finished me, for I am romantic, and do enjoy love stories with all my heart, even if the lovers are only a skinny spinster and a master carpenter. So I just resolved to see what I could do for poor Almiry and the peppery old lady. I didn't promise anything but my bits, and, taking the things I bought, went home to talk it over with Mamma. I found she had often got pins and tape, and such small wares, at the little shop, and found it very convenient, though she knew nothing about the Millers. She was willing I should help if I could, but advised going slowly, and seeing what they could do first. We did not dare to treat them like beggars, and send them money and clothes, and tea and sugar, as we do the Irish, for they were evidently respectable people, and proud as poor. So I took my bundle of odds and ends, and Mamma added some nice large pieces of dresses we had done with, and gave a fine order for aprons and holders and balls for our church fair.

"It would have done your hearts good, girls, to see those poor old faces light up as I showed my scraps, and asked if the work would be ready by Christmas. Grammer fairly swam in the gay colors I strewed over her bed, and enjoyed them like a child, while Almiry tried to be grim, but had to give it up, as she began at once to cut out aprons, and dropped tears all over the muslin when her back was turned to me. I didn't know a washed-out old maid COULD be so pathetic."

Ella stopped to give a regretful sigh over her past blindness, while her hearers made a sympathetic murmur; for young hearts are very tender, and take an innocent interest in lovers' sorrows, no matter how humble.

"Well, that was the beginning of it. I got so absorbed in making things go well that I didn't look any further, but just 'buckled to' with Miss Miller and helped run that little shop. No one knew me in that street, so I slipped in and out, and did what I liked. The old lady and I got to be great friends; though she often pecked and croaked like a cross raven, and was very wearing. I kept her busy with her 'pin-balls and knittin'-work, and supplied Almiry with pretty materials for the various things I found she could make. You wouldn't believe what dainty bows those long fingers could tie, what ravishing doll's hats she would make out of a scrap of silk and lace, or the ingenious things she concocted with cones and shells and fans and baskets. I love such work, and used to go and help her often, for I wanted her window and shop to be full for Christmas, and lure in plenty of customers. Our new toys and the little cases of sewing silk sold well, and people began to come more, after I lent Almiry some money to lay in a stock of better goods. Papa enjoyed my business venture immensely, and was never tired of joking about it. He actually went and bought balls for four small black boys who were gluing their noses to the window one day, spellbound by the orange, red, and blue treasures displayed there. He liked my partner's looks, though he teased me by saying that we'd better add lemonade to our stock, as poor, dear Almiry's acid face would make lemons unnecessary, and sugar and water were cheap.

"Well, Christmas came, and we did a great business, for Mamma came and sent others, and our fancy things were as pretty and cheaper than those at the art stores, so they went well, and the Millers were cheered up, and I felt encouraged, and we took a fresh start after the holidays. One of my gifts at New Year was my own glove-case, - you remember the apple-blossom thing I began last autumn? I put it in our window to fill up, and Mamma bought it, and gave it to me full of elegant gloves, with a sweet note, and Papa sent a check to 'Miller, Warren & Co.' I was so pleased and proud I could hardly help telling you all. But the best joke was the day you girls came in and bought our goods, and I peeped at you through the crack of the door, being in the back room dying with laughter to see you look round, and praise our 'nice assortment of useful and pretty articles.'"

"That's all very well, and we can bear to be laughed at if you succeeded, Miss. But I don't believe you did, for no Millers are there now. Have you taken a palatial store on Boylston Street for this year, intending to run it alone? We'll all patronize it, and your name will look well on a sign," said Maggie, wondering what the end of Ella's experience had been.

"Ah! I still have the best of it, for my romance finished up delightfully, as you shall hear. We did well all winter, and no wonder. What was needed was a little 'boost' in the right direction, and I could give it; so my Millers were much comforted, and we were good friends. But in March Grammer died suddenly, and poor Almiry mourned as if she had been the sweetest mother in the world. The old lady's last wishes were to be 'laid out harnsome in a cap with a pale blue satin ribbin, white wasn't becomin', to hev at least three carriages to the funeral, and be sure a paper with her death in it was sent to N. Baxter, Westminster, Vermont.'

"I faithfully obeyed her commands, put on the ugly cap myself, gave a party of old ladies from the home a drive in the hacks, and carefully directed a marked paper to Nathan, hoping that he HAD proved 'faithful and true.' I didn't expect he would, so was not surprised when no answer came. But I WAS rather amazed when Almiry told me she didn't care to keep on with the store now she was free. She wanted to visit her friends a spell this spring, and in the fall would go back to her trade in some milliner's store.

"I was sorry, for I really enjoyed my partnership. It seemed a little bit ungrateful after all my trouble in getting her customers, but I didn't say anything, and we sold out to the Widow Bates, who is a good soul with six children, and will profit by our efforts.

"Almiry bid me good-by with all the grim look gone out of her face, many thanks, and a hearty promise to write soon. That was in April. A week ago I got a short letter saying, -

"'DEAR FRIEND, - You will be pleased to hear that I am married to Mr. Baxter, and shall remain here. He was away when the paper came with mother's death, but as soon as he got home he wrote. I couldn't make up my mind till I got home and see him. Now it's all right. and I am very happy. Many thanks for all you done for me and mother. I shall never forget it My husband sends respects, and I remain Yours gratefully, ALMIRA M. BAXTER.'"

"That's splendid! You did well, and next winter you can look up another sour spinster and cranky old lady and make them happy," said Anna, with the approving smile all loved to receive from her.

"My adventures are not a bit romantic, or even interesting, and yet I've been as busy as a bee all winter, and enjoyed my work very much," began Elizabeth, as the President gave her a nod.

"The plan I had in mind was to go and carry books and papers to the people in hospitals, as one of Mamma's friends has done for years. I went once to the City Hospital with her, and it was very interesting, but I didn't dare to go to the grown people all alone, so I went to the Children's Hospital, and soon loved to help amuse the poor little dears. I saved all the picture-books and papers I could find for them, dressed dolls, and mended toys, and got new ones, and made bibs and night-gowns, and felt like the mother of a large family.

"I had my pets, of course, and did my best for them, reading and singing and amusing them, for many suffered very much. One little girl was so dreadfully burned she could not use her hands, and would lie and look at a gay dolly tied to the bedpost by the hour together, and talk to it and love it, and died with it on her pillow when I 'sung lullaby' to her for the last time. I keep it among my treasures, for I learned a lesson in patience from little Norah that I never can forget.

"Then Jimmy Dolan with hip disease was a great delight to me, for he was as gay as a lark in spite of pain, and a real little hero in the way he bore the hard things that had to be done to him. He never can get well, and he is at home now; but I still see to him, and he is learning to make toy furniture very nicely, so that by and by, if he gets able to work at all, he may be able to learn a cabinet-maker's trade, or some easy work.

"But my pet of pets was Johnny, the blind boy. His poor eyes had to be taken out, and there he was left so helpless and pathetic, all his life before him, and no one to help him, for his people were poor and he had to go away from the hospital since he was incurable. He seemed almost given to me, for the first time I saw him I was singing to Jimmy, when the door opened and a small boy came fumbling in.

"'I hear a pretty voice, I want to find it,' he said, stopping as I stopped with both hands out as if begging for more.

"'Come on. Johnny, and the lady will sing to you like a bobolink,' called Jimmy, as proud as Barnum showing off Jumbo.

"The poor little thing came and stood at my knee, without stirring, while I sang all the nursery jingles I knew. Then he put such a thin little finger on my lips as if to feel where the music came from, and said, smiling all over his white face, 'More, please more, lots of 'em! I love it!'

"So I sang away till I was as hoarse as a crow, and Johnny drank it all in like water; kept time with his head, stamped when I gave him 'Marching through Georgia,' and hurrahed feebly in the chorus of 'Red, White, and Blue.' It was lovely to see how he enjoyed it, and I was so glad I had a voice to comfort those poor babies with. He cried when I had to go, and so touched my heart that I asked all about him, and resolved to get him into the Blind School as the only place where he could be taught and made happy."

"I thought you were bound there the day I met you, Lizzie; but you looked as solemn as if all your friends had lost their sight," cried Marion.

"I did feel solemn, for if Johnny could not go there he would be badly off. Fortunately he was ten, and dear Mrs. Russell helped me, and those good people took him in though they were crowded. 'We cannot turn one away,' said kind Mr. Parpatharges.

"So there my boy is, as happy as a king with his little mates, learning all sorts of useful lessons and pretty plays. He models nicely in clay. Here is one of his little works. Could you do as well without eyes?" and Lizzie proudly produced a very one-sided pear with a long straw for a stem. "I don't expect he will ever be a sculptor, but I hope he will do something with music he loves it so, and is already piping away on a fife very cleverly. Whatever his gift may prove, if he lives, he will be taught to be a useful, independent man, not a helpless burden, nor an unhappy creature sitting alone in the dark. I feel very happy about my lads, and am surprised to find how well I get on with them. I shall look up some more next year, for I really think I have quite a gift that way, though you wouldn't expect it, as I have no brothers, and always had a fancy boys were little imps."

The girls were much amused at Lizzie's discovery of her own powers, for she was a stately damsel, who never indulged in romps, but lived for her music. Now it was evident that she had found the key to unlock childish hearts, and was learning to use it, quite unconscious that the sweet voice she valued so highly was much improved by the tender tones singing lullabies gave it. The fat pear was passed round like refreshments, receiving much praise and no harsh criticism; and when it was safely returned to its proud possessor, Ida began her tale in a lively tone.

"I waited for MY chore, and it came tumbling down our basement steps one rainy day in the shape of a large dilapidated umbrella with a pair of small boots below it. A mild howl made me run to open the door, for I was at lunch in the dining-room, all alone, and rather blue because I couldn't go over to see Ella. A very small girl lay with her head in a puddle at the foot of the steps, the boots waving in the air, and the umbrella brooding over her like a draggled green bird.

"'Are you hurt, child?' said I.

"'No, I thank you, ma'am,' said the mite quite calmly, as she sat up and settled a woman's shabby black hat on her head.

"'Did you come begging?' I asked.

"'No, ma'am, I came for some things Mrs. Grover's got for us. She told me to. I don't beg.' And up rose the sopping thing with great dignity.

"So I asked her to sit down, and ran up to call Mrs. Grover. She was busy with Grandpa just then, and when I went back to my lunch there sat my lady with her arms folded, water dripping out of the toes of her old boots as they hung down from the high chair, and the biggest blue eyes I ever saw fixed upon the cake and oranges on the table. I gave her a piece, and she sighed with rapture, but only picked at it till I asked if she didn't like it.

"'Oh yes, 'm, it's elegant! Only I was wishin' I could take it to Caddy and Tot, if you didn't mind. They never had frostin' in all their lives, and I did once.'

"Of course I put up a little basket of cake and oranges and figs, and while Lotty feasted, we talked. I found that their mother washed dishes all day in a restaurant over by the Albany Station, leaving the three children alone in the room they have on Berry Street. Think of that poor thing going off before light these winter mornings to stand over horrid dishes all day long, and those three scraps of children alone till night! Sometimes they had a fire, and when they hadn't they stayed in bed. Broken food and four dollars a week was all the woman got, and on that they tried to live. Good Mrs. Grover happened to be nursing a poor soul near Berry Street last summer, and used to see the three little things trailing round the streets with no one to look after them.

"Lotty is nine, though she looks about six, but is as old as most girls of fourteen, and takes good care of 'the babies,' as she calls the younger ones. Mrs. Grover went to see them, and, though a hard-working creature, did all she could for them. This winter she has plenty of time to sew, for Grandpapa needs little done for him except at night and morning, and that kind woman spent her own money, and got warm flannel and cotton and stuff, and made each child a good suit. Lotty had come for hers, and when the bundle was in her arms she hugged it close, and put up her little face to kiss Grover so prettily, I felt that I wanted to do something too. So I hunted up Min's old waterproof and rubbers, and a hood, and sent Lotty home as happy as a queen, promising to go and see her. I did go, and there was my work all ready for me. Oh, girls! such a bare, cold room, without a spark of fire, and no food but a pan of bits of pie and bread and meat, not fit for any one to eat, and in the bed, with an old carpet for cover, lay the three children. Tot and Caddy cuddled in the warmest place, while Lotty, with her little blue hands, was trying to patch up some old stockings with bits of cotton. I didn't know how to begin, but Lotty did, and I just took her orders; for that wise little woman told me where to buy a bushel of coal and some kindlings, and milk and meal, and all I wanted. I worked like a beaver for an hour or two, and was so glad I'd been to a cooking-class, for I could make a fire, with Lotty to do the grubby part, and start a nice soup with the cold meat and potatoes, and an onion or so. Soon the room was warm, and full of a nice smell, and out of bed tumbled 'the babies,' to dance round the stove and sniff at the soup, and drink milk like hungry kittens, till I could get bread and butter ready.

"It was great fun! and when we had cleared things up a bit, and I'd put food for supper in the closet, and told Lotty to warm a bowl of soup for her mother and keep the fire going, I went home tired and dirty, but very glad I'd found something to do. It is perfectly amazing how little poor people's things cost, and yet they can't get the small amount of money needed without working themselves to death. Why, all I bought didn't cost more than I often spend for flowers, or theatre tickets, or lunches, and it made those poor babies so comfortable I could have cried to think I'd never done it before."

Ida paused to shake her head remorsefully, then went on with her story, sewing busily all the while on an unbleached cotton night-gown which looked about fit for a large doll.

"I have no romantic things to tell, for poor Mrs. Kennedy was a shiftless, broken-down woman, who could only 'sozzle round,' as Mrs. Grover said, and rub along with help from any one who would lend a hand. She had lived out, married young, and had no faculty about anything; so when her husband died, and she was left with three little children, it was hard to get on, with no trade, feeble health, and a discouraged mind. She does her best, loves the girls, and works hard at the only thing she can find to do; but when she gives out, they will all have to part, - she to a hospital, and the babies to some home. She dreads that, and tugs away, trying to keep together and get ahead. Thanks to Mrs. Grover, who is very sensible, and knows how to help poor people, we have made things comfortable, and the winter has gone nicely.

Louisa May Alcott

"The mother has got work nearer home, Lotty and Caddy go to school, and Tot is safe and warm, with Miss Parsons to look after her. Miss Parsons is a young woman who was freezing and starving in a little room upstairs, too proud to beg and too shy and sick to get much work. I found her warming her hands one day in Mrs. Kennedy's room, and hanging over the soup-pot as if she was eating the smell. It reminded me of the picture in Punch where the two beggar boys look in at a kitchen, sniffing at the nice dinner cooking there. One says, 'I don't care for the meat, Bill, but I don't mind if I takes a smell at the pudd'n' when it's dished.' I proposed a lunch at once, and we all sat down, and ate soup out of yellow bowls with pewter spoons with such a relish it was fun to see. I had on my old rig; so poor Parsons thought I was some dressmaker or work-girl, and opened her heart to me as she never would have done if I'd gone and demanded her confidence, and patronized her, as some people do when they want to help. I promised her some work, and proposed that she should do it in Mrs. K.'s room, as a favor, mind you, so that the older girls could go to school and Tot have some one to look after her. She agreed, and that saved her fire, and made the K.'s all right. Sarah (that's Miss P.) tried to stiffen up when she learned where I lived; but she wanted the work, and soon found I didn't put on airs, but lent her books, and brought her and Tot my bouquets and favors after a german, and told her pleasant things as she sat cooking her poor chilblainy feet in the oven, as if she never could get thawed out.

"This summer the whole batch are to go to Uncle Frank's farm and pick berries, and get strong. He hires dozens of women and children during the fruit season, and Mrs. Grover said it was just what they all needed. So off they go in June, as merry as grigs, and I shall be able to look after them now and then, as I always go to the farm in July. That's all, - not a bit interesting, but it came to me, and I did it, though only a small chore."

"I'm sure the helping of five poor souls is a fine work, and you may well be proud of it, Ida. Now I know why you wouldn't go to matinees with me, and buy every pretty thing we saw as you used to. The pocket money went for coal and food, and your fancy work was little clothes for these live dolls of yours. You dear thing! how good you were to cook, and grub, and prick your fingers rough, and give up fun, for this kind work!"

Maggie's hearty kiss, and the faces of her friends, made Ida feel that her humble task had its worth in their eyes, as well as in her own; and when the others had expressed their interest in her work, all composed themselves to hear what Marion had to tell.

"I have been taking care of a scarlet runner, - a poor old frost-bitten, neglected thing; it is transplanted now, and doing well, I'm happy to say."

"What do you mean?" asked Ella, while the rest looked very curious.

Marion picked up a dropped stitch in the large blue sock she was knitting, and continued, with a laugh in her eyes: "My dears, that is what we call the Soldiers' Messenger Corps, with their red caps and busy legs trotting all day. I've had one of them to care for, and a gorgeous time of it, I do assure you. But before I exult over my success, I must honestly confess my failures, for they were sad ones. I was so anxious to begin my work at once, that I did go out and collar the first pauper I saw. It was an old man, who sometimes stands at the corners of streets to sell bunches of ugly paper flowers. You've seen him, I dare say, and his magenta daisies and yellow peonies. Well, he was rather a forlorn object, with his poor old red nose, and bleary eyes, and white hair, standing at the windy corners silently holding out those horrid flowers. I bought all he had that day, and gave them to some colored children on my way home, and told him to come to our house and get an old coat Mamma was waiting to get rid of. He told a pitiful story of himself and his old wife, who made the paper horrors in her bed, and how they needed everything, but didn't wish to beg. I was much touched, and flew home to look up the coat and some shoes, and when my old Lear came creeping in the back way, I ordered cook to give him a warm dinner and something nice for the old woman.

"I was called upstairs while he was mumbling his food, and blessing me in the most lovely manner; and he went away much comforted, I flattered myself. But an hour later, up came the cook in a great panic to report that my venerable and pious beggar had carried off several of Papa's shirts and pairs of socks out of the clothes-basket in the laundry, and the nice warm hood we keep for the girl to hang out clothes in.

"I was VERY angry, and, taking Harry with me, went at once to the address the old rascal gave me, a dirty court out of Hanover Street No such person had ever lived there, and my white-haired saint was a humbug. Harry laughed at me, and Mamma forbade me to bring any more thieves to the house, and the girls scolded awfully.

"Well, I recovered from the shock, and, nothing daunted, went off to the little Irishwoman who sells apples on the Common, - not the fat, tosey one with the stall near West Street, but the dried-up one who sits by the path, nodding over an old basket with six apples and four sticks of candy in it. No one ever seems to buy anything, but she sits there and trusts to kind souls dropping a dime now and then; she looks so feeble and forlorn, 'on the cold, cold ground.'

"She told me another sad tale of being all alone and unable to work, and 'as wake as wather-grewl, without a hap-worth av flesh upon me bones, and for the love of Heaven gimme a thrifle to kape the breath av loife in a poor soul, with a bitter hard winter over me, and niver a chick or child to do a hand's turn.' I hadn't much faith in her, remembering my other humbug, but I did pity the old mummy; so I got some tea and sugar, and a shawl, and used to give her my odd pennies as I passed. I never told at home, they made such fun of my efforts to be charitable. I thought I really was getting on pretty well after a time, as my old Biddy seemed quite cheered up, and I was planning to give her some coal, when she disappeared all of a sudden. I feared she was ill, and asked Mrs. Maloney, the fat woman, about her.

"'Lord love ye, Miss dear, it's tuk up and sint to the Island for tree months she is; for a drunken ould craythur is Biddy Ryan, and niver a cint but goes for whiskey, - more shame to her, wid a fine bye av her own ready to kape her daycint.'

"Then I WAS discouraged, and went home to fold my hands, and see what fate would send me, my own efforts being such failures."

"Poor thing, it WAS hard luck!" said Elizabeth, as they sobered down after the gale of merriment caused by Marion's mishaps, and her clever imitation of the brogue.

"Now tell of your success, and the scarlet runner," added Maggie.

"Ah! that was SENT, and so I prospered. I must begin ever so far back, in war times, or I can't introduce my hero properly. You know Papa was in the army, and fought all through the war till Gettysburg, where he was wounded. He was engaged just before he went; so when his father hurried to him after that awful battle, Mamma went also, and helped nurse him till he could come home. He wouldn't go to an officer's hospital, but kept with his men in a poor sort of place, for many of his boys were hit, and he wouldn't leave them. Sergeant Joe Collins was one of the bravest, and lost his right arm saving the flag in one of the hottest struggles of that great fight. He had been a Maine lumberman, and was over six feet tall, but as gentle as a child, and as jolly as a boy, and very fond of his colonel.

"Papa left first, but made Joe promise to let him know how he got on, and Joe did so till he too went home. Then Papa lost sight of him, and in the excitement of his own illness, and the end of the war, and being married, Joe Collins was forgotten, till we children came along, and used to love to hear the story of Papa's battles, and how the brave sergeant caught the flag when the bearer was shot, and held it in the rush till one arm was blown off and the other wounded. We have fighting blood in us, you know, so we were never tired of that story, though twenty-five years or more make it all as far away to us as the old Revolution, where OUR ancestor was killed, at OUR Bunker Hill!

"Last December, just after my sad disappointments, Papa came home to dinner one day, exclaiming, in great glee: 'I've found old Joe! A messenger came with a letter to me, and when I looked up to give my answer, there stood a tall, grizzled fellow, as straight as a ramrod, grinning from ear to ear, with his hand to his temple, saluting me in regular style. "Don't you remember Joe Collins, Colonel? Awful glad to see you, sir," said he. And then it all came back, and we had a good talk, and I found out that the poor old boy was down on his luck, and almost friendless, but as proud and independent as ever, and bound to take care of himself while he had a leg to stand on. I've got his address, and mean to keep an eye on him, for he looks feeble and can't make much, I'm sure.'

"We were all very glad, and Joe came to see us, and Papa sent him on endless errands, and helped him in that way till he went to New York. Then, in the fun and flurry of the holidays, we forgot all about Joe, till Papa came home and missed him from his post. I said I'd go and find him; so Harry and I rummaged about till we did find him, in a little house at the North End, laid up with rheumatic fever in a stuffy back room, with no one to look after him but the washerwoman with whom he boarded.

"I was SO sorry we had forgotten him! but HE never complained, only said, with his cheerful grin,' I kinder mistrusted the Colonel was away, but I wasn't goin' to pester him.' He tried to be jolly, though in dreadful pain; called Harry 'Major,' and was so grateful for all we brought him, though he didn't want oranges and tea, and made us shout when I said, like a goose, thinking that was the proper thing to do, 'Shall I bathe your brow, you are so feverish?'

"'No, thanky, miss, it was swabbed pretty stiddy to the horsepittle, and I reckon a trifle of tobaccer would do more good and be a sight more relishin', ef you'll excuse my mentionin' it.'

"Harry rushed off and got a great lump and a pipe, and Joe lay blissfully puffing, in a cloud of smoke, when we left him, promising to come again. We did go nearly every day, and had lovely times; for Joe told us his adventures, and we got so interested in the war that I began to read up evenings, and Papa was pleased, and fought all his battles over again for us, and Harry and I were great friends reading together, and Papa was charmed to see the old General's spirit in us, as we got excited and discussed all our wars in a fever of patriotism that made Mamma laugh. Joe said I 'brustled up' at the word BATTLE like a war-horse at the smell of powder, and I'd ought to have been a drummer, the sound of martial music made me so 'skittish.'

"It was all new and charming to us young ones, but poor old Joe had a hard time, and was very ill. Exposure and fatigue, and scanty food, and loneliness, and his wounds, were too much for him, and it was plain his working days were over. He hated the thought of the poor-house at home, which was all his own town could offer him, and he had no friends to live with, and he could not get a pension, something being wrong about his papers; so he would have been badly off, but for the Soldiers' Home at Chelsea. As soon as he was able, Papa got him in there, and he was glad to go, for that seemed the proper place, and a charity the proudest man might accept, after risking his life for his country.

"There is where I used to be going when you saw me, and I was SO afraid you'd smell the cigars in my basket. The dear old boys always want them, and Papa says they MUST have them, though it isn't half so romantic as flowers, and jelly, and wine, and the dainty messes we women always want to carry. I've learned about different kinds of tobacco and cigars, and you'd laugh to see me deal out my gifts, which are received as gratefully as the Victoria Cross, when the Queen decorates HER brave men. I'm quite a great gun over there, and the boys salute when I come, tell me their woes, and think that Papa and I can run the whole concern. I like it immensely, and am as proud and fond of my dear old wrecks as if I'd been a Rigoletto, and ridden on a cannon from my babyhood. That's MY story, but I can't begin to tell how interesting it all is, nor how glad I am that it led me to look into the history of American wars, in which brave men of our name did their parts so well."

A hearty round of applause greeted Marion's tale, for her glowing face and excited voice stirred the patriotic spirit of the Boston girls, and made them beam approvingly upon her.

"Now, Maggie, dear, last but not least, I'm sure," said Anna, with an encouraging glance, for SHE had discovered the secret of this friend, and loved her more than ever for it.

Maggie blushed and hesitated, as she put down the delicate muslin cap-strings she was hemming with such care. Then, looking about her with a face in which both humility and pride contended, she said with an effort, "After the other lively experiences, mine will sound very flat. In fact, I have no story to tell, for MY charity began at home, and stopped there."

"Tell it, dear. I know it is interesting, and will do us all good," said Anna, quickly; and, thus supported, Maggie went on.

"I planned great things, and talked about what I meant to do, till Papa said one day, when things were in a mess, as they often are at our house, 'If the little girls who want to help the world along would remember that charity be gins at home, they would soon find enough to do.'

"I was rather taken aback, and said no more, but after Papa

had gone to the office, I began to think, and looked round to see what there was to be done at that particular moment. I found enough for that day, and took hold at once; for poor Mamma had one of her bad headaches, the children could not go out because it rained, and so were howling in the nursery, cook was on a rampage, and Maria had the toothache. Well, I began by making Mamma lie down for a good long sleep. I kept the children quiet by giving them my ribbon box and jewelry to dress up with, put a poultice on Maria's face, and offered to wash the glass and silver for her, to appease cook, who was as cross as two sticks over extra work washing-day. It wasn't much fun, as you may imagine, but I got through the afternoon, and kept the house still, and at dusk crept into Mamma's room and softly built up the fire, so it should be cheery when she waked. Then I went trembling to the kitchen for some tea, and there found three girls calling, and high jinks going on; for one whisked a plate of cake into the table drawer, another put a cup under her shawl, and cook hid the teapot, as I stirred round in the china closet before opening the slide, through a crack of which I'd seen, heard, and smelt 'the party,' as the children call it.

"I was angry enough to scold the whole set, but I wisely held my tongue, shut my eyes, and politely asked for some hot water, nodded to the guests, and told cook Maria was better, and would do her work if she wanted to go out.

"So peace reigned, and as I settled the tray, I heard cook say in her balmiest tone, for I suspect the cake and tea lay heavy on her conscience, 'The mistress is very poorly, and Miss takes nice care of her, the dear.'

"All blarney, but it pleased me and made me remember how feeble poor Mamma was, and how little I really did. So I wept a repentant weep as I toiled upstairs with my tea and toast, and found Mamma all ready for them, and so pleased to find things going well. I saw by that what a relief it would be to her if I did it oftener, as I ought, and as I resolved that I would.

"I didn't say anything, but I kept on doing whatever came along, and before I knew it ever so many duties slipped out of Mamma's hands into mine, and seemed to belong to me. I don't mean that I liked them, and didn't grumble to myself; I did, and felt regularly crushed and injured sometimes when I wanted to go and have my own fun. Duty is right, but it isn't easy, and the only comfort about it is a sort of quiet feeling you get after a while, and a strong feeling, as if you'd found something to hold on to and keep you steady. I can't express it, but you know?" And Maggie looked wistfully at the other faces, some of which answered her with a quick flash of sympathy, and some only wore a puzzled yet respectful expression, as if they felt they ought to know, but did not.

"I need not tire you with all my humdrum doings," continued Maggie. "I made no plans, but just said each day, 'I'll take what comes, and try to be cheerful and contented.' So I looked after the children, and that left Maria more time to sew and help round. I did errands, and went to market, and saw that Papa had his meals comfortably when Mamma was not able to come down. I made calls for her, and received visitors, and soon went on as if I were the lady of the house, not 'a chit of a girl,' as Cousin Tom used to call me.

"The best of all were the cosey talks we had in the twilight, Mamma and I, when she was rested, and all the day's worry was over, and we were waiting for Papa. Now, when he came, I didn't have to go away, for they wanted to ask and tell me things, and consult about affairs, and make me feel that I was really the eldest daughter. Oh, it was just lovely to sit between them and know that they needed me, and loved to have me with them! That made up for the hard and disagreeable things, and not long ago I got my reward. Mamma is better, and I was rejoicing over it, when she said,' Yes, I really am mending now, and hope soon to be able to relieve my good girl. But I want to tell you, dear, that when I was most discouraged my greatest comfort was, that if I had to leave my poor babies they would find such a faithful little mother in you.'

"I was SO pleased I wanted to cry, for the children DO love me, and run to me for everything now, and think the world of Sister, and they didn't use to care much for me. But that wasn't all. I ought not to tell these things, perhaps, but I'm so proud of them I can't help it. When I asked Papa privately, if Mamma was REALLY better and in no danger of falling ill again, he said, with his arms round me, and such a tender kiss, -

"'No danger now, for this brave little girl put her shoulder to the wheel so splendidly, that the dear woman got the relief from care she needed just at the right time, and now she really rests sure that we are not neglected. You couldn't have devoted yourself to a better charity, or done it more sweetly, my darling. God bless you!'"

Here Maggie's voice gave out, and she hid her face, with a happy sob, that finished her story eloquently. Marion flew to wipe her tears away with the blue sock, and the others gave a sympathetic murmur, looking much touched; forgotten duties of their own rose before them, and sudden resolutions were made to attend to them at once, seeing how great Maggie's reward had been.

"I didn't mean to be silly; but I wanted you to know that I hadn't been idle all winter, and that, though I haven't much to tell, I'm quite satisfied with my chore," she said, looking up with smiles shining through the tears till her face resembled a rose in a sun-shower.

"Many daughters have done well, but thou excellest them all," answered Anna, with a kiss that completed her satisfaction.

"Now, as it is after our usual time, and we must break up," continued the President, producing a basket of flowers from its hiding-place, "I will merely say that I think we have all learned a good deal, and will be able to work better next winter; for I am sure we shall want to try again, it adds so much sweetness to our own lives to put even a little comfort into the hard lives

Louisa May Alcott

of the poor. As a farewell token, I sent for some real Plymouth mayflowers, and here they are, a posy apiece, with my love and many thanks for your help in carrying out my plan so beautifully."

So the nosegays were bestowed, the last lively chat enjoyed, new plans suggested, and goodbyes said; then the club separated, each member going gayly away with the rosy flowers on her bosom, and in it a clearer knowledge of the sad side of life, a fresh desire to see and help still more, and a sweet satisfaction in the thought that each had done what she could.

AN IVY SPRAY AND LADIES' SLIPPERS

"IT can't be done! So I may as well give it I up and get a new pair. I long for them, but I'm afraid my nice little plan for Laura will be spoilt," said Jessie Delano to herself, as she shook her head over a pair of small, dilapidated slippers almost past mending. While she vainly pricked her fingers over them for the last time, her mind was full of girlish hopes and fears, as well as of anxieties far too serious for a light-hearted creature of sixteen.

A year ago the sisters had been the petted daughters of a rich man; but death and misfortune came suddenly, and now they were left to face poverty alone. They had few relations, and had offended the rich uncle who offered Jessie a home, because she refused to be separated from her sister. Poor Laura was an invalid, and no one wanted her; but Jessie would not leave her, so they clung together and lived on in the humble rooms where their father died, trying to earn their bread by the only accomplishments they possessed. Laura painted well, and after many disappointments was beginning to find a sale for her dainty designs and delicate flowers. Jessie had a natural gift for dancing; and her former teacher, a kind-hearted French-woman, offered her favorite pupil the post of assistant teacher in her classes for children.

It cost the girl a struggle to accept a place of this sort and be a humble teacher, patiently twirling stupid little boys and girls round and round over the smooth floor where she used to dance so happily when she was the pride of the class and the queen of the closing balls. But for Laura's sake she gratefully accepted the offer, glad to add her mite to their small store, and to feel that she could help keep the wolf from the door. They had seemed to hear the howl of this dreaded phantom more than once during that year, and looked forward to the long hard winter with an anxiety which neither would confess to the other. Laura feared to fall ill if she worked too hard, and then what would become of this pretty young sister who loved her so tenderly and would not be tempted to leave her? And Jessie could do very little except rebel against their hard fate and make impracticable plans. But each worked bravely, talked cheerfully, and waited hopefully for some good fortune to befall them, while doubt and pain and poverty and care made the young hearts so heavy that the poor girls often fell asleep on pillows wet with secret tears.

The smaller trials of life beset Jessie at this particular moment, and her bright wits were trying to solve the problem how to spend her treasured five dollars on slippers for herself and paints for Laura. Both were much needed, and she had gone in shabby shoes to save up money for the little surprise on which she had set her heart; but now dismay fell upon her when the holes refused to be cobbled, and the largest of bows would not hide the worn-out toes in spite of ink and blacking lavishly applied.

"These are the last of my dear French slippers, and I can't afford any more. I hate cheap things! But I shall have to get them; for my boots are shabby, and every one has to look at my feet when I lead. Oh dear, what a horrid thing it is to be poor!" and Jessie surveyed the shabby little shoes affectionately, as her eyes filled with tears; for the road looked very rough and steep now. when she remembered how she used to dance through life as happy as a butterfly in a garden full of sunshine and flowers.

"Now, Jess , no nonsense, no red eyes to tell tales! Go and do your errands, and come in as gay as a lark, or Laura will be worried." And springing up, the girl began to sing instead of sob, as she stirred about her dismal little room, cleaning her old gloves, mending her one white dress, and wishing with a sigh of intense longing that she could afford some flowers to wear, every ornament having been sold long ago. Then, with a kiss and a smile to her patient sister, she hurried away to get the necessary slippers and the much-desired paints, which Laura would not ask for, though her work waited for want of them.

Having been reared in luxury, poor little Jessie's tastes were all of the daintiest sort; and her hardest trial, after Laura's feeble health, was the daily sacrifice of the many comforts and elegances to which she had been accustomed. Faded gowns, cleaned gloves, and mended boots cost her many a pang, and the constant temptation of seeing pretty, useful, and unattainable things was a very hard one. Laura rarely went out, and so was spared this cross; then she was three years older, had always been delicate, and lived much in a happy world of her own. So Jessie bore her trials silently, but sometimes felt very covetous and resentful to see so much pleasure, money, and beauty in the world, and yet have so little of it fall to her lot.

"I feel as if I could pick a pocket to-day and not mind a bit, if it were a rich person's. It's a shame, when papa was always so generous, that no one remembers us. If ever I'm rich again, I'll just hunt up all the poor girls I can find, and give them nice shoes, if nothing else," she thought, as she went along the crowded streets, pausing involuntarily at the shop windows to look with longing eyes at the treasures within.

Resisting the allurements of French slippers with bows and buckles, she wisely bought a plain, serviceable pair, and trudged away, finding balm for her wounds in the fact that they were very cheap. More balm came when she met a young friend, who joined her as she stood wistfully eying the piles of grapes in a window and longing to buy some for Laura.

This warm-hearted schoolmate read the wish before Jessie saw her, and gratified it so adroitly that the girl could accept the pretty basketful sent to her sister without feeling like a spendthrift or a beggar. It comforted her very much, and the world began to look brighter after that little touch of kindness, as it always does when genuine sympathy makes sunshine in shady places.

At the art store she was told that more of Laura's autumn-flowers were in demand; and her face was so full of innocent delight and gratitude it quite touched the old man who sold her the paints, and gave her more than her money's worth, remembering his own hard times and pitying the pretty young girl whose father he had known.

So Jessie did not have to pretend very hard at being "as gay as a lark" when she got home and showed her treasures. Laura was so happy over the unexpected gifts that the dinner of bread and milk and grapes was quite a picnic; and Jessie found a smile on her face when she went to dress for her party.

It was only a child's party at the house of one of Mademoiselle's pupils, and Jessie was merely invited to help the little people through their dancing. She did not like to go in this way, as she was sure to meet familiar faces there, full of the pity, curiosity, or indifference so hard for a girl to bear. But Mademoiselle asked it as a favor, and Jessie was grateful; so she went, expecting no pleasure and certain of much weariness, if not annoyance.

When she was ready, - and it did not take long to slip on the white woollen dress, brush out the curly dark hair, and fold up slippers and gloves, - she stood before her glass looking at herself, quite conscious that she was very pretty, with her large eyes, blooming cheeks, and the lofty little air which nothing could change. She was also painfully conscious that her dress was neither fresh nor becoming without a bit of ribbon or a knot of flowers to give it the touch of color it needed. She had an artistic eye, and used to delight in ordering charming costumes for herself in the happy days when all her wishes were granted as if fairies still lived. She tossed over her very small store of ribbons in vain; everything had been worn till neither beauty nor freshness remained.

"Oh dear! where CAN I find something to make me look less like a nun, - and a very shabby one, too?" she said, longing for the pink corals she sold to pay Laura's doctor's bill.

The sound of a soft tap, tap, tap, startled her, and she ran to open the door. No one was there but Laura, fast asleep on the sofa. Tap, tap, tap! went the invisible hand; and as the sound seemed to come from the window, Jessie glanced that way, thinking her tame dove had corne to be fed. Neither hungry dove nor bold sparrow appeared, - only a spray of Japanese ivy waving in the wind. A very pretty spray it was, covered with tiny crimson leaves; and it tapped impatiently, as if it answered her question by saying, "Here is a garland for you; come and take it."

Jessie's quick eye was caught at once by the fine color, and running to the window she looked out as eagerly as if a new idea had come into her head. It was a dull November day, and the prospect of sheds, ash-barrels, and old brooms was a gloomy one; but the whole back of the house glowed with the red tendrils of the hardy vine that clung to and covered the dingy bricks with a royal mantle, as if eager to cheer the eyes and hearts of all who looked. It preached a little sermon of courage, aspiration, and content to those who had the skill to read it, and bade them see how, springing from the scanty soil of that back yard full of the commonest objects, the humblest work, it set its little creepers in the crannies of the stone, and struggled up to find the sun and air, till it grew strong and beautiful, - making the blank wall green in summer, glorious in autumn, and a refuge in winter, when it welcomed the sparrows to the shelter of its branches where the sun lay warmest.

Jessie loved this beautiful neighbor, and had enjoyed it all that summer, - the first she ever spent in the hot city. She felt the

Louisa May Alcott

grace its greenness gave to all it touched, and half unconsciously imitated it in trying to be brave and bright, as she also climbed up from the dismal place where she seemed shut away from everything lovely, till she was beginning to discover that the blue sky was over all, the sun still shone for her, and heaven's fresh air kissed her cheeks as kindly as ever. Many a night she had leaned from the high window when Laura was asleep, dreaming innocent dreams, living over her short past, or trying to look into the future bravely and trustfully. The little vine had felt warmer drops than rain or dew fall on it when things went badly, had heard whispered prayers when the lonely child asked the Father of the fatherless for help and comfort, had peeped in to see her sleeping peacefully when the hard hour was over, and been the first to greet her with a tap on the window-pane as she woke full of new hope in the morning. It seemed to know all her moods and troubles, to be her friend and confidante, and now came with help like a fairy godmother when our Cinderella wanted to be fine for the little ball.

"Just the thing! Why didn't I think of it? So bright and delicate and becoming? It will last better than flowers; and no one can think I'm extravagant, since it costs nothing."

As she spoke, Jessie was gathering long sprays of the rosy vine, with its glossy leaves so beattifully shaded that it was evident Jack Frost had done his best for it. Going to her glass, she fastened a wreath of the smallest leaves about her head, set a cluster of larger ones in her bosom, and then surveyed herself with girlish pleasure, as well she might; for the effect of the simple decoration was charming. Quite satisfied now, she tied on her cloud and slipped away without waking Laura, little dreaming what good fortune the ivy spray was to bring them both.

She found the children prancing with impatience to begin their ballet, much excited by the music, gaslight, and gay dresses, which made it seem like "a truly ball." All welcomed Jessie, and she soon forgot the cheap slippers, mended gloves, and old dress, as she gayly led her troop through the pretty dance with so much grace and skill that the admiring mammas who lined the walls declared it was the sweetest thing they ever saw.

"Who is that little person?" asked one of the few gentlemen who hovered about the doorways.

His hostess told Jessie's story in a few words, and was surprised to hear him say in a satisfied tone, -

"I'm glad she is poor. I want her head, and now there is some chance of getting it."

"My dear Mr. Vane, what DO you mean?" asked the lady, laughing.

"I came to study young faces; I want one for a picture, and that little girl with the red leaves is charming. Please present me."

"No use; you may ask for her hand by-and-by, if you like, but not for her head. She is very proud, and never would consent to sit as a model, I'm sure."

"I think I can manage it, if you will kindly give me a start."

"Very well. The children are just going down to supper, and Miss Delano will rest. You can make your bold proposal now, if you dare."

A moment later, as she stood watching the little ones troop away, Jessie found herself bowing to the tall gentleman, who begged to know what he could bring her with as much interest as if she had been the finest lady in the room. Of course she chose ice-cream, and slipped into a corner to rest her tired feet, preferring the deserted parlor to the noisy dining-room, - not being quite sure where she belonged now.

Mr. Vane brought her a salver full of the dainties girls best love, and drawing up a table began to eat and talk in such a simple, comfortable way that Jessie could not feel shy, but was soon quite at her ease. She knew that he was a famous artist, and longed to tell him about poor Laura, who admired his pictures so much and would have enjoyed every moment of this chance interview. He was not a very young man, nor a handsome one, but he had a genial face, and the friendly manners which are so charming; and in ten minutes Jessie was chatting freely, quite unconscious that the artist was studying her in a mirror all the while. They naturally talked of the children, and after praising the pretty dance Mr. Vane quietly added, -

"I've been trying - to find a face among them for a picture I'm doing; but the little dears are all too young, and I must look elsewhere for a model for my wood-nymph."

"Are models hard to find?" asked Jessie, eating her ice with the relish of a girl who does not often taste it.

"What I want is very hard to find. I can get plenty of beggar-girls, but this must be a refined face, young and blooming, but with poetry in it; and that does not come without a different training from any my usual models get. It will be difficult to suit me, for I'm in a hurry and don't know where to look," - which last sentence was not quite true, for the long glass showed him exactly what he wanted.

"I help Mademoiselle with her classes, and she has pupils of all ages; perhaps you could find some one there."

Jessie looked so interested that the artist felt that he had begun well, and ventured a step further as he passed the cake-basket for the third time.

"You are very kind; but the trouble there is, that I fear none of the young ladies would consent to sit to me if I dared to ask them. I will confide to you that I HAVE seen a head which quite suits me; but I fear I cannot get it. Give me your advice, please. Should you think this pretty creature would be offended, if I made the request most respectfully?"

"No, indeed; I should think she would be proud to help with one of your pictures, sir. My sister thinks they are very lovely; and we kept one of them when we had to sell all the rest," said Jessie, in her eager, frank way.

"That was a beautiful compliment, and I am proud of it. Please tell her so, with my thanks. Which was it?"

"The woman's head, - the sad, sweet one people call a Madonna. We call it Mother, and love it very much, for Laura says it is like our mother. I never saw her, but my sister remembers the dear face very well."

Jessie's eyes dropped, as if tears were near; and Mr. Vane said, in a voice which showed he understood and shared her feeling, -

"I am very glad that anything of mine has been a comfort to you. I thought of my own mother when I painted that picture years ago; so you see you read it truly, and gave it the right name. Now, about the other head; you think I may venture to propose the idea to its owner, do you?"

"Why not, sir? She would be very silly to refuse, I think."

"Then YOU wouldn't be offended if asked to sit in this way?"

"Oh, no. I've sat for Laura many a time, and she says I make a very good model. But then, she only paints simple little things that I am fit for."

"That is just what I want to do. Would you mind asking the young lady for me? She is just behind you."

Jessie turned with a start, wondering who had come in; but all she saw was her own curious face in the mirror, and Mr.

Vane's smiling one above it.

"Do you mean me?" she cried, so surprised and pleased and half ashamed that she could only blush and laugh and look prettier than ever.

"Indeed I do. Mrs. Murray thought the request would annoy you; but I fancied you would grant it, you wore such a graceful little garland, and seemed so interested in the pictures here."

"It is only a bit of ivy, but so pretty I wanted to wear it, as I had nothing else," said the girl, glad that her simple ornament found favor in such eyes.

"It is most artistic, and caught my eye at once. I said to myself,' That is the head I want, and I MUST secure it if possible.' Can I?" asked Mr. Vane, smiling persuasively as he saw what a frank and artless young person he had to deal with.

"With pleasure, if Laura doesn't mind. I'll ask her, and if she is willing I shall be very proud to have even my wreath in a famous picture," answered Jessie, so full of innocent delight at being thus honored that it was a pretty sight to see.

"A thousand thanks! Now I can exult over Mrs. Murray, and get my palette ready. When can we begin? As your sister is an invalid and cannot come to my studio with you, perhaps you will allow me to make my sketch at your own house," said Mr. Vane, as pleased with his success as only a perplexed artist could be.

"Did Mrs. Murray tell you about us?" asked Jessie quickly, as her smiles faded away and the proud look came into her face; for she was sure their misfortunes were known, since he spoke of poor Laura's health.

"A little," began the new friend, with a sympathetic glance.

"I know models are paid for sitting; did you wish to do it with me because I'm poor?" asked Jessie, with an irrepressible frown and a glance at the thrice-cleaned dress and the neatly mended gloves.

Mr. Vane knew what thorn pricked the sensitive little girl, and answered in his friendliest tone, -

"I never thought of such a thing. I wanted YOU to help ME, because I am poor in what artists so much need, - real grace and beauty. I hoped you would allow me to give your sister a copy of the sketch as a token of my gratitude for four great kindness."

The frown vanished and the smile returned as the soft answer turned away Jessie's wrath and made her hasten to say penitently, -

"I was very rude; but I haven't learned to be humble yet, and often forget that I am poor. Please come to us any time. Laura will enjoy seeing you work, and be delighted with anything you give her. So shall I, though I don't deserve it."

"I won't punish you by painting the frown that quite frightened me just now, but do my best to keep the happy face, and so heap coals of fire on your head. They won't burn any more than the pretty red leaves that brought me this good fortune," answered the artist, seeing that his peace was made.

"I'm SO glad I wore them!" and as if trying to make amends for her little flash of temper, Jessie told him about the ivy, and how she loved it, - unconsciously betraying more of her pathetic little story than she knew, and increasing her hearer's interest in his new model.

The children came back in riotous spirits, and Jessie was called to lead the revels again. But now her heart was as light as her heels; for she had something pleasant to think of, - a hope of help for Laura, and the memory of kind words to make hard duties easier. Mr. Vane soon slipped away, promising to come the next day; and at eight o'clock Jessie ran home to tell her sister the good news, and to press the little wreath which had served her so well.

With the sanguine spirit of girlhood, she felt sure that something delightful would happen, and built fine castles in the air for her sister, with a small corner for herself, where she could watch Laura bloom into a healthy woman and a great artist. The desire of Jessie's heart was to earn eneugh money to enable them to spend a month or two at the seashore when summer came, as that was the surest cure for Laura's weak nerves and muscles. She had cherished the wild idea of being a ballet-girl, as dancing was her delight; but every one frowned upon that plan, and her own refined nature told her that it was not the life for a young girl. Mr. Vane's request for her head suggested a splendid hope; and after getting angry with him for hinting at her being a model, she suddenly decided to try it, - with the charming inconsistency of her sex. The more she thought of it, the better she liked the idea, and resolved to ask her new friend all about it, fondly hoping that much money could be made in this way.

She said nothing to her sister, but while she sat patiently to Mr. Vane when he came next day, she asked many questions; and though somewhat discouraged by his replies, confided to him her hopes and begged his advice. Being a wise man as well as a good and kindly one, he saw at once that this life would not be safe for the pretty, impulsive, and tenderly reared girl, left so unprotected in a world full of trials and temptations. So he told her it would not do, except so far as she would allow him to make several studies of her head in various characters and pay for them.

She consented, and though much disappointed found some consolation in hoarding a part of the handsome sum so earned for the desire of her heart.

The artist seemed in no haste to finish his work, and for some weeks came often to the sittings in that quiet room; for it grew more and more attractive to him, and while he painted the younger sister's changeful face he studied the beautiful nature of the elder and learned to love it. But no one guessed that secret for a long time; and Jessie was so busy racking her brain for a way to earn more money that she was as blind and deaf to much that went on before her as if she had been a wooden dummy.

Suddenly, when she least expected it, help came, and in such a delightful way that she long remembered the little episode with girlish satisfaction. One day as she sat wearily waiting till the dressing-room was cleared of maids and children after the dancing-class was over, a former friend came sauntering up to her, saying In the tone which always nettled Jessie, -

"You poor thing! aren't you tired to death trying to teach these stupid babies?"

"No; I love to dance, and we had new figures to-day. See! isn't this pretty?" and Jessie, who knew her own skill and loved to display it, twirled away as lightly as if her feet were not aching with two hours of hard work.

"Lovely! I do wish I ever could learn to keep time and not jerk and bounce. Being plump is a dreadful trial," sighed Fanny Fletcher, as Jessie came back beaming and breathless.

"Perhaps I can teach you. I think of making this my profession since I must do something. Mademoiselle earns heaps of money by it," she said, sitting down to rest, resolved not to be ashamed of her work or to let Fanny pity her,

"I wish you COULD teach me, for I know I shall disgrace myself at the Kirmess. You've heard about it, of course? So sorry you can't take a part, for it's going to be great fun and very splendid. I am in the Hungarian dance, and it's one of the hardest; but the dress is lovely, and I would be in it. Mamma is the matron of it; so I had my way, though I know the girls don't want me, and the boys make fun of me. Just see if this isn't the queerest step you ever beheld!"

Fanny started bravely across the wide smooth floor, with a stamp, a slide, and a twirl which was certainly odd, but might have been lively and graceful if she had not unfortunately been a very plump, awkward girl, with no more elasticity than a feather-bed. Jessie found it impossible not to laugh when Fanny ended her display with a sprawl upon the floor, and sat rubbing her elbows in an attitude of despair.

"I know that dance! It is the tzardas, and I can show you how it should be done. Jump up and try it with me!" she said good-naturedly, running to help her friend up, glad to have a partner of her own size for once.

Away they went, but soon stopped; for Fanny could not keep step, and Jessie pulled and stamped and hummed in vain.

"Do it alone; then I can see how it goes, and manage better next time," panted the poor girl, dropping down upon the velvet seat which ran round the hall.

Mademoiselle had come in and watched them for a moment. She saw at once what was needed, and as Mrs. Fletcher was one of her best patrons, she was glad to oblige the oldest daughter; so she went to the piano and struck up the proper air just as Jessie, with one arm on her hip, the other on the shoulder of an invisible partner, went down the hall with a martial stamp, a quick slide, and a graceful turn, in perfect time to the stirring music that made her nerves tingle and her feet fly. To and fro, round and round, with all manner of graceful gestures, intricate steps, and active bounds went the happy girl, quite carried away by the music and motion of the pastime she loved so much.

Fanny clapped her hands with admiration, and Mademoiselle cried, "Bien, tres bien, charmante, ma cherie!" as she paused at last, rosy and smiling, with one hand on her heart and the other at her temple with the salute that closed the dance.

"I MUST learn it! Do come and give me lessons at our house. I called for Maud and must go now. Will you come, Jessie? I'll be glad to pay you if you don't mind. I hate to be laughed at; and I know if some one would just help me alone I should do as well as the rest, for Professor Ludwig raves at us all."

Fanny seemed in such a sad strait, and Jessie sympathized so heartily with her, that she could not refuse a request which flattered her vanity and tempted her with a prospect of some addition to the "Sister-fund," as she called her little savings. So she graciously consented, and after a few laborious lessons prospered so well that her grateful pupil proposed to several other unsuccessful dancers in the set to invite Jessie to the private rehearsals held in various parlors as the festival drew near.

Some of these young people knew Jessie Delano, had missed the bright girl, and gladly welcomed her back when, after much persuasion, she agreed to go and help them with the difficult figures of the tzardas. Once among them she felt in her element, and trained the awkward squad so well that Professor Ludwig complimented them on their improvement at the public rehearsals, and raved no more, to the great delight of the timid damsels, who lost their wits when the fiery little man shouted and wrung his hands over their mistakes.

The young gentlemen needed help also, as several of them looked very much like galvanized grasshoppers in their efforts to manage long legs or awkward elbows. Jessie willingly danced with them, and showed them how to move with grace and spirit, and handle their partners less like dolls and more like peasant maidens with whom the martial Hungarians were supposed to be disporting themselves at the fair. Merry meetings were these; and all enjoyed them, as young people do whatever is lively, dramatic, and social. Every one was full of the brilliant Kirmess, which was the talk of the city, and to which every one intended to go as actor or spectator. Jessie was sadly tempted to spend three of her cherished dollars for a ticket, and perhaps would have done so if there had been any one to take care of her. Laura could not go, and Mr. Vane was away; no other friend appeared, and no one remembered to invite her, so she bravely hid her girlish longing, and got all the pleasure out of the rehearsals that she could.

At the last of these, which was a full-dress affair at Fanny's house, something happened which not only tried Jessie's temper sorely, but brought her a reward for many small sacrifices. So much dancing was very hard upon her slippers, the new pair were worn out long ago, and a second pair were in a dangerous condition; but Jessie hoped that they would last that evening, and then she would indulge in better ones with what Fanny would pay her. She hated to take it, but her salary at Mademoiselle's was needed at home; all she could spare from other sources was sacredly kept for Laura's jaunt, and only now and then did the good little girl buy some very necessary article for herself. She was learning to be humble, to love work, and be grateful for her small wages for her sister's sake; and while she hid her trials, withstood her temptations, and bravely tugged away at her hard tasks, the kind Providence, who teaches us the sweetness of adversity, was preparing a more beautiful and helpful surprise than any she could plan or execute.

That night all were much excited, and great was the energy displayed as the scarlet, blue, and silver couples went through the rapid figures with unusual spirit and success. The brass-heeled boots stamped in perfect time, the furred caps waved, and the braided jackets glittered as the gay troop swung to and fro or marched to the barbaric music of an impromptu band. Jessie looked on with such longing in her eyes that Fanny, who was ill with a bad cold, kindly begged her to take her place, as motion made her cough, and putting on the red and silver cap sent her joyfully away to lead them all.

The fun grew rather fast and furious toward the end, and when the dance broke up there lay in the middle of the floor a shabby little slipper, burst at the side, trodden down at the heel, and utterly demoralized as to the bow with a broken buckle in it. Such a disreputable little shoe was it that no one claimed it when one of the young men held it up on the point of his sword, exclaiming gayly, -

"Where is Cinderella? Here's her shoe, and it's quite time she had a new pair. Glass evidently doesn't wear well now-a-days."

They all laughed and looked about to find the shoeless foot. The girls with small feet displayed them readily; those less blessed hid them at once, and no Cinderella appeared to claim the old slipper. Jessie turned as red as her cap, and glanced imploringly at Fanny as she slipped through a convenient door and flew up-stairs, knowing that in a moment all would see that it must be hers, since the other girls wore red boots as a part of their costume.

Fanny understood; and though awkward and slow with her feet, she was kind-hearted and quick to spare her friend the mortification which a poor and proud girl could not help feeling at such a moment. The unfortunate slipper was flying from hand to hand as the youths indulged in a boyish game of ball to tease the laughing girls, who hastened to disclaim all knowledge of "the horrid thing."

"Please give it to me!" cried Fanny, trying to catch it, and glad Jessie was safe.

"No; Cinderella must come and put it on. Here's the Prince all ready to help her," said the finder of the shoe, holding it up.

"And here are lots of proud sisters ready to cut off their toes and heels if they could only get on such a small slipper," added another young Mygar, enjoying the fun immensely.

"Listen, and let me tell you something. It's Jessie Delano's, and she has run away because she lost it. Don't laugh and make fun of it, because it was worn out in helping us. You all know what a hard time she has had, but you don't know how good and brave and patient she is, trying to help poor Laura and to earn her living. I asked her to teach me, and I shall pay her well for it, because I couldn't have gone on if she hadn't. If any of you feel as grateful as I do, and as sorry for her, you can show it in any kind way you please, for it must be dreadful to be so poor."

Fanny had spoken quickly, and at the last Words hid the tremble in her voice with a cough, being rather scared at what she had done on the impulse of the moment. But it was a true impulse, and the generous young hearts were quick to answer it. The old slipper was respectfully handed to her with many apologies and various penitent suggestions. None were adopted just then, however, for Fanny ran off to find Jessie with her things on waiting - for a chance to slip away unseen. No persuasions would keep her to supper; and at last, with many thanks, she was allowed to go, while Fanny returned to lay plans with her guests as they disturbed their digestions with lobster salad, ice-cream, and strong coffee.

Feeling more than ever like Cinderella as she hurried out into the winter night, leaving all the good times behind her, Jessie stood waiting for a car on the windy street-corner, with the ragged slippers under her arm, tears of weariness and vexation in her eyes, and a resentful feeling against an unjust fate lying heavy at her heart. The glimpses of her old gay, easy life, which these rehearsals had given her, made the real hardship and loneliness of her present life all the more irksome, and that night she felt as if she could not bear it much longer. She longed with all a girl's love of gayety to go to the Kirmess, and no one thought to invite her. She could not go alone even if she yielded to temptation and spent her own money. Laura would have to hire a carriage if she ventured to try it; so it was impossible, for six or seven dollars was a fortune to the poor girls now. To have been one of the happy creatures who were to take part in it, to dance on the green in a dainty costume to the music of a full band, - to see and do and enjoy all the delights of those two enchanting evenings, would have filled Jessie's cup to overflowing. But since she might as well cry for the moon she tried to get some comfort out of imagining it all as she rumbled home in a snowstorm, and cried herself to sleep after giving Laura a cheerful account of the rehearsal, omitting the catastrophe.

The sun shone next morning, hope woke again, and as she dressed Jessie sung to keep her heart up, still trusting that some one would remember her before the day was over. As she opened her windows the sparrows welcomed her with shrill chirpings, and the sun turned the snow-covered vine to a glittering network very beautiful to see as it hung like a veil of lace over the dingy wall. Jessie smiled as she saw it, while taking a long breath of the keen air, feeling cheered and refreshed by these familiar comforters; then with a brave, bright glance up at the clear blue sky she went away to the day's duties, little guessing what pleasant surprises were on their way to reward her for the little sacrifices which were teaching her strength, patience, and courage for greater ones by-and-by.

All the morning she listened eagerly for the bell, but nothing came; and at two o'clock she went away to the dancing-class, saying to herself with a sigh, -

"Every one is so busy, it is no wonder I'm forgotten. I shall hear about the fun in the papers, and try to be contented with that."

Though she never felt less like dancing, she was very patient with her little pupils, and when the lesson was over sat resting a moment, with her head still full of the glories of the Kirmess. Suddenly Mademoiselle came to her, and in a few kind words gave her the first of the pleasant surprises by offering her a larger salary, an older class, and many commendations for her skill and faithfulness. Of course she gratefully accepted the welcome offer, and hurried home to tell Laura, forgetting her heavy heart, tired feet, and disappointed hopes.

At her own door the second surprise stood waiting for her, in the person of Mrs. Fletcher's servant with a large box and a note from Miss Fanny. How she ever got herself and her parcel up the long stairs Jessie never knew, she was in such a frantic hurry to see what that vast box could contain. She startled her sister by bursting into the room breathless, flushed, and beaming, with the mysterious cry of, -

"Scissors! quick, the scissors!"

Off went cords and papers, up flew the cover, and with a shriek of rapture Jessie saw the well-known Hungarian costume lying there before her. What it all meant she could not guess, till she tore open the note and read these delightful words: -

DEAR JESS, - My cold is worse, and the doctor won't let me go to-night. Isn't it dreadful? Our dance will be ruined unless you will take my place. I know you will to oblige us, and have a lovely time. Every one will be glad, you do it so much better than I can. My dress will fit you, with tucks and reefs here and there; and the hoots won't be much too large, for though I'm fat I have small feet, thank goodness! Mamma will call for you at seven, and bring you safely home; and you must come early to-morrow and tell me all about it.

In the small box you will find a little token of our gratitude to you for your kindness in helping us all so much. Yours ever,

FAN.

As soon as Jessie could get her breath and recover from this first delightful shock, she opened the dainty parcel carefully tied up with pink ribbons. It proved to be a crystal slipper, apparently full of rosebuds; but under the flowers lay five-and-twenty shining gold dollars. A little card with these words was tucked in one corner, as if, with all their devices to make the offering as delicate and pretty as possible, the givers feared to offend: -

"We return to our dear Princess the glass slipper which she lost at the ball, full of thanks and good wishes."

If the kind young persons who sent the fanciful gift could have seen how it was received, their doubts would soon have been set at rest; for Jessie laughed and cried as she told the story, counted the precious coins, and filled the pretty shoe with water that the buds might keep fresh for Laura. Then, while the needles flew and the gay garments were fitted, the happy voices talked and the sisters rejoiced together over this unexpected pleasure as only loving girls could do.

"The sweetest part of all the splendid surprise is that they remembered me just at the busiest time, and thanked me in such a lovely way. I shall keep that glass slipper all my life, if I can, to remind me not to despair; for just when everything seemed darkest, all this good luck came," said Jessie, with ecstatic skips as she clanked the brass heels of her boots and thought of the proud moment when she would join in the tzardas before all Boston.

Gentle Laura rejoiced and sympathized heartily, sewed like a busy bee, and sent her happy sister away at seven o'clock with her sweetest smile, never letting her suspect what tender hopes and fears were hidden in her own heart, what longing and disappointment made her days doubly sad and lonely, or how very poor a consolation all the glories of the Kirmess would be for the loss of a friend who had grown very near and dear to her.

No need to tell the raptures of that evening to little Jessie, who enjoyed every moment, played her part well, and was brought home at midnight ready to begin all over again, so inexhaustible is youth's appetite for pleasure.

To her great surprise, Laura was up and waiting to welcome her, with a face so full of a new and lovely happiness that Jessie guessed at once some good fortune had come to her also. Yes, Laura's well-earned reward and beautiful surprise had arrived at last; and she told it all in a few words as she held out her arms exclaiming, -

"He has come back! He loves me, and I am so happy! Dear little sister, all your hard times are over now, and you shall have a home again."

So the dreams came true, as they sometimes do even in this work-a-day world of ours, when the dreamers strive as well as hope, and earn their rewards.

Laura had a restful summer at the seaside, with a stronger arm than Jessie's to lean upon, and more magical medicine to help her back to health than any mortal doctor could prescribe. Jessie danced again with a light heart, - for pleasure, not for pay, - and found the new life all the sweeter for the trials of the old one. In the autumn there was a quiet wedding, before three very happy people sailed away to Italy, the artist's heaven on earth.

"No roses for me," said Jessie, smiling at herself in the mirror as she fastened a spray of rosy ivy-leaves in the bosom of her fresh white gown that October morning. "I'll be true to my old friend; for it helped me in my dark days, and now it shall rejoice with me in my bright ones, and go on teaching me to climb bravely and patiently toward the light"

PANSIES

They are never alone that are accompanied with noble thoughts. - SIR PHILIP SIDNEY.

"I'VE finished my book, and now what CAN I do till this tiresome rain is over?" exclaimed Carrie, as she lay back on the couch with a yawn of weariness.

"Take another and a better book; the house is full of them, and this is a rare chance for a feast on the best," answered Alice, looking over the pile of volumes in her lap, as she sat on the floor before one of the tall book-cases that lined the room.

"Not being a book-worm like you, I can't read forever, and you needn't sniff at 'Wanda,' for it's perfectly thrilling!" cried Carrie, regretfully turning the crumpled leaves of the Seaside Library copy of that interminable and impossible tale.

"We should read to improve our minds, and that rubbish is only a waste of time," began Alice, in a warning tone, as she looked up from "Romola," over which she had been poring with the delight one feels in meeting an old friend.

"I don't WISH to improve my mind, thank you: I read for amusement in vacation time, and don't want to see any moral works till next autumn. I get enough of them in school. This isn't 'rubbish'! It's full of fine descriptions of scenery -"

"Which you skip by the page, I've seen you do it," said Eva, the third young girl in the library, as she shut up the stout book on her knee and began to knit as if this sudden outburst of chat disturbed her enjoyment of "The Dove in the Eagle's Nest."

"I do at first, being carried away by my interest in the people, but I almost always go back and read them afterward," protested Carrie. "You know YOU like to hear about nice clothes, Eva, and Wanda's were simply gorgeous; white velvet and a rope of pearls is one costume; gray velvet and a silver girdle another; and Idalia was all a 'shower of perfumed laces,' and scarlet and gold satin mask dresses, or primrose silk with violets, so lovely! I do revel in 'em!"

Both girls laughed as Carrie reeled off this list of elegances, with the relish of a French modiste.

"Well, I'm poor and can't have as many pretty things as I want, so it IS delightful to read about women who wear white quilted satin dressing-gowns and olive velvet trains with Mechlin lace sweepers to them. Diamonds as large as nuts, and rivers of opals and sapphires, and rubies and pearls, are great fun to read of, if you never even get a look at real ones. I don't believe the love part does me a bit of harm, for we never see such languid swells in America, nor such lovely, naughty ladies; and Ouida scolds them all, so of course she doesn't approve of them, and that's moral, I'm sure."

But Alice shook her head again, as Carrie paused out of breath, and said in her serious way: "That's the harm of it all. False and foolish things are made interesting, and we read for that, not for any lesson there may be hidden under the velvet and jewels and fine words of your splendid men and women. Now, THIS book is a wonderful picture of Florence in old times, and the famous people who really lived are painted in it, and it has a true and clean moral that we can all see, and one feels wiser and better for reading it. I do wish you'd leave those trashy things and try something really good."

"I hate George Eliot, - so awfully wise and preachy and dismal! I really couldn't wade through 'Daniel Deronda,' though 'The Mill on the Floss' wasn't bad," answered Carrie, with another yawn, as she recalled the Jew Mordecai's long speeches, and Daniel's meditations.

"I know you'd like this," said Eva, patting her book with an air of calm content; for she was a modest, common-sense little body, full of innocent fancies and the mildest sort of romance. "I love dear Miss Yonge, with her nice, large families, and their trials, and their pious ways, and pleasant homes full of brothers and sisters, and good fathers and mothers. I'm never tired of them, and have read 'Daisy Chain' nine times at least."

"I used to like them, and still think them good for young girls, with our own 'Queechy' and 'Wide, Wide World,' and books of that kind. Now I'm eighteen I prefer stronger novels, and books by great men and women, because these are always talked about by cultivated people, and when I go into society next winter I wish to be able to listen intelligently, and know what to admire."

"That's all very well for you, Alice; you were always poking over books, and I dare say you will write them some day, or be a blue-stocking. But I've got another year to study and fuss over my education, and I'm going to enjoy myself all I can, and leave the wise books till I come out."

"But, Carrie, there won't be any time to read them; you'll be so busy with parties, and beaux, and travelling, and such things. I WOULD take Alice's advice and read up a little now; it's so nice to know useful things, and be able to find help and comfort in good books when trouble comes, as Ellen Montgomery and Fleda did, and Ethel, and the other girls in Miss Yonge's stories," said Eva, earnestly, remembering how much the efforts of those natural little heroines had helped her in her own struggles tor self-control and the cheerful bearing of the burden which come to all.

Louisa May Alcott

"I don't want to be a priggish Ellen, or a moral Fleda, and I do detest bothering about self-improvement all the time. I know I ought, but I'd rather wait another year or two, and enjoy my vanities in peace just a LITTLE longer." And Carrie tucked Wanda under the sofa pillow, as if a trifle ashamed of her society, with Eva's innocent eyes upon her own, and Alice sadly regarding her over the rampart of wise books, which kept growing higher as the eager girl found more and more treasures in this richly stored library.

A little silence followed, broken only by the patter of the rain without, the crackle of the wood fire within, and the scratch of a busy pen from a curtained recess at the end of the long room. In the sudden hush the girls heard it and remembered that they were not alone.

"She must have heard every word we said!" and Carrie sat up with a dismayed face as she spoke in a whisper.

Eva laughed, but Alice shrugged her shoulders, and said tranquilly, "I don't mind. She wouldn't expect much wisdom from school-girls."

This was cold comfort to Carrie, who was painfully conscious of having been a particularly silly school-girl just then. So she gave a groan and lay down again, wishing she had not expressed her views quite so freely, and had kept Wanda for the privacy of her own room.

The three girls were the guests of a delightful old lady, who had know their mothers and was fond of renewing her acquaintance with them through their daughters. She loved young people, and each summer invited parties of them to enjoy the delights of her beautiful country house, where she lived alone now, being the childless widow of a somewhat celebrated man. She made it very pleasant for her guests, leaving them free to employ a part of the day as they liked, providing the best of company at dinner, gay revels in the evening, and a large house full of curious and interesting things to examine at their leisure.

The rain had spoiled a pleasant plan, and business letters had made it necessary for Mrs. Warburton to leave the three to their own devices after lunch. They had read quietly for several hours, and their hostess was just finishing her last letter when fragments of the conversation reached her ear. She listened with amusement, unconscious that they had forgotten her presence, finding the different views very characteristic, and easily explained by the difference of the homes out of which the three friends came.

Alice was the only daughter of a scholarly man and a brilliant woman; therefore her love of books and desire to cultivate her mind was very natural, but the danger in her case would be in the neglect of other things equally important, too varied reading, and a superficial knowledge of many authors rather than a true appreciation of a few of the best and greatest. Eva was one of many children in a happy home, with a busy father, a pious mother, and many domestic cares, as well as joys, already falling to the dutiful girl's lot. Her instincts were sweet and unspoiled, and she only needed to be shown where to find new and better helpers for the real trials of life, when the childish heroines she loved could no longer serve her in the years to come.

Carrie was one of the ambitious yet commonplace girls who wish to shine, without knowing the difference between the glitter of a candle which attracts moths, and the serene light of a star, or the cheery glow of a fire round which all love to gather. Her mother's aims were not high, and the two pretty daughters knew that she desired good matches for them, educated them for that end, and expected them to do their parts when the time came. The elder sister was now at a watering-place with her mother, and Carrie hoped that a letter would soon come telling her that Mary was settled. During her stay with Mrs. Warburton she had learned a good deal, and was unconsciously contrasting the life here with the frivolous one at home, made up of public show and private sacrifice of comfort, dignity, and peace. Here were people who dressed simply, enjoyed conversation, kept up their accomplishments even when old, and were so busy, lovable, and charming, that poor Carrie often felt vulgar, ignorant, and mortified among them, in spite of their fine breeding and kindliness. The society Mrs. Warburton drew about her was the best, and old and young, rich and poor, wise and simple, all seemed genuine, - glad to give or receive, enjoy and rest, and then go out to their work refreshed by the influences of the place and the sweet old lady who made it what it was. The girls would soon begin life for themselves, and it was well that they had this little glimpse of really good society before they left the shelter of home to choose friends, pleasures, and pursuits for themselves, as all young women do when once launched.

The sudden silence and then the whispers suggested to the listener that she had perhaps heard something not meant for her ears; so she presently emerged with her letters, and said, as she came smiling toward the group about the fire, -

"How are you getting through this long, dull afternoon, my dears? Quiet as mice till just now. What woke you up? A battle of the books? Alice looks as if she had laid in plenty of ammunition, and you were preparing to besiege her."

The girls laughed, and all rose, for Madam Warburton was a stately old lady, and people involuntarily treated her with great respect, even in this mannerless age.

"We were only talking about books," began Carrie, deeply grateful that Wanda was safely out of sight.

"And we couldn't agree," added Eva, running to ring the bell for the man to take the letters, for she was used to these little offices at home, and loved to wait on Madam.

"Thanks, my love. Now let us talk a little, if you are tired of reading, and if you like to let me share the discussion. Comparing tastes in literature is always a pleasure, and I used to enjoy talking over books with my girl friends more than anything else."

As she spoke, Mrs. Warburton sat down in the chair which Alice rolled up, drew Eva to the cushion at her feet, and nodded to the others as they settled again, with interested faces, one at the table where the pile of chosen volumes now lay, the other erect upon the couch where she had been practising the poses "full of languid grace," so much affected by her favorite heroines.

"Carrie was laughing at me for liking wise books and wanting to improve my mind. Is it foolish and a waste of time?" asked Alice, eager to convince her friend and secure so powerful an ally.

"No, my dear, it is a very sensible desire, and I wish more girls had it. Only don't be greedy, and read too much; cramming and smattering is as bad as promiscuous novel-reading, or no reading at all. Choose carefully, read intelligently, and digest thoroughly each book, and then you make it your own," answered Mrs. Warburton, quite in her element now, for she loved to give advice, as most old ladies do.

"But how can we know WHAT to read if we mayn't follow our tastes?" said Carrie, trying to be interested and "intelligent" in spite of her fear that a "school-marmy" lecture was in store for her.

"Ask advice, and so cultivate a true and refined taste. I always judge people's characters a good deal by the books they like, as well as by the company they keep; so one should be careful, for this is a pretty good test. Another is, be sure that whatever will not bear reading aloud is not fit to read to one's self. Many young girls ignorantly or curiously take up books quite worthless, and really harmful, because under the fine writing and brilliant color lurks immorality or the false sentiment which gives wrong ideas of life and things which should be sacred. They think, perhaps, that no one knows this taste of theirs; but they are mistaken, for it shows itself in many ways, and betrays them. Attitudes, looks, careless words, and a morbid or foolishly romantic view of certain things, show plainly that the maidenly instincts are blunted, and harm done that perhaps can never be repaired."

Mrs. Warburton kept her eyes fixed upon the tall andirons as if gravely reproving them, which was a great relief to Carrie, whose cheeks glowed as she stirred uneasily and took up a screen as if to guard them from the fire. But conscience pricked her sharply, and memory, like a traitor, recalled many a passage or scene in her favorite books which she could not have read aloud even to that old lady, though she enjoyed them in private. Nothing very bad, but false and foolish, poor food for a lively fancy and young mind to feed on, as the weariness or excitement which always followed plainly proved, since one should feel refreshed, not cloyed, with an intellectual feast.

Alice, with both elbows on the table, listened with wide-awake eyes, and Eva watched the raindrops trickle clown the pane with an intent expression, as if asking herself if she had ever done this naughty thing.

"Then there is another fault," continued Mrs. Warburton, well knowing that her first shot had hit its mark, and anxious to be just. "Some book-loving lassies have a mania for trying to read everything, and dip into works far beyond their powers, or try too many different kinds of self-improvement at once. So they get a muddle of useless things into their heads, instead of well-assorted ideas and real knowledge. They must learn to wait and select; for each age has its proper class of books, and what is Greek to us at eighteen may be just what we need at thirty. One can get mental dyspepsia on meat and wine as well as on ice-cream and frosted cake, you know."

Alice smiled, and pushed away four of the eight books she had selected, as if afraid she had been greedy, and now felt that it was best to wait a little.

Eva looked up with some anxiety in her frank eyes as she said, "Now it is my turn. Must I give up my dear homely books, and take to Ruskin, Kant, or Plato?"

Mrs. Warburton laughed, as she stroked the pretty brown head at her knee.

"Not yet, my love, perhaps never, for those are not the masters you need, I fancy. Since you like stories about every-day people, try some of the fine biographies of real men and women about whom you should know something. You will find their lives full of stirring, helpful, and lovely experiences, and in reading of these you will get courage and hope and faith to bear your own trials as they come. True stories suit you, and are the best, for there we get real tragedy and comedy, and the lessons all must learn."

"Thank you! I will begin at once if you will kindly give me a list of such as would be good for me," cried Eva, with the sweet docility of one eager to be all that is lovable and wise in woman.

"Give us a list, and we will try to improve in the best way. You know what we need, and love to help foolish girls, or you wouldn't be so kind and patient with us," said Alice, going to sit beside Carrie, hoping for much discussion of this, to her, very interesting subject.

"I will, with pleasure; but I read few modern novels, so I may not be a good judge there. Most of them seem very poor stuff, and I cannot waste time even to skim them as some people do. I still like the old-fashioned ones I read as a girl, though you would laugh at them. Did any of you ever read 'Thaddeus of Warsaw'?"

"I have, and thought it very funny; so were 'Evelina' and 'Cecilia.' I wanted to try Smollett and Fielding, after reading some fine essays about them, but Papa told me I must wait," said Alice.

"Ah, my dears, in my day, Thaddeus was our hero, and we thought the scene where he and Miss Beaufort are in the Park a most thrilling one. Two fops ask Thaddeus where he got his boots, and he replies, with withering dignity, 'Where I got my sword, gentlemen.' I treasured the picture of that episode for a long time. Thaddeus wears a hat as full of black plumes as a hearse, Hessian boots with tassels, and leans over Mary, who languishes on the seat in a short-waisted gown, limp scarf, poke bonnet, and large bag, - the height of elegance then, but very funny now. Then William Wallace in 'Scottish Chiefs.' Bless me! we cried over him as much as you do over your 'Heir of Clifton,' or whatever the boy's name is. You wouldn't get through it, I fancy; and as for poor, dear, prosy Richardson, his letter-writing heroines would bore you to death. Just imagine a lover saying to a friend, 'I begged my angel to stay and sip one dish of tea. She sipped one dish and flew.'"

"Now, I'm sure that's sillier than anything the Duchess ever wrote with her five-o'clock teas and flirtations over plum-cake on lawns," cried Carrie, as they all laughed at the immortal Lovelace.

"I never read Richardson, but he couldn't be duller than Henry James, with his everlasting stories, full of people who talk a great deal and amount to nothing. *I* like the older novels best, and enjoy some of Scott's and Miss Edgeworth's better than Howells's, or any of the modern realistic writers, with their elevators, and paint-pots, and every-day people," said Alice, who wasted little time on light literature.

"I'm glad to hear you say so, for I have an old-fashioned fancy that I'd rather read about people as they were, for that is history, or as they might and should be, for that helps us in our own efforts; not as they are, for that we know, and are all sufficiently commonplace ourselves, to be the better for a nobler and wider view of life and men than any we are apt to get, so busy are we earning daily bread, or running after fortune, honor or some other bubble. But I mustn't lecture, or I shall bore you, and forget that I am your hostess, whose duty it is to amuse."

As Mrs. Warburton paused, Carrie, anxious to change the subject, said, with her eyes on a curious jewel which the old lady wore, "I also like true stories, and you promised to tell us about that lovely pin some day. This is just the time for it, - please do."

"With pleasure, for the little romance is quite apropos to our present chat. It is a very simple tale, and rather sad, but it had a great influence on my life, and this brooch is very dear to me."

As Mrs. Warburton sat silent a moment, the girls all looked with interest at the quaint pin which clasped the soft folds of muslin over the black silk dress which was as becoming to the still handsome woman as the cap on her white hair and the winter roses in her cheeks. The ornament was in the shape of a pansy; its purple leaves were of amethyst, the yellow of topaz, and in the middle lay a diamond drop of dew. Several letters were delicately cut on its golden stem, and a guard pin showed how much its wearer valued it.

"My sister Lucretia was a good deal older than I, for the three boys came between," began Mrs. Warburton, still gazing at the fire, as if from its ashes the past rose up bright and warm again. "She was a very lovely and superior girl, and I looked up to her with wonder as well as adoration. Others did the same, and at eighteen she was engaged to a charming man, who would have made his mark had he lived. She was too young to marry then, and Frank Lyman had a fine opening to practise his profession at the South. So they parted for two years, and it was then that he gave her the brooch, saying to her, as she whispered how lonely she should be without him, 'This PENSEE is a happy, faithful THOUGHT of me. Wear it, dearest girl, and don't pine while we are separated. Read and study, write much to me, and remember, "They never are alone that are accompanied with noble thoughts."'"

"Wasn't that sweet?" cried Eva, pleased with the beginning of the tale.

"So romantic!" added Carrie, recalling the "amber amulet" one of her pet heroes wore for years, and died kissing, after he had killed some fifty Arabs in the desert.

"Did she read and study?" asked Alice, with a soft color in her cheek, and eager eyes, for a budding romance was folded away in the depths of her maidenly heart, and she liked a love story.

"I'll tell you what she did, for it was rather remarkable at that day, when girls had little schooling, and picked up accomplishments as they could. The first winter she read and studied at home, and wrote much to Mr. Lyman. I have their letters now, and very fine ones they are, though they would seem old-fashioned to you young things. Curious love letters, - full of advice, the discussion of books, report of progress, glad praise, modest gratitude, happy plans. and a faithful affection that never wavered, though Lucretia was beautiful and much admired, and the dear fellow a great favorite among the brilliant Southern women.

"The second spring, Lucretia, anxious to waste no time, and ambitious to surprise Lyman decided to go and study with old Dr. Gardener at Portland. He fitted young men for college, was a friend of our father's, and had a daughter who was a very wise and accomplished woman. That was a very happy summer, and Lu got on so well that she begged to stay all winter. It was a rare chance, for there were no colleges for girls then, and very few advantages to be had, and the dear creature burned to improve every faculty, that she might be more worthy of her lover. She fitted herself for college with the youths there, and did wonders; for love sharpened her wits, and the thought of that happy meeting spurred her on to untiring exertion. Lyman was expected in May, and the wedding was to be in June; but, alas for the poor girl! the yellow-fever came, and he was one of the first victims. They never met again, and nothing was left her of all that happy time but his letters, his library, and the pansy."

Mrs. Warburton paused to wipe a few quiet tears from her eyes, while the girls sat in sympathetic silence.

"We thought it would kill her, that sudden change from love, hope, and happiness to sorrow, death, and solitude. But hearts don't break, my dears, if they know where to go for strength. Lucretia did, and after the first shock was over found comfort in her books, saying, with a brave, bright look, and the sweetest resignation, 'I must go on trying to be more worthy of him, for we shall meet again in God's good time and he shall see that I do not forget.'

"That was better than tears and lamentation, and the long years that followed were beautiful and busy ones, full of dutiful care for us at home after our mother died, of interest in all the good works of her time, and a steady, quiet effort to improve every faculty of her fine mind, till she was felt to be one of the noblest women in our city. Her influence was wide-spread; all the intelligent people sought her, and when she travelled she was welcome everywhere, for cultivated persons have a free-masonry of their own, and are recognized at once."

"Did she ever marry?" asked Carrie, feeling that no life could be quite successful without that great event.

"Never. She felt herself a widow, and wore black to the day of her death. Many men asked her hand, but she refused them all, and was the sweetest 'old maid' ever seen, - cheerful and serene to the very last, for she was ill a long time, and found her solace and stay still in the beloved books. Even when she could no longer read them, her memory supplied her with the mental food that kept her soul strong while her body failed. It was wonderful to see and hear her repeating fine lines, heroic sayings, and comforting psalms through the weary nights when no sleep would come, making friends and helpers of the poets, philosophers, and saints whom she knew and loved so well. It made death beautiful, and taught me how victorious an immortal soul can be over the ills that vex our mortal flesh.

"She died at dawn on Easter Sunday, after a quiet night, when she had given me her little legacy of letters, books, and the one jewel she had always worn, repeating her lover's words to comfort me. I had read the Commendatory Prayer, and as I finished she whispered, with a look of perfect peace, 'Shut the book, dear, I need study no more; I have hoped and believed, now I shall know;' and so went happily away to meet her lover after patient waiting."

The sigh of the wind was the only sound that broke the silence till the quiet voice went on again, as if it loved to tell the story, for the thought of soon seeing the beloved sister took the sadness from the memory of the past.

"I also found my solace in books, for I was very lonely when she was gone, my father being dead, the brothers married, and home desolate. I took to study and reading as a congenial employment, feeling no inclination to marry, and for many years was quite contented among my books. But in trying to follow in dear Lucretia's footsteps, I unconsciously fitted myself for the great honor and happiness of my life, and curiously enough I owed it to a book."

Mrs. Warburton smiled as she took up a shabby little volume from the table where Alice had laid it, and, quick to divine another romance, Eva said, like a story-loving child, "Do tell about it! The other was so sad."

"This begins merrily, and has a wedding in it, as young girls think all tales should. Well, when I was about thirty-five, I was invited to join a party of friends on a trip to Canada, that being the favorite jaunt in my young days. I'd been studying hard for some years, and needed rest, so I was glad to go. As a good book for an excursion, I took this Wordsworth in my bag. It is full of fine passages, you know, and I loved it, for it was one of the books given to Lucretia by her lover. We had a charming time, and were on our way to Quebec when my little adventure happened. I was in raptures over the grand St. Lawrence as we steamed slowly from Montreal that lovely summer day. I could not read, but sat on the upper deck, feasting my eyes and dreaming dreams as even staid maiden ladies will when out on a holiday. Suddenly I caught the sound of voices in earnest discussion on the lower deck, and, glancing down, saw several gentlemen leaning against the rail as they talked over certain events of great public interest at that moment. I knew that a party of distinguished persons were on board, as my friend's husband, Dr. Tracy, knew some of them, and pointed out Mr. Warburton as one of the rising scientific men of the day. I remembered that my sister had met him years ago, and much admired him both for his own gifts and because he had known Lyman. As other people were listening, I felt no delicacy about doing the same, for the conversation was an eloquent one, and well worth catching. So interested did I become that I forgot the great rafts floating by, the picturesque shores, the splendid river, and leaned nearer and nearer that no word might be lost, till my book slid out of my lap and fell straight down upon the head of one of the gentlemen, giving him a smart blow, and knocking his hat overboard."

"Oh, what DID you do?" cried the girls, much amused at this unromantic catastrophe.

Mrs. Warburton clasped her hands dramatically, as her eyes twinkled and a pretty color came into her cheeks at the memory of that exciting moment.

"My dears, I could have dropped with mortification! What COULD I do but dodge and peep as I waited to see the end of this most untoward accident? Fortunately I was alone on that side of the deck, so none of the ladies saw my mishap and, slipping along the seat to a distant corner, I hid my face behind a convenient newspaper, as I watched the little flurry of fishing up the hat by a man in a boat near by, and the merriment of the gentlemen over this assault of William Wordsworth upon Samuel Warburton. The poor book passed from hand to hand,

and many jokes were made upon the 'fair Helen' whose name was written on the paper cover which projected it.

"'I knew a Miss Harper once, - a lovely woman, but her name was not Helen, and she is dead, - God bless her!' I heard Mr. Warburton say, as he flapped his straw hat to dry it, and rubbed his head, which fortunately was well covered with thick gray hair at that time.

"I longed to go down and tell him who I was, but I had not the courage to face all those men. It really was MOST embarrassing; so I waited for a more private moment to claim my book, as I knew we should not land till night, so there was no danger of losing it.

"'This is rather unusual stuff for a woman to be reading. Some literary lady doubtless. Better look her up, Warburton. You'll know her by the color of her stockings when she comes down to lunch,' said a jolly old gentlenoan, in a tone that made me 'rouge high,' as Evelina says.

"'I shall know her by her intelligent face and conversation, if this book belongs to a lady. It will be an honor and a pleasure to meet a woman who enjoys Wordsworth, for in my opinion he is one of our truest poets,' answered Mr. Warburton, putting the book in his pocket, with a look and a tone that were most respectful and comforting to me just then.

"I hoped he would examine the volume, for Lucretia's and Lyman's names were on the fly leaf, and that would be a delightful introduction for me. So I said nothing and bided my time, feeling rather foolish when we all filed in to lunch, and I saw the other party glancing at the ladies at the table. Mr. Warburton's eye paused a moment as it passed from Mrs. Tracy to me, and I fear I blushed like a girl, my dears, for Samuel had very fine eyes, and I remembered the stout gentleman's unseemly joke about the stockings. Mine were white as snow, for I had a neat foot, and was fond of nice hose and well-made shoes. I am so still, as you see." Here the old lady displayed a small foot in a black silk stocking and delicate slipper, with the artless pride a woman feels, at any age, in one of her best points. The girls gratified her by a murmur of admiration, and, decorously readjusting the folds of her gown, she went on with the most romantic episode of her quiet life.

"I retired to my state-room after lunch to compose myself, and when I emerged, in the cool of the afternoon, my first glance showed me that the hour had come, for there on deck was Mr. Warburton, talking to Mrs. Tracy, with my book in his hand. I hesitated a moment, for in spite of my age I was rather shy, and really it was not an easy thing to apologize to a strange gentle-man for dropping books on his head and spoiling his hat. Men think so much of their hats you know. I was spared embarrassment, however, for he saw me and came to me at once, saying, in the most cordial manner, as he showed the names on the fly leaf of my Wordsworth, 'I am sure we need no other introduction but the names of these two dear friends of ours. I am very glad to find that Miss Helen Harper is the little girl I saw once or twice at your father's house some years ago, and to meet her so pleasantly again.'

"That made everything easy and delightful, and when I had apologized and been laughingly assured that he considered it rather an honor than otherwise to be assaulted by so great a man, we fell to talking of old times, and soon forgot that we were strangers. He was twenty years older than I, but a hand-some man, and a most interesting and excellent one, as we all know. He had lost a young wife long ago, and had lived for science ever since, but it had not made him dry, or cold, or selfish. He was very young at heart for all his wisdom, and enjoyed that holiday like a boy out of school. So did I, and never dreamed that anything would come of it but a pleasant friendship founded on our love for those now dead and gone. Dear me! how strangely things turn out in this world of ours, and how the dropping of that book changed my life! Well, that was our introduction, and that first long conversation was followed by many more equally charming, during the three weeks our parties were much together, as both were taking the same trip, and Dr. Tracy was glad to meet his old friend.

"I need not tell you how delightful such society was to me, nor how surprised I was when, on the last day before we parted, Mr. Warburton, who had answered many questions of mine during these long chats of ours, asked me a very serious one, and I found that I could answer it as he wished. It brought me great honor as well as happiness. I fear I was not worthy of it, but I tried to be, and felt a tender satisfaction in thinking that I owed it to dear Lucretia, in part at least; for my effort to imitate her made me fitter to become a wise man's wife, and thirty years of very sweet companionship was my reward."

As she spoke, Mrs. Warburton bowed her head before the portrait of a venerable old man which hung above the mantelpiece.

It was a pretty, old-fashioned expression of wifely pride and womanly tenderness in the fine old lady, who forgot her own gifts, and felt only humility and gratitude to the man who had found in her a comrade in intellectual pursuits, as well as a helpmeet at home and a gentle prop for his declining years.

The girls looked up with eyes full of something softer than mere curiosity, and felt in their young hearts how precious and honorable such a memory must be, how true and beautiful such a marriage was, and how sweet wisdom might become when it went hand in hand with love.

Alice spoke first, saying, as she touched the worn cover of the little book with a new sort of respect, "Thank you very much! Perhaps I ought not to have taken this from the corner shelves in your sanctum? I wanted to find the rest of the lines Mr. Thornton quoted last night, and didn't stop to ask leave."

"You are welcome, my love, for you know how to treat books. Yes, those in that little case are my precious relics. I keep them all, from my childish hymn-book to my great-grandfather's brass-bound Bible, for by and by when I sit 'Looking towards

Sunset,' as dear Lydia Maria Child calls our last days, I shall lose my interest in other books, and take comfort in these. At the end as at the beginning of life we are all children again, and love the songs our mothers sung us, and find the one true Book our best teacher as we draw near to God."

As the reverent voice paused, a ray of sunshine broke through the parting clouds, and shone full on the serene old face turned to meet it, with a smile that welcomed the herald of a lovely sunset.

"The rain is over; there will be just time for a run in the garden before dinner, girls. I must go and change my cap, for literary ladies should not neglect to look well after the ways of their household and keep themseves tidy, no matter how old they may be." And with a nod Mrs. Warburton left them, wondering what the effect of the conversation would be on the minds of her young guests.

Alice went away to the garden, thinking of Lucretia and her lover, as she gathered flowers in the sunshine. Conscientious Eva took the Life of Mary Somerville to her room, and read diligently for half an hour, that no time might be lost in her new course of study, Carrie sent Wanda and her finery up the chimney in a lively blaze, and, as she watched the book burn, decided to take her blue and gold volume of Tennyson with her on her next trip to Nahant, in case any eligible learned or literary man's head should offer itself as a shining mark. Since a good marriage was the end of life, why not follow Mrs. Warburton's example, and make a really excellent one?

When they all met at dinner-time the old lady was pleased to see a nosegay of fresh pansies in the bosoms of her three youngest guests, and to hear Alice whisper, with grateful eyes, -

"We wear your flower to show you that we don't mean to forget the lesson you so kindly gave us, and to fortify ourselves with 'noble thoughts,' as you and she did."

Louisa May Alcott

WATER-LILIES

A PARTY of people, young and old, sat on the piazza of a seaside hotel one summer morning, discussing plans for the day as they waited for the mail.

"Hullo! here comes Christie Johnstone," exclaimed one of the young men perched on the railing, who was poisoning the fresh air with the sickly scent of a cigarette.

"So 'tis, with 'Flucker, the baddish boy,' in tow, as large as life," added another, with a pleasant laugh as he turned to look.

The new-comers certainly looked somewhat like Charles Reade's picturesque pair, and every one watched them with idle interest as they drew nearer. A tall, robust girl of seventeen, with dark eyes and hair, a fine color on her brown cheek, and vigor in every movement, came up the rocky path from the beach with a basket of lobsters on one arm, of fish on the other, and a wicker tray of water-lilies on her head. The scarlet and silver of the fish contrasted prettily with the dark blue of her rough dress, and the pile of water flowers made a fitting crown for this bonny young fish-wife. A sturdy lad of twelve came lurching after her in a pair of very large rubber boots, with a dilapidated straw hat on the back of his head and a pail on either arm.

Straight on went the girl , never turning head or eyes as she passed the group on the piazza and vanished round the corner, though it was evident that she heard the laugh the last speech produced, for the color deepened in her cheeks and her step quickened. The boy, however, returned the glances bent upon him, and answered the smiles with such a cheerful grin that the youth with the cigarette called out, -

"Good-morning, Skipper! Where do you hail from?"

"Island, yender," answered the boy, with a gesture of his thumb over his shoulder.

"Oh, you are the lighthouse-keeper, are you?"

"No, I ain't; me and Gramper's fishermen now."

"Your name is Flucker Johnstone, and your sister's Christie, I think?" added the youth, enjoying the amusement of the young ladies about him.

"It's Sammy Bowen, and hern's Ruth."

"Have you got a Boaz over there for her?"

"No, we've got a devil-fish, a real whacker."

This unexpected reply produced a roar from the gentlemen, while the boy grinned good-naturedly, though without the least idea what the joke was. Pretty Miss Ellery, who had been told that she had "a rippling laugh," rippled sweetly as she leaned over the railing to ask,

"Are those lilies in your pails? I want some if they are for sale."

"Sister'll fetch 'em round when she's left the lobs. I ain't got none; this is bait for them fellers." And, as if reminded of business by the yells of several boys who had just caught sight of him, Sammy abruptly weighed anchor and ran before the wind toward the stable.

"Funny lot, these natives! Act as if they owned the place and are as stupid as their own fish," said the youth in the white yachting suit, as he flung away his cigarette end.

"Don't agree with you, Fred. I've known people of this sort all my life and a finer set of honest, hardworking, independent men I never met, - brave as lions and tender as women in spite of their rough ways," answered the other young man, who wore blue flannel and had a gold band on his cap.

"Sailors and soldiers always stand by one another; so of course you see the best side of these fellows, Captain. The girls are fine creatures, I grant you; but their good looks don't last long, more's the pity!"

"Few women's would with the life they lead, so full of hard work, suspense, and sorrow. No one knows till one is tried, how much courage and faith it takes to keep young and happy when the men one loves are on the great sea," said quiet, gray-haired lady, as she laid her hand on the knee of the young man in blue with a look that made him smile affectionately at her, with his own brown hand on hers.

"Shouldn't wonder if Ben Bowen was laid up, since the girl brings the fish. He's a fine old fellow. I've been to No Man's Land many a time blue-fishing with him; must ask after him," said an elderly gentleman who was pacing to and fro yearning for the morning papers.

"We might go over to the island and have a chowder-party or a fish-fry some moonlight night. I haven't been here for several years, but it used to be great fun, and I suppose we can do it now," suggested Miss Ellery with the laugh.

"By Jove, we will! And look up Christie; ask her when she comes round," said Mr. Fred, the youthful dude, untwining his languid legs as if the prospect put a little life into him.

"Of course we pay for any trouble we give; these people will do anything for money," began Miss Ellery; but Captain John, as they called the sailor, held up his hand with a warning, "Hush! she's coming," as Ruth's weather-beaten brown hat turned the corner.

She paused a moment to drop the empty baskets, shake her skirts, and put up a black braid that had fallen down; then, with the air of one resolved to do a distasteful task as quickly as possible, she came up the steps, held out the rough basket cover, and said in a clear voice, -

"Would any of the ladies like some fresh lilies? Ten cents a bunch."

A murmur from the ladies expressed their admiration of the beautiful flowers, and the gentlemen pressed forward to buy and present every bunch with gallant haste. Ruth's eyes shone as the money fell into her hand, and several voices begged her to bring more lilies while they lasted.

"I didn't know the darlings would grow in salt water," said Miss Ellery, as she fondly gazed upon the cluster Mr. Fred had just offered her.

"They don't. There's a little fresh-water pond on our island, and they grow there, - only place for miles round;" and Ruth looked at the delicate girl in ruffled white lawn and a mull hat, with a glance of mingled pity for her ignorance and admiration for her beauty.

"How silly of me! I am SUCH a goose;" and Miss Ellery gurgled as she hid her face behind her red parasol.

"Ask about the fish-fry," whispered Mr. Fred, putting his head behind the rosy screen to assure the pretty creature that he didn't know any better himself.

"Oh yes, I will!" and, quite consoled, Miss Ellery called out, "Girl, will you tell me if we can have chower-parties on your rocks as we used to a few seasons ago?"

"If you bring your own fish. Grandpa is sick and can't get 'em
for you."

"We will provide them, but who will cook them for us? It's
such horrid work."

"Any one can fry fish! I will if you want me to;" and Ruth half
smiled, remembering that this girl who shuddered at the idea
of pork and a hot frying-pan, used to eat as heartily as any one
when the crisp brown cunners were served up.

"Very good; then we'll engage you as cook, and come over to-
night if it's clear and our fishing prospers. Don't forget a dozen
of the finest lilies for this lady to-morrow morning. Pay you
now, may not be up;" and Mr. Fred dropped a bright silver
dollar into the basket with a patronizing air, intended to
impress this rather too independent young person with a
proper sense of inferiority.

Ruth quietly shook the money out upon the door-mat, and
said with a sudden sparkle in her black eyes, -

"It's doubtful if I bring any more. Better wait till I do."

"I'm sorry your grandfather is sick. I'll come over and see him
by-and-by, and bring the papers if he would like some," said
the elderly gentleman as he came up with a friendly nod and
real interest in his face.

"Very much, thank you, sir. He is very feeble now;" and Ruth
turned with a bright smile to welcome kind Mr. Wallace, who
had not forgotten the old man.

"Christie has got a nice little temper of her own, and don't
know how to treat a fellow when he wants to do her a favor,"
growled Mr. Fred, pocketing his dollar with a disgusted air.

"She appears to know how to treat a gentleman when HE offers one," answered Blue Jacket, with a twinkle of the eye as if he enjoyed the other's discomfiture.

"Girls of that class always put on airs if they are the least bit pretty, - so absurd!" said Miss Ellery, pulling up her long gloves as she glanced at the brown arms of the fisher maiden.

"Girls of any class like to be treated with respect. Modesty in linsey-woolsey is as sweet as in muslin, my dear, and should be even more admired, according to my old-fashioned way of thinking," said the gray-haired lady.

"Hear! hear!" murmured her sailor nephew with an approving nod.

It was evident that Ruth had heard also, as she turned to go, for with a quick gesture she pulled three great lilies from her hat and laid them on the old lady's lap, saying with a grateful look, "Thank you, ma'am."

She had seen Miss Scott hand her bunch to a meek little governess who had been forgotten, and this was all she had to offer in return for the kindness which is so sweet to poor girls whose sensitive pride gets often wounded by trifles like these.

She was going without her baskets when Captain John swung himself over the railing, and ran after her with them. He touched his cap as he met her, and was thanked with as bright a smile as that the elder gentleman had received; for his respectful "Miss Bowen" pleased her much after the rude "Girl!" and the money tossed to her as if she were a beggar. When he came back the mail had arrived, and all scattered at once, - Mr. Fred to spend the dollar in more cigarettes, and Captain John to settle carefully in his button-hole the water-lily Aunt Mary gave him, before both young men went off to play tennis as if their bread depended on it.

As it bid fair to be a moonlight night, the party of a dozen young people, with Miss Scott and Mr. Wallace to act as matron and admiral of the fleet, set off to the Island about sunset. Fish in abundance had been caught, and a picnic supper provided to be eaten on the rocks when the proper time arrived. They found Sammy, in a clean blue shirt and a hat less like a Feejee headpiece, willing to do the honors of the Island, beaming like a freckled young merman as he paddled out to pull up the boats.

"Fire's all ready for kindlin', and Ruth's slicin' the pertaters. Hope them fish is cleaned?" he added with a face of deep anxiety; for that weary task would fall to him if not already done, and the thought desolated his boyish soul.

"All ready, Sam! Lend a hand with these baskets, and then steer for the lighthouse; the ladies want to see that first," answered Captain John, as he tossed a stray cookie into Sammy's mouth with a smile that caused that youth to cleave to him like a burr all the evening.

The young people scattered over the rocks, and hastened to visit the points of interest before dark. They climbed the lighthouse tower, and paid Aunt Nabby and Grandpa a call at the weather-beaten little house, where the old woman lent them a mammoth coffee-pot, and promised that Ruth would "dish up them fish in good shape at eight punctooal." Then they strolled away to see the fresh-water pond where the lilies grew.

"How curious that such a thing should be here right in the middle of the salt sea!" said one of the girls, as they stood looking at the quiet pool while the tide dashed high upon the rocks all about them.

"Not more curious than how it is possible for anything so beautiful and pure as one of those lilies to grow from the mud at the bottom of the pond. The ugly yellow ones are not so out of place; but no one cares for them, and they smell horridly," added another girl in a reflective tone.

"Instinct sends the white lily straight up to the sun and air, and the strong slender stem anchors it to the rich earth below, out of which it has power to draw the nourishment that makes it so lovely and keeps it spotless - unless slugs and flies and boys spoil it," added Miss Scott as she watched Mr, Fred poke and splash with his cane after a half-closed flower.

"The naughty things have all shut up and spoilt the pretty sight; I'm so disappointed," sighed Miss Ellery, surveying the green buds with great disfavor as she had planned to wear some in her hair and act Undine.

"You must come early in the morning if you want to see them at their best. I've read somewhere that when the sun first strikes them they open rapidly, and it is a lovely sight. I shall try to see it some day if I can get here in time," said Miss Scott.

"How romantic old maids are!" whispered one girl to another.

"So are young ones; hear what Floss Ellery is saying," answered the other; and both giggled under their big hats as they caught these words followed by the rippling laugh, -

"All flowers open and show their hearts when the sun shines on them at the right moment."

"I wish human flowers would," murmured Mr. Fred; and then, as if rather alarmed at his own remark, he added hastily, "I'll get that big lily out there and MAKE it bloom for you."

Trusting to an old log that lay in the pond, he went to the end and bent to pull in the half-shut flower; but this too ardent sun was not to make it blossom, for his foot slipped and down he went up to his knees in mud and water.

"Save him! oh, save him!" shrieked Miss Ellery, clutching Captain John, who was laughing like a boy, while the other lads shouted and the girls added their shrill merriment as poor Fred scrambled to the shore a wreck of the gallant craft that

Louisa May Alcott

had set sail in spotless white.

"What the deuce shall I do?" he asked in a tone of despair as they flocked about him to condole even while they laughed.

"Roll up your trousers and borrow Sam's boots. The old lady will dry your shoes and socks while you are at supper, and have them ready to wear home," suggested Captain John, who was used to duckings and made light of them.

The word "supper" made one carnal-minded youth sniff the air and announce that he smelt "something good;" and at once every one turned toward the picnic ground, like chickens hurrying to the barn at feeding-time. Fred vanished into the cottage, and the rest gathered about the great fire of driftwood fast turning to clear coals, over which Ruth was beginning her long hot task. She wore a big apron, a red handkerchief over her head, had her sleeves rolled up, and was so intent on her work that she merely nodded and smiled as the new-comers greeted her with varying degrees of courtesy.

"She looks like a handsome gypsy, with her dark face and that red thing in the firelight. I wish I could paint her," said Miss Scott, who was very young at heart in spite of her fifty years and gray head.

"So do I, but we can remember it. I do like to see a girl work with a will, even at frying fish. Most of 'em dawdle so at the few things they try to do. There's a piece of energy for you!" and Captain John leaned forward from his rocky seat to watch Ruth, who just then caught up the coffee-pot about to boil over, and with the other hand saved her frying-pan from capsizing on its unsteady bed of coals.

"She is a nice girl, and I'm much interested in her. Mr. Wallace says he will tell us her story by-and-by if we care to hear it. He has known the old man a long time."

"Don't forget to remind him, Aunty. I like a yarn after mess;"

and Captain John went off to bring the first plate of fish to the dear old lady who had been a mother to him for many years.

It was a merry supper, and the moon was up before it ended; for everything "tasted so good" the hearty young appetites sharpened by sea air were hard to satisfy. When the last cunner had vanished and nothing but olives and oyster crackers remained, the party settled on a sloping rock out of range of the fire, and reposed for a brief period to recover from the exertions of the feast, having, like the heroes in the old story, "eaten mightily for the space of an hour."

Mr. Fred in the capacious boots was a never-failing source of amusement, and consequently somewhat subdued. But Miss Ellery consoled him, and much food sustained him till his shoes were dry. Ruth remained to clear up, and Sammy to gorge himself on the remnants of "sweet cake" which he could not bear to see wasted. So, when some one proposed telling stories till they were ready to sing, Mr. Wallace was begged to begin.

"It is only something about this island, but you may like to hear it just now," said the genial old gentleman, settling his handkerchief over his bald head for fear of cold, and glancing at the attentive young faces grouped about him in the moonlight.

"Some twenty years ago there was a wreck over there on those great rocks; you fellows have heard about it, so I'll only say that a very brave sailor, a native of the Port here, swam out with a rope and saved a dozen men and women. I'll call him Sam. Well, one of the women was an English governess, and when the lady she was with went on her way after the wreck, this pretty girl (who by the way was a good deal hurt trying to save the child she had in charge) was left behind to recover, and -"

"Marry the brave sailor of course," cried one of the girls.

"Exactly! and a very happy pair they were. She had no family who wanted her at home; her father had been a clergyman, I believe, and she was well born, but Sam was a fine fellow and earned his living honestly, fishing off the Banks, as half the men do here. Well, they were very happy, had two children, and were saving up a bit, when poor Sam and two brothers were lost in one of the great storms which now and then make widows and orphans by the dozen. It killed the wife; but Sam's father, who kept the lighthouse here then, took the poor children and supported them for ten years. The boy was a mere baby; the girl a fine creature, brave like her father, handsome like her mother, and with a good deal of the lady about her, though every one didn't find it out."

"Ahem!" cried the sharp girl, who began to understand the point of the story now, but would not spoil it, as the others seemed still in the dark, though Miss Scott was smiling, and Captain John staring hard at the old gentleman in the blue silk nightcap.

"Got a fly in your throat?" asked a neighbor; but Kate only laughed and begged pardon for interrupting.

"There's not much more; only that affair was rather romantic, and one can't help wondering how the children turned out. Storms seem to have been their doom, for in the terrible one we had two winters ago, the old lighthouse keeper had a bad fall on the icy rocks, and if it had not been for the girl, the light would have gone out and more ships been lost on this dangerous point. The keeper's mate had gone ashore and couldn't get back for two days, the gale raged so fiercely; but he knew Ben could get on without him, as he had the girl and boy over for a visit. In winter they lived with a friend and went to school at the Port. It would have been all right if Ben hadn't broken his ribs. But he was a stout old salt; so he told the girl what to do, and she did it, while the boy waited on the sick man. For two days and nights that brave creature lived in the tower, that often rocked as if it would come down, while the sleet and snow dimmed the lantern, and sea-birds were beaten to death against the glass. But the light burned steadily, and people said, 'All is well,' as ships steered away in time, when the clear light warned them of danger, and grateful sailors blessed the hands that kept it burning faithfully."

"I hope she got rewarded," cried an eager voice, as the story-teller paused for breath.

"'I only did my duty; that is reward enough,' she said, when some of the rich men at the Port heard of it and sent her money and thanks. She took the money, however, for Ben had to give up the place, being too lame to do the work. He earns his living by fishing now, and puts away most of his pension for the children. He won't last long, and then they must take care of themselves; for the old woman is no relation, and the girl is too proud to hunt up the forgetful English friends, if they have any. But I don't fear for her; a brave lass like that will make her own way anywhere."

"Is that all?" asked several voices, as Mr. Wallace leaned back and fanned himself with his hat.

"That's all of the first and second parts; the third is yet to come. When I know it, I'll tell you; perhaps next summer, if we meet here again."

"Then you know the girl? What is she doing now?" asked Miss Ellery, who had lost a part of the story as she sat in a shadowy nook with the pensive Fred.

"We all know her. She is washing a coffee-pot at this moment, I believe;" and Mr. Wallace pointed to a figure on the beach, energetically shaking a large tin article that shone in the moonlight.

"Ruth? Really? How romantic and interesting!" exclaimed Miss Ellery, who was just of the age, as were most of the other girls, to enjoy tales of this sort and imagine sensational denouements.

"There is a great deal of untold romance in the lives of these toilers of the sea, and I am sure this good girl will find her reward for the care she takes of the old man and the boy. It costs her something, I've discovered, for she wants an education, and could get it if she left this poor place and lived for herself; but she won't go, and works hard to get money for Grandpa's comfort, instead of buying the books she longs for. I think, young ladies, that there is real heroism in cheerfully selling lilies and frying fish for duty's sake when one longs to be studying, and enjoying a little of the youth that comes but once," said Mr. Wallace.

"Oh dear, yes, so nice of her! We might take up a contribution for her when we get home. I'll head the paper with pleasure and give all I can afford, for it must be so horrid to be ignorant at her age. I dare say the poor thing can't even read; just fancy!" and Miss Ellery clasped her hands with a sigh of pity.

"Very few girls can read fit to be heard now-a-days," murmured Miss Scott.

"Don't let them affront her with their money; she will fling it in their faces as she did that donkey's dollar. You see to her in your nice, delicate way, Aunty, and give her a lift if she will let you," whispered Captain John in the old lady's ear.

"Don't waste your pity, Miss Florence. Ruth reads a newspaper better than any woman I ever knew. I've heard her doing it to the old man, getting through shipping news, money-market, and politics in fine style. I wouldn't offer her money if I were you, though it is a kind thought. These people have an honest pride in earning things for themselves, and I respect them for it," added Mr. Wallace.

"Dear me! I should as soon think of a sand skipper having pride as one of these fishy folks in this stupid little place," observed Mr. Fred, moving his legs into the shadow as the creeping moonlight began to reveal the hideous boots.

"Why not? I think they have more to be proud of, these brave, honest, independent people, than many who never earn a cent and swell round on the money their fathers made out of pork, rum, or - any other rather unpleasant or disreputable business," said Captain John, with the twinkle in his eye, as he changed the end of his sentence, for the word "pickles" was on his lips when Aunt Mary's quick touch checked it. Some saucy girl laughed, and Mr. Fred squirmed, for it was well known that his respectable grandfather whom he never mentioned had made his large fortune in a pickle-factory.

"We all rise from the mud in one sense, and all may be handsome flowers if we choose before we go back, after blooming, to ripen our seeds at the bottom of the water where we began," said Miss Scott's refined voice, sounding softly after the masculine ones.

"I like that idea! Thank you, Aunt Mary, for giving me such a pretty fancy to add to my love for water-lilies. I shall remember it, and try to be a lovely one, not a bit ashamed to own that I came from honest farmer stock," exclaimed the thoughtful girl who had learned to know and love the sweet, wise woman who was so motherly to all girls.

"Hear! hear!" cried Captain John, heartily; for he was very proud of his own brave name kept clean and bright through a long line of sailor kin.

"Now let us sing or we shall have no time," suggested Miss Ellery, who warbled as well as rippled, and did not wish to lose this opportunity of singing certain sentimental songs appropriate to the hour.

So they tuned their pipes and made "music in the air" for an hour, to the great delight of Sammy, who joined in every song, and was easily persuaded to give sundry nautical melodies in a shrill small voice which convulsed his hearers with merriment.

"Ruth sings awful well, but she won't afore folks," he said, as he paused after a roaring ditty.

"She will for me;" and Mr. Wallace went slowly up to the rock not far away, where Ruth sat alone listening to the music as she rested after her long day's work.

"Such airs!" said Miss Ellery, in a sharp tone; for her "Wind of the Summer Night" had not gone well, owing to a too copious supper. "Posing for Lorelei," she added, as Ruth began to sing, glad to oblige the kind old gentleman. They expected some queer ballad or droning hymn, and were surprised when a clear sweet voice gave them "The Three Fishers" and "Mary on the Sands of Dee" with a simple pathos that made real music-lovers thrill with pleasure, and filled several pairs of eyes with tears.

"More, please, more!" called Captain John, as she paused; and as if encouraged by the hearty applause her one gift excited, she sang on as easily as a bird till her small store was exhausted.

"I call THAT music," said Miss Scott, as she wiped her eyes with a sigh of satisfaction. "It comes from the heart and goes to the heart, as it should. Now we don't want anything else, and had better go home while the spell lasts."

Most of the party followed her example, and went to thank and say good-night to Ruth, who felt as rich and happy as a queen with the money Mr. Wallace had slipped into her pocket, and the pleasure which even this short glimpse of a higher, happier life had brought her hungry nature.

As the boats floated away, leaving her alone on the shore, she sent her farewell ringing over the water in the words of the old song, "A Life on the Ocean Wave;" and every one joined in it with a will, especially Mr. Wallace and Captain John; and so the evening picnic ended tunefully and pleasantly for all, and was long remembered by several.

After that day many "good times" came to Ruth and Sammy;

and even poor old Grandpa had his share, finding the last summer of his life very smooth sailing as he slowly drifted into port. It seemed quite natural that Captain John, being a sailor, should like to go and read and "yarn" with the old fisherman; so no one wondered when he fell into the way of rowing over to the Island very often with his pocket full of newspapers, and whiling away the long hours in the little house as full of sea smells and salt breezes as a shell on the shore.

Miss Scott also took a fancy to go with her nephew; for, being an ardent botanist, she discovered that the Island possessed many plants which she could not find on the rocky point of land where the hotel and cottages stood. The fresh-water pond was her especial delight, and it became a sort of joke to ask, when she came home brown and beaming with her treasures in tin boxes, bottles, and bunches, -

"Well, Aunt Mary, have you seen the water-lilies bloom yet?" and she always answered with that wise smile of hers, -

"Not yet, but I'm biding my time, and am watching a very fine one with especial interest. When the right moment comes, it will bloom and show its golden heart to me, I hope."

Ruth never quite knew how it came about, but books seemed to find their way to the Island and stay there, to her great delight. A demand for lilies sprang up, and when their day was over marsh-rosemary became the rage. Sammy found a market for all the shells and gulls' wings he could furnish, and certain old curiosities brought from many voyages were sold for sums which added many comforts to the old sailor's last cruise.

Now the daily row to the Point was a pleasure, not a trial, to Ruth, - for Mr. Wallace was always ready with a kind word or gift, the ladies nodded as she passed, and asked how the old Skipper was to-day; Miss Scott often told her to stop at the cottage for some new book or a moment's chat on her way to the boat, and Captain John helped Sammy with his fishing so much that the baskets were always full when they came home.

All this help and friendliness put a wonderful energy and sweetness into Ruth's hard life, and made her work seem light, her patient waiting for freedom easier to bear cheerfully. She sang as she stood over her wash-tub, cheered the long nights of watching with the precious books, and found the few moments of rest that came to her when the day's work was done very pleasant, as she sat on her rock, watching the lights from the Point, catching the sound of gay music as the young people danced, and thinking over the delightful talks she had with Miss Scott. Perhaps the presence of a blue jacket in Grandpa's little bedroom, the sight of a friendly brown face smiling when she came in, and the sonorous murmur of a man's voice reading aloud, added a charm to the girl's humdrum life. She was too innocent and frank to deny that she enjoyed these new friends, and welcomed both with the same eagerness, saw both go with the same regret, and often wondered how she ever had got on without them.

But the modest fisher-maiden never dreamed of any warmer feeling than kindness on the one side and gratitude on the other; and this unconsciousness was her greatest charm, especially to Captain John, who hated coquettes, and shunned the silly girls who wasted time in idle flirtation when they had far better and wholesomer pastimes to enjoy. The handsome sailor was a favorite, being handy at all sorts of fun, and the oldest of the young men at the Point. He was very courteous in his hearty way to every woman he met, from the stateliest dowager to the dowdiest waiter-girl, but devoted himself entirely to Aunt Mary, and seemed to have no eyes for younger fairer faces.

"He must have a sweetheart over the sea somewhere," the damsels said among themselves, as they watched him pace the long piazzas alone, or saw him swinging in his hammock with eyes dreamily fixed on the blue bay before him.

Miss Scott only smiled when curious questions were asked her, and said she hoped John would find his mate some time, for he deserved the best wife in the world, having been a good son and an honest boy for six-and-twenty years.

"What is it, Captain, - a steamer?" asked Mr. Fred, as he came by the cottage one August afternoon, with his usual escort of girls, all talking at once about some very interesting affair.

"Only a sail-boat; no steamers to-day," answered Captain John, dropping the glass from his eye with a start.

"Can you see people on the Island with that thing? We want to know if Ruth is at home, because if she isn't we can't waste time going over," said Miss Ellery, with her sweetest smile.

"I think not. That boat is Sammy's, and as there is a speck of red aboard, I fancy Miss Ruth is with him. They are coming this way, so you can hail them if you like," answered the sailor, with "a speck of red" on his own sunburnt cheek if any one had cared to look.

"Then we'll wait here if we may. We ordered her to bring us a quantity of bulrushes and flowers for our tableaux to-night, and we want her to be Rebecca at the well. She is so dark, and with her hair down, and gold bangles and scarlet shawls, I think she would do nicely. It takes so long to arrange the 'Lily Maid of Astolat' we MUST have an easy one to come just before that, and the boys are wild to make a camel of themselves, so we planned this. Won't you be Jacob or Abraham or whoever the man with the bracelets was?" asked Miss Ellery, as they all settled on the steps in the free-and-easy way which prevailed at the Point.

"No, thank you, I don't act. Used to dance hornpipes in my young days, but gave up that sort of thing some time ago."

"How unfortunate! Every one acts; it's all the fashion," began Miss Ellery, rolling up her blue eyes imploringly.

"So I see; but I never cared much for theatricals, I like natural things better."

"How unkind you are! I quite depended on you for that, since you wouldn't be a corsair."

"Fred's the man for such fun. He's going to startle the crowd with a regular Captain Kidd rig, pistols and cutlasses enough for a whole crew, and a terrific beard."

"I know Ruth won't do it, Floss, for she looked amazed when I showed her my Undine costume, and told her what I wanted the sea-weed for. 'Why, you won't stand before all those folks dressed that way, will you?' she said, "as much scandalized as if she'd never seen a low-necked dress and silk stockings before;" and Miss Perry tossed her head with an air of pity for a girl who could be surprised at the display of a pretty neck and arms and ankles.

"We'll HIRE her, then; she's a mercenary wretch and will do anything for money. I won't be scrambled into my boat in a hurry, and we MUST have Rebecca because I've borrowed a fine pitcher and promised the boys their camel," said Miss Ellery, who considered herself the queen of the place and ruled like one, in virtue of being the prettiest girl there and the richest.

"She has landed, I think, for the boat is off again to the wharf. Better run down and help her with the bulrushes, Fred, and the rest of the stuff you ordered," suggested Captain John, longing to go himself but kept by his duty as host, Aunt Mary being asleep upstairs.

"Too tired. Won't hurt her; she's used to work, and we mustn't pamper her up, as old ladies say," answered Mr. Fred, enjoying his favorite lounge on the grass.

"I wouldn't ask her to act, if you'll allow me to say so," said Captain John, in his quiet way. "That sort of thing might unsettle her and make her discontented. She steers that little craft over there and is happy now; let her shape her own course, and remember it isn't well to talk to the man at the wheel."

Miss Perry stared; Miss Ray, the sharp girl, nodded, and Miss Ellery said petulantly, -

"As if it mattered what SHE thought or said or did! It's her place to be useful if we want her, and we needn't worry about spoiling a girl like that. She can't be any prouder or more saucy than she is, and I shall ask her if only to see the airs she will put on."

As she spoke Ruth came up the sandy path from the beach laden with rushes and weeds, sun-flowers and shells, looking warm and tired but more picturesque than ever, in her blue gown and the red handkerchief she wore since her old hat blew away. Seeing the party on the cottage steps, she stopped to ask if the things were right, and Miss Ellery at once made her request in a commanding tone which caused Ruth to grow very straight and cool and sober all at once, and answer decidedly, -

"I couldn't anyway."

"Why not?"

"Well, one reason is I don't think it's right to act things out of the Bible just to show off and amuse folks."

"The idea of minding!" and Miss Ellery frowned, adding angrily, "We will pay you for it. I find people will do anything for money down here."

"We are poor and need it, and this is our best time to make it. I'd do most anything to earn a little, but not that;" and Ruth looked as proud as the young lady herself.

"Then we'll say no more if you are too elegant to do what WE don't mind at all. I'll pay you for this stuff now, as I ordered it, and you needn't bring me any more. How much do I owe you?" asked the offended beauty, taking out her purse in a pet.

"Nothing. I'm gad to oblige the ladies if I can, for they have been very kind to me. Perhaps if you knew why I want to earn money, you'd understand me better. Grandpa can't last long, and I don't want the town to bury him. I'm working and saving so he can be buried decently, as he wants to be, not like a pauper."

There was something in Ruth's face and voice as she said this, standing there shabby, tired, and heavy-laden, yet honest, dutiful and patient for love's sake, that touched the hearts of those who looked and listened; but she left no time for any answer, for with the last word she went on quickly, as if to hide the tears that dimmed her clear eyes and the quiver of her lips.

"Floss, how could you!" cried Miss Ray, and ran to take the sheaf of bulrushes from Ruth's arms, followed by the rest, all ashamed and repentant now that a word had shown them the hard life going on beside their idle, care-free ones.

Captain John longed to follow, but walked into the house, growling to himself with a grim look, -

"That girl has no more heart than a butterfly, and I'd like to see her squirm on a pin! Poor Ruth! we'll settle that matter, and bury old Ben like an admiral, hang me if we don't!"

He was so busy talking the affair over with Aunt Mary that he did not see the girl flit by to wait for her boat on the beach, having steadily refused the money offered her, though she accepted the apologies in the kindest spirit.

The beach at this hour of the day was left to the nurses and maids who bathed and gossiped while the little people played in the sand or paddled in the sea. Several were splashing about, and one German governess was scolding violently because while she was in the bath-house her charge, a little girl of six, had rashly ventured out in a flat-bottomed tub, as they called the small boats used by the gentlemen to reach the yachts anchored in deep water.

Ruth saw the child's danger at a glance, for the tide was going out, carrying the frail cockleshell rapidly away, while the child risked an upset every moment by stretching her arms to the women on the shore and calling them to help her.

None dared to try, but all stood and wrung their hands, screaming like sea-gulls, till the girl, throwing off shoes and heavy skirt plunged in, calling cheerily, "Sit still! I'll come and get you, Milly!"

She could swim like a fish, but encumbered with her clothes and weary with an unusually hard day's work, she soon found that she did not gain as rapidly as she expected upon the receding boat. She did not lose courage, but a thrill of anxiety shot through her as she felt her breath grow short, her limbs heavy, and the tide sweep her farther and farther from the shore.

"If they would only stop screaming and go for help, I could keep up and push the boat in; but the child will be out presently and then we are lost, for I can't get back with her, I'm afraid."

As these thoughts passed through her mind Ruth was swimming stoutly, and trying by cheerful words to keep the frightened child from risking their main chance of safety. A few more strokes and she would reach the boat, rest a moment, then, clinging to it, push it leisurely to shore. Feeling that the danger was over, she hurried on and was just putting up her hands to seize the frail raft and get her breath when Milly, thinking she was to be taken in her arms, leaned forward. In rushed the water, down went the boat, and out splashed the screaming child to cling to Ruth with the desperate clutch she dreaded.

Louisa May Alcott

Both went under for a moment, but rose again; and with all her wits sharpened by the peril of the moment, Ruth cried, as she kept herself afloat, -

"On my back, quick! quick! Don't touch my arms; hold tight to my hair, and keep still."

Not realizing all the danger, and full of faith in Ruth's power to do anything, after the feats of diving and floating she had seen her perform, Milly scrambled up as often before, and clung spluttering and gasping to Ruth's strong shoulders. So burdened, and conscious of fast-failing strength, Ruth turned toward the shore, and bent every power of mind and body to her task. How far away it seemed! how still the women were, - not one even venturing out a little way to help her, and no man in sight! Her heart seemed to stop beating, her temples throbbed, her breath was checked by the clinging arms, and the child, seemed to grow heavier every moment.

"I'll do what I can, but, oh, why don't some one come?"

That was the last thought Ruth was conscious of, as she panted and ploughed slowly back, with such a set white face and wide eyes fixed on the flag that fluttered from the nearest cottage, that it was no wonder the women grew still as they watched her. One good Catholic nurse fell on her knees to pray; the maids cried, the governess murmured, "Mein Gott, I am lost if the child go drowned!" and clear and sweet came the sound of Captain John's whistle as he stood on his piazza waiting to row Ruth home.

They were nearly in, a few more strokes and she could touch the bottom, when suddenly all grew black before her eyes, and whispering, "I'll float. Call, Milly, and don't mind me," Ruth turned over, still holding the child fast, and with nothing but her face out of water, feebly struggled on.

"Come and get me! She's going down! Oh, come, quick!" called the child in a tone of such distress that the selfish

German bestirred herself at last, and began to wade cautiously in. Seeing help at hand, brave little Milly soon let go, and struck out like an energetic young frog, while Ruth, quite spent, sank quietly down, with a dim sense that her last duty was done and rest had come.

The shrill cries of the women when they saw the steady white face disappear and rise no more, reached Captain John's ear, and sent him flying down the path, sure that some one was in danger.

"Ruth - gone down - out there!" was all he caught, as many voices tried to tell the tale; and waiting for no more, he threw off hat and coat, and dashed into the sea as if ready to search the Atlantic till he found her.

She was safe in a moment, and pausing only to send one girl flying for the doctor, he carried his streaming burden straight home to Aunt Mary, who had her between blankets before a soul arrived, and was rubbing for dear life while John fired up the spirit lamp for hot brandy and water, with hands that trembled as he splashed about like an agitated Newfoundland fresh from a swim.

Ruth was soon conscious, but too much exhausted to do or say anything, and lay quietly suffering the discomforts of resuscitation till she fell asleep.

"Is Milly safe?" was all she asked, and being assured that the child was in her mother's arms, and Sammy had gone to tell Grandpa all about it, she smiled and shut her eyes with a whispered, "Then it's all right, thank God!"

All that evening Captain John paced the piazza, and warned away the eager callers, who flocked down to ask about the heroine of the hour; for she was more interesting than Undine, the Lily Maid, or any of the pretty creatures attitudinizing behind the red curtains in the hot hotel parlor. All that night Aunt Mary watched the deep sleep that restored the girl, and now and then crept out to tell her nephew there was nothing to fear for one so strong and healthful. And all night Ruth dreamed strange dreams, some weird and dim, some full of pain and fear; but as the fever of reaction passed away, lovely visions of a happy place came to her, where faces she loved were near, and rest, and all she longed for was hers at last. So clear and beautiful was this dream that she waked in the early dawn to lie and think of it, with such a look of peace upon her face that Aunt Mary could not but kiss it tenderly when she came in to see if all was well.

"How are you, dear? Has this nice long sleep set you up again as I hoped?"

"Oh yes, I'm quite well, thank you, and I must go home. Grandpa will worry so till he sees me," answered Ruth, sitting up with her wet hair on her shoulders, and a little shiver of pain as she stretched her tired arms.

"Not yet, my dear; rest another hour or two and have some breakfast. Then, if you like, John shall take you home before any one comes to plague you with idle questions. I'm not going to say a word, except that I'm proud of my brave girl, and mean to take care of her if she will let me."

With that and a motherly embrace, the old lady bustled away to stir up her maid and wakt John from his first nap with the smell of coffee. a most unromantic but satisfying perfume to all the weary watchers in the house.

An hour later, dressed in Miss Scott's gray wrapper and rose-colored shawl, Ruth came slowly to the beach leaning on Captain John's arm, while Aunt Mary waved her napkin from the rocks above, and sent kind messages after them as they pushed off.

It was the loveliest hour of all the day. The sun had not yet risen, but sea and sky were rosy with the flush of dawn; the small waves rippled up the sand, the wind blew fresh and fragrant from hayfields far away, and in the grove the birds were singing, as they only sing at peep of day. A still, soft, happy time before the work and worry of the world began, the peaceful moment which is so precious to those who have learned to love its balm and consecrate its beauty with their prayers.

Ruth sat silent, looking about her as if she saw a new heaven and earth, and had no words in which to tell the feeling that made her eyes so soft, sent the fresh color back into her cheeks, and touched her lips with something sweeter than a smile.

Captain John rowed very slowly, watching her with a new expression in his face; and when she drew a long breath, a happy sort of sigh, he leaned forward to ask, as if he knew what brought it, -

"You are glad to be alive, Ruth?"

"Oh, so glad! I didn't want to die; life's very pleasant now," she answered, with her frank eyes meeting his so gratefully.

"Even though it's hard?"

"It's easier lately; you and dear Miss Mary have helped so much, I see my way clear, and mean to go right on, real brave and cheerful, sure I'll get my wish at last."

"So do I!" and Captain John laughed a queer, happy laugh, as he bent to his oars again, with the look of a man who knew where he was going and longed to get there as soon as possible.

"I hope you will. I wish I could help anyway to pay for all you've done for me. I know you don't want to be thanked for fishing me up, but I mean to do it all the same, if I can, some time;" and Ruth's voice was full of tender energy as she looked down into the deep green water where her life would have ended but for him.

"What did you think of when you went down so quietly? Those women said you never called for help once."

"I had no breath to call. I knew you were near, I hoped you'd come, and I thought of poor Grandpa and Sammy as I gave up and seemed to go to sleep."

A very simple answer, but it made Captain John beam with delight; and the morning red seemed to glow all over his brown face as he rowed across the quiet bay, looking at Ruth sitting opposite, so changed by the soft becoming colors of her dress, the late danger, and the dreams that still lingered in her mind, making it hard to feel that she was the same girl who went that way only a day ago.

Presently the Captain spoke again in a tone that was both eager and anxious, -

"I'm glad my idle summer hasn't been quite wasted. It's over now, and I'm off in a few days for a year's cruise, you know."

"Yes, Miss Mary told me you were going soon. I'll miss you both, but maybe you'll come next year?"

"I will, please God!"

"So will I; for even if I get away this fall, I'd love to come again in summer and rest a little while, no matter what I find to do."

"Come and stay with Aunt Mary if this home is gone. I shall want Sammy next time. I've settled that with the Skipper, you know, and I'll take good care of the little chap. He's not much younger than I was when I shipped for my first voyage. You'll let him go?"

"Anywhere with you. He's set his heart on being a sailor, and Grandpa likes it. All our men are, and I'd be one if I were a boy. I love the sea so, I couldn't be happy long away from it."

"Even though it nearly drowned you?"

"Yes, I'd rather die that way than any other. But it was my fault; I shouldn't have failed if I hadn't been so tired. I've often swum farther; but I'd been three hours in the marsh getting those things for the girls, and it was washing-day, and I'd been up nearly all night with Grandpa; so don't blame the sea, please, Captain John."

"You should have called me; I was waiting for you, Ruth."

"I didn't know it. I'm used to doing things myself. It might have been too late for Milly if I'd waited."

"Thank God, I wasn't too late for you."

The boat was at the shore now; and as he spoke Captain John held out his hands to help Ruth down, for, encumbered with her long dress, and still weak from past suffering, she could not spring to land as she used to do in her short gown. For the first time the color deepened in her cheek as she looked into the face before her and read the meaning of the eyes that found her beautiful and dear, and the lips that thanked God for her salvation so fervently.

She did not speak, but let him lift her down, draw her hand through his arm, and lead her up the rocky slope to the little pool that lay waiting for the sun's first rays to wake from its sleep. He paused there, and with his hand on hers said quietly, -

"Ruth, before I go I want to tell you something, and this is a good time and place. While Aunt Mary watched the flowers, I've watched you, and found the girl I've always wanted for my wife. Modest and brave, dutiful and true, that's what I love; could you give me all this, dear, for the little I can offer, and next year sail with Sammy and a very happy man if you say yes?"

"I'm not half good and wise enough for that! Remember what I am," began Ruth, bending her head as if the thought were more than she could bear.

"I do remember, and I'm proud of it! Why, dear heart, I've worked my way up from a common sailor, and am the better for it. Now I've got my ship, and I want a mate to make a home for me aboard and ashore. Look up and tell me that I didn't read those true eyes wrong."

Then Ruth lifted up her face, and the sunshine showed him all he asked to know, as she answered with her heart in her voice and the "true eyes" fixed on his, -

"I tried not to love you, knowing what a poor ignorant girl I am; but you were so kind to me, how could I help it, John?"

That satisfied him, and he sealed his happy thanks on the innocent lips none had kissed but the little brother, the old man, and the fresh winds of the sea.

One can imagine the welcome they met at the small brown house, and what went on inside as Grandpa blessed the lovers, and Sammy so overflowed with joy at his enchanting prospects, that he was obliged to vent his feelings in ecstatic jigs upon the beach, to the great amazement of the gulls and sandpipers at breakfast there.

No one at the Point, except a certain dear old lady, knew the pleasant secret, though many curious or friendly visitors went to the Island that day to see the heroine and express their wonder, thanks, and admiration. All agreed that partial drowning seemed to suit the girl, for a new Ruth had risen like Venus from the sea. A softer beauty was in her fresh face now, a gentler sort of pride possessed her, and a still more modest shrinking from praise and publicity became her well. No one guessed the cause, and she was soon forgotten; for the season was over, the summer guests departed, and the Point was left to the few cottagers who loved to linger into golden September.

Miss Mary was one of these, and Captain John another; for he remained as long as he dared, to make things comfortable for the old man, and to sit among the rocks with Ruth when her day's work was done, listening while his "Mermaid," as he called her, sang as she had never sung before, and let him read the heart he had made his own, for the lily was wide open now, and its gold all his.

With the first frosts Grandpa died, and was carried to his grave by his old comrades, owing no man a cent, thanks to his dutiful granddaughter and the new son she had given him. Then the little house was deserted, and all winter Ruth was happy with Aunt Mary, while Sammy studied bravely, and lived on dreams of the joys in store for him when the Captain came sailing home again.

Another summer brought the happy day when the little brown house was set in order for a sailor's honeymoon, when the flag floated gayly over Miss Mary's cottage, and Ruth in a white gown with her chosen flowers in her hair and bosom, shipped with her dear Captain for the long cruise which had its storms and calms, but never any shipwreck of the love that grew and blossomed with the water-lilies by the sea.

Louisa May Alcott

POPPIES AND WHEAT

AS the great steamer swung round into the stream the cloud of white handkerchiefs waving on the wharf melted away, the last good-byes grew fainter, and those who went and those who stayed felt that the parting was over, -

"It may be for years, and it may be forever,"

as the song says.

With only one of the many groups on the deck need we concern ourselves, and a few words will introduce our fellow-travellers. A brisk middle-aged lady leaned on the arm of a middle-aged gentleman in spectacles, both wearing the calmly cheerful air of people used to such scenes, and conscious only of the relief change of place brings to active minds and busy lives.

Before them stood two girls, evidently their charges, and as evidently not sisters, for in all respects they were a great contrast. The younger was a gay creature of seventeen, in an effective costume of navy-blue and white, with bright hair blowing in the wind, sparkling eyes roving everywhere, lively tongue going, and an air of girlish excitement pleasant to see. Both hands were full of farewell bouquets, which she surveyed with more pride than tenderness as she glanced at another group of girls less blessed with floral offerings.

Her companion was a small, quiet person, some years older

than herself, very simply dressed, laden with wraps, and apparently conscious just then of nothing but three dark specks on the wharf, as she still waved her little white flag, and looked shoreward with eyes too dim for seeing. A sweet, modest face it was, with intelligent eyes, a firm mouth, and the look of one who had early learned self-reliance and self-control.

The lady and gentleman watched the pair with interest and amusement; for both liked young people, and were anxious to know these two better, since they were to be their guides and guardians for six months. Professor Homer was going abroad to look up certain important facts for his great historical work, and as usual took his wife with him; for they had no family, and the good lady was ready to march to any quarter of the globe at short notice. Fearing to be lonely while her husband pored over old papers in foreign libraries, Mrs. Homer had invited Ethel Amory, a friend's daughter, to accompany her. Of course the invitation was gladly accepted, for it was a rare opportunity to travel in such company, and Ethel was wild with delight at the idea. One thorn, however, vexed her, among the roses with which her way seemed strewn. Mamma would not let her take a French maid, but preferred a young lady as companion; for, three being an awkward number, a fourth party would be not only convenient, but necessary on the girl's account, since she was not used to take care of herself and Mrs. Homer could only be expected to act as chaperone.

"Jane Bassett is just the person I want, and Jane shall go. She needs a change after teaching all these years; it will do her a world of good, for she will improve and enjoy every moment, and the salary I shall offer her will make it worth her while," said Mrs. Amory, as she discussed the plan with her daughter.

"She is only three years older than I am, and I hate to be taken care of, and watched, and fussed over. I can order a maid round, but a companion is worse than a governess; such people are always sensitive and proud, and hard to get on with. Every one takes a maid, and I'd set my heart on that nice Marie who wants to go home, and talks such lovely French. Do let me

Louisa May Alcott

have her, Mamma!" begged Ethel, who was a spoiled child and usually got her own way.

But for once Mamma stood firm, having a strong desire to benefit her daughter by the society of better companions than the gay girls of her own set, also to give a great pleasure to good little Jane Bassett, who had been governessing ever since she was sixteen, with very few vacations in her hard, dutiful life.

"No, darling, I have asked Jane, and if her mother can spare her, Jane it shall be. She is just what you need, - sensible and kind, intelligent and capable; not ashamed to do anything for you, and able to teach you a great deal in a pleasant way. Mrs. Homer approves of her, and I am sure you will be glad by-and-by; for travelling is not all 'fun,' as you expect, and I don't want you to be a burden on our friends. You two young things can take care of each other while the Professor and his wife are busy with their own affairs; and Jane is a far better companion for you than that coquettish French woman, who will probably leave you in the lurch as soon as you reach Paris. I shouldn't have a moment's peace if you were left with her, but I have entire confidence in Jane Bassett because she is faithful, discreet, and a true lady in all things."

There was no more to be said, and Ethel pouted in vain. Jane accepted the place with joy; and after a month of delightful hurry they were off, one all eagerness for the new world, the other full of tender regret for the dear souls left behind. How they got on, and what they learned, remains to be told.

"Come, Miss Bassett, we can't see them any longer, so we may as well begin to enjoy ourselves. You might take those things down below, and settle the stateroom a bit; I'm going to walk about and get my bearings before lunch. You will find me somewhere round."

Ethel spoke with a little tone of command, having made up her mind to be mistress and keep Jane Bassett in her place, though she did know three languages and sketched much better than Miss Amory.

Jenny, as we who are going to be her bosom friends will call her, nodded cheerfully, and looked about for the stairway; for, never having been on a steamer before, she was rather bewildered.

"I'll show you the way, my dear. I always get my things settled at once, as one never knows when one may have to turn in. The Professor will go with you, Ethel; it is not proper for you to roam about alone;" and with that hint Mrs. Homer led the way below, privately wondering how these young persons were going to get on together.

Jane swallowed her "heimweh" in silence, and bestirred herself so well that soon the stateroom looked very cosy with the wrappers laid ready, the hanging bags tacked up, and all made ship-shape for the ten days' trip.

"But where are YOUR comforts? You have given Ethel all the room, the lower berth, and the best of everything," said Mrs. Homer, popping in her head to see how her quiet neighbor got on.

"Oh, I live in my trunk; I didn't bring half as many little luxuries as Ethel did, so I don't need as much room. I'm used to living in corners like a mouse, and I get on very well," answered Jane, looking very like a mouse just then, as she peeped out of the upper berth, with her gray gown, bright eyes, and quick nod of contentment.

"Well, my dear, I've just one word of advice to give you. Don't let that child tyrannize over you. She means well, but is wilful and thoughtless, and it is NOT your duty to be made a slave of. Assert yourself and she will obey and respect you, and you will help her a great deal. I know all about it; I was a companion in my youth, and had a hard time of it till I revolted and took my proper place. Now let us go up and enjoy the fine air while we can."

"Thank you, I will remember;" and Jane offered the good lady her arm, with a feeling of gratitude for such friendliness, all being new and strange to her, and many doubts of her own fitness for the position lying heavy at her heart.

But soon all was forgotten as she sat on deck watching the islands, lighthouses, ships, and shores glide by as she went swiftly out to sea that bright June day. Here was the long-cherished desire of her life come to pass at last, and now the parting with mother and sisters was over, nothing but pleasure remained, and a very earnest purpose to improve this unexpected opportunity to the uttermost. The cares of life had begun early for little Jane, she being the eldest of the three girls, and her mother a widow. First came hard study, then a timid beginning as nursery governess; and as year by year the teaching of others taught her, she ventured on till here she was companion to a fine young lady "going abroad," where every facility for acquiring languages, studying history, seeing the best pictures, and enjoying good society would all be hers. No wonder the quiet face under the modest gray hat beamed, as it turned wistfully toward the unknown world before her, and that her thoughts were so far away, she was quite unconscious of the kind eyes watching her, as Mrs. Homer sat placidly knitting beside her.

"I shall like the Mouse, I'm quite sure. Hope Lemuel will be as well satisfied. Ethel is charming when she chooses, but will need looking after, that's plain," thought the lady as she glanced down the deck to where her husband stood talking with several gentlemen, while his charge was already making friends with the gay girls who were to be her fellow-passengers.

"Daisy Millers, I fear," went on Mrs. Homer, who had a keen eye for character, and was as fond of studying the people about her as the Professor was of looking up dead statesmen, kings, and warriors. The young ladies certainly bore some resemblance to the type of American girl which one never fails to meet in travelling. They were dressed in the height of the fashion, pretty with the delicate evanescent beauty of too many of our girls, and all gifted with the loud voices, shrill laughter, and free-and-easy manners which so astonish decorous English matrons and maids. Ethel was evidently impressed with their style, as they had a man and maid at their beck and call, and every sign of ostentatious wealth about them. A stout papa, a thin mamma, evidently worn out with the cares of the past winter, three half-grown girls, and a lad of sixteen made up the party; and a very lively one it was, as the Professor soon found, for he presently bowed himself away, and left Ethel to her new friends, since she smilingly refused to leave them.

"Ought I to go to her?" asked Jenny, waking from her happy reverie to a sudden sense of duty as the gentleman sat down beside her.

"Oh dear, no, she is all right. Those are the Sibleys of New York. Her father knows them, and she will find them a congenial refuge when she tires of us quiet folk; and you too, perhaps?" added the Professor as he glanced at the girl.

"I think not. I should not be welcome to them, nor are they the sort of people I like. I shall be very happy with the 'quiet folk,' if they won't let me be in the way," answered Jenny, in the cheerful voice that reminded one of the chirp of a robin.

"We won't; we'll toss you overboard as soon as you begin to scream and bounce in that style," he answered, laughing at the idea of this demure young person's ever dreaming of such a thing. Jenny laughed also, and ran to pick up Mrs. Homer's ball, as it set out for a roll into the lee-scuppers. As she brought it back she found the Professor examining the book she left behind her.

"Like all young travellers you cling to your 'Baedeker,' I see, even in the first excitement of the start. He is a useful fellow, but I know my Europe so well now, I don't need him."

"I thought it would be wise to read up our route a little, then I needn't ask questions. They must be very tiresome to people who know all about it," said Jenny, regarding him with an expression of deep respect for she considered him a sort of walking encyclopaedia of universal knowledge.

It pleased the learned man, who was kindly as well as wise, and loved to let his knowledge overflow into any thirsty mind, however small the cup might be. He liked the intelligent face before him, and a timid question or two set him off on his favorite hobby at a pleasant amble, with Jenny on the pillion behind, as it were. She enjoyed it immensely, and was deep in French history, when the lunch gong recalled her from Francis I. and his sister Margaret to chops and English ale.

Ethel came prancing back to her own party, full of praises of the Sibleys, and the fun they meant to have together.

"They are going to the Langham; so we shall be able to go about with them, and they know all the best shops, and some lords and ladies, and expect to be in Paris when we are, and that will be a great help with our dresses and things."

"But we are not going to shop and have new dresses till we are on our way home, you know. Now we haven't time for such things, and can't trouble the Homers with more trunks," answered Jenny, as they followed their elders to the table.

"I shall buy what I like, and have ten trunks if it suits me. I'm not going to poke round over old books and ruins, and live in a travelling-dress all the time. You can do as you like; it's different with me, and *I* know what is proper."

With which naughty speech Ethel took her seat first at the table, and began to nod and smile at the Sibleys opposite. Jenny set her lips and made no answer, but ate her lunch with what appetite she could, trying to forget her troubles in listening to the chat going on around her.

All that afternoon Ethel left her to herself, and enjoyed the more congenial society of the new acquaintances. Jenny was tired, and glad to read and dream in the comfortable seat Mrs. Homer left her when she went for her nap.

By sunset the sea grew rough and people began to vanish below. There were many empty places at dinner-time, and those who appeared seemed to have lost their appetites suddenly. The Homers were, good sailors, but Jenny looked pale, and Ethel said her head ached, though both kept up bravely till nine o'clock, when the Sibleys precipitately retired after supper, and Ethel thought she might as well go to bed early to be ready for another pleasant day to-morrow.

Jenny had a bad night, but disturbed no one. Ethel slept soundly, and sprang up in the morning, eager to be the first on deck. But a sudden lurch sent her and her hair-brush into a corner: and when she rose, everything in the stateroom seemed to be turning somersaults, while a deathly faintness crept over her.

"Oh, wake up, Jane! We are sinking! What is it? Help me, help me!" and with a dismal wail Ethel tumbled into her berth in the first anguish of seasickness.

We will draw the curtain for three days, during which rough weather and general despair reigned. Mrs. Homer took care of the girls till Jenny was able to sit up and amuse Ethel; but the latter had a hard time of it, for a series of farewell lunches had left her in a bad state for a sea-voyage, and the poor girl could not lift her head for days. The new-made friends did not trouble themselves about her after a call of condolence, but faithful Jenny sat by her hour after hour, reading and talking by day, singing her to sleep at night, and often creeping from her bed on the sofa to light her little candle and see that her charge was warmly covered and quite comfortable. Ethel was used to being petted, so she was not very grateful; but she felt the watchful care about her, and thought Jane almost as handy a person as a maid, and told her so.

Jenny thanked her and said nothing of her own discomforts; but Mrs. Homer saw them, and wrote to Mrs. Amory that so far the companion was doing admirably and all that could be desired. A few days later she added more commendations to the journal-letters she kept for the anxious mothers at home, and this serio-comical event was the cause of her fresh praises.

The occupants of the deck staterooms were wakened in the middle of the night by a crash and a cry, and starting up found that the engines were still, and something was evidently the matter somewhere. A momentary panic took place; ladies screamed, children cried, and gentlemen in queer costumes burst out of their rooms, excitedly demanding, "What is the matter?"

As no lamps are allowed in the rooms at night, darkness added to the alarm, and it was some time before the real state of the case was known. Mrs. Homer went at once to the frightened girls, and found Ethel clinging to Jenny, who was trying to find the life-preservers lashed to the wall.

"We've struck! Don't leave me! Let us die together! Oh, why did I come? why did I come?" she wailed; while the other girl answered with a brave attempt at cheerfulness, as she put over Ethel's head the only life-preserver she could find, - .

"I will! I will! Be calm, dear! I guess there is no immediate danger. Hold fast to this while I try to find something warm for you to put on."

In a moment Jenny's candle shone like a star of hope in the gloom, and by the time the three had got into wrappers and shawls, a peal of laughter from the Professor assured them that the danger could not be great. Other sounds of merriment, as well as Mrs. Sibley's voice scolding violently, was heard; and presently Mr. Homer came to tell them to be calm, for the stoppage was only to cool the engines, and the noise was occasioned by Joe Sibley's tumbling out of his berth in a fit of nightmare caused by Welsh rarebits and poached eggs at eleven at night.

Much relieved, and a little ashamed now of their fright, every one subsided; but Ethel could not sleep, and clung to Jenny in an hysterical state till a soft voice began to sing "Abide with me" so sweetly that more than one agitated listener blessed the singer and fell asleep before the comforting hymn ended.

Ethel was up next day, and lay on the Professor's bearskin rug on deck, looking pale and interesting, while the Sibleys sat by her talking over the exciting event of the night, to poor Joe's great disgust. Jenny crept to her usual corner. and sat with a book on her lap, quietly reviving in the fresh air till she was able to enjoy the pleasant chat of the Homers, who established themselves near by and took care of her, learning each day to love and respect the faithful little soul who kept her worries to herself, and looked brightly forward no matter how black the sky might be.

Only one other incident of the voyage need be told; but as that marked a change in the relations between the two girls it is worth recording.

As she prepared for bed late one evening, Mrs. Homer heard Jenny say in a tone never used before, -

"My dear, I must say something to you or I shall not feel as if I were doing my duty. I promised your mother that you should keep early hours, as you are not very strong and excitement is bad for you. Now, you WON'T come to bed at ten, as I ask you to every night, but stay up playing cards or sitting on deck till nearly every one but the Sibleys is gone. Mrs. Homer waits for us, and is tired, and it is very rude to keep her up. Will you PLEASE do as you ought, and not oblige me to say you must?"

Ethel was sleepy and cross, and answered pettishly, as she held out her foot to have her boot unbuttoned, - for Jenny, anxious to please, refused no service asked of her, -

"I shall do as I like, and you and Mrs. Homer needn't trouble yourselves about me. Mamma wished me to have a good time, and I shall! There is no harm in staying up to enjoy the moonlight, and sing and tell stories. Mrs. Sibley knows what is proper better than you do."

"I don't think she does, for she goes to bed and leaves the girls to flirt with those officers in a way that I know is NOT proper," answered Jenny, firmly. "I should be very sorry to hear them say of you as they did of the Sibley girls, 'They are a wild lot, but great fun.'"

"Did they say that? How impertinent!" and Ethel bridled up like a ruffled chicken, for she was not out yet, and had not lost the modest instincts that so soon get blunted when a frivolous fashionable life begins.

"I heard them, and I know that the well-bred people on board do not like the Sibleys' noisy ways and bad manners. Now, you, my dear, are young and unused to this sort of life; so you cannot be too careful what you say and do, and with whom you go."

"Good gracious! any one would think YOU were as wise as Solomon and as old as the hills. YOU are young, and YOU haven't travelled, and don't know any more of the world than I do, - not so much of some things; so you needn't preach."

"I'm not wise nor old, but I DO know more of the world than you, for I began to take care of myself and earn my living at sixteen, and four years of hard work have taught me a great deal. I am to watch over you, and I intend to do it faithfully, no matter what you say, nor how hard you make it for me; because I promised, and I shall keep my word. We are not to trouble Mrs. Homer with our little worries, but try to help each other and have a really good time. I will do anything for you that I can, but I shall NOT let you do things which I wouldn't allow my own sisters to do, and if you refuse to mind me, I shall write to your mother and ask to go home. My conscience won't let me take money and pleasure unless I earn them and do my duty."

"Well, upon my word!" cried Ethel, much impressed by such a decided speech from gentle Jane, and dismayed at the idea of being taken home in disgrace.

"We won't talk any more now, because we may get angry and say what we should be sorry for. I am sure you will see that I am right when you think it over quietly. So good-night, dear."

"Good-night," was all the reply Ethel gave, and a long silence followed.

Mrs. Homer could not help hearing as the staterooms were close together, and the well-ventilated doors made all conversation beyond a whisper audible.

"I didn't think Jane had the spirit to talk like that. She has taken my hint and asserted herself, and I'm very glad, for Ethel must be set right at once or we shall have no peace. She will respect and obey Jane after this, or I shall be obliged to say MY word."

Mrs. Homer was right, and before her first nap set in she heard a meek voice say, -

"Are you asleep, Miss Bassett?"

"No, dear."

"Then I want to say, I've thought it over. Please DON'T write to mamma. I'll be good. I'm sorry I was rude to you; do forgive -"

The sentence was not ended, for a sudden rustle, a little sob, and several hearty kisses plainly told that Jenny had flown to pardon, comfort, and caress her naughty child, and that all was well.

After that Ethel's behavior was painfully decorous for the rest of the voyage, which, fortunately for her good resolutions, ended at Queenstown, much to her regret. The Homers thought a glimpse at Ireland and Scotland would be good for the girls; and as the Professor had business in Edinburgh this was the better route for all parties. But Ethel longed for London, and refused to see any beauty in the Lakes of Killarney, turned up her nose at jaunting-cars, and pronounced Dublin a stupid place.

Scotland suited her better, and she could not help enjoying the fine scenery with such companions as the Homers; for the Professor knew all about the relics and ruins, and his wife had a memory richly stored with the legends, poetry, and romance which make dull facts memorable and history enchanting.

But Jenny's quiet rapture was pleasant to behold. She had not scorned Scott's novels as old-fashioned, and she peopled the cottages and castles with his heroes and heroines; she crooned Burns's sweet songs to herself as she visited his haunts, and went about in a happy sort of dream, with her head full of Highland Mary, Tam o' Shanter, field-mice and daisies, or fought terrific battles with Fitz-James and Marmion, and tried if "the light harebell" would "raise its head, elastic from her airy tread," as it did from the Lady of the Lake's famous foot.

Ethel told her she was "clean daft;" but Jenny said, "Let me enjoy it while I can. I've dreamed of it so long I can hardly realize that it has come, and I cannot lose a minute of it;" so she absorbed Scotch poetry and romance with the mist and the keen air from the moors, and bloomed like the bonnie heather which she loved to wear.

"What shall we do this rainy day in this stupid place?" said Ethel, one morning when bad weather kept them from an excursion to Stirling Castle.

"Write our journals and read up for the visit; then we shall know all about the castle, and need not tire people with our questions," answered Jenny, already established in a deep window-seat of their parlor at the hotel with her books and portfolio.

"I don't keep a journal, and I hate to read guide-books; it's much easier to ask, though there is very little I care for about these mouldy old places," said Ethel with a yawn, as she looked out into the muddy street.

"How can you say so? Don't you care for poor Mary, and Prince Charlie, and all the other sad and romantic memories that haunt the country? Why, it seems as real to me as if it happened yesterday, and I never can forget anything about the place or the people now. Really, dear, I think you ought to take more interest and improve this fine chance. Just see how helpful and lovely Mrs. Homer is, with a quotation for every famous spot we see. It adds so much to our pleasure, and makes her so interesting. I'm going to learn some of the fine bits in this book of hers, and make them my own, since I cannot buy the beautiful little set this Burns belongs to. Don't you want to try it, and while away the dull day by hearing each other recite and talking over the beautiful places we have seen?"

"No, thank you; no study for me. It is to be all play now. Why tire my wits with that Scotch stuff when Mrs. Homer is here to do it for me?" and lazy Ethel turned to the papers on the table for amusement more to her taste.

"But we shouldn't think only of our own pleasure, you know. It is so sweet to be able to teach, amuse, or help others in any way. I'm glad to learn this new accomplishment, so that I may be to some one by-and-by what dear Mrs. Homer is to us now, if I ever can. Didn't you see how charmed those English people were at Holyrood when she was reciting those fine lines to us? The old gentleman bowed and thanked her, and the handsome lady called her 'a book of elegant extracts.' I thought it was such a pretty and pleasant thing that I described it all to mother and the girls."

"So it was; but did you know that the party was Lord Cumberland and his family? The guide told me afterward. I never guessed they were anybody, in such plain tweed gowns and thick boots; did you?"

"I knew they were ladies and gentlemen by their manners and conversation; did you expect they would travel in coronets and ermine mantles?" laughed Jenny.

"I'm not such a goose! But I'm glad we met them, because I can tell the Sibleys of it. They think so much of titles, and brag about Lady Watts Barclay, whose husband is only a brewer knighted. I shall buy a plaid like the one the lord's daughter wore, and wave it in the faces of those girls; they do put on SUCH airs because they have been in Europe before."

Jenny was soon absorbed in her books; so Ethel curled herself up in the window-seat with an illustrated London paper full of some royal event, and silence reigned for an hour. Neither had seen the Professor's glasses rise like two full moons above his paper now and then to peep at them as they chatted at the other end of the room; neither saw him smile as he made a memorandum in his note-book, nor guessed how pleased he was at Jenny's girlish admiration of his plain but accomplished and excellent wife. It was one of the trifles which went to form his opinion of the two lasses, and in time to suggest a plan which ended in great joy for one of them.

"Now the real fun begins, and I shall be perfectly contented," cried Ethel as they rolled through the London streets towards the dingy Langham Hotel, where Americans love to congregate.

Jenny's eyes were sparkling also, and she looked as if quite ready for the new scenes and excitements which the famous old city promised them, though she had private doubts as to whether anything could be more delightful than Scotland.

The Sibleys were at the hotel; and the ladies of both parties at once began a round of shopping and sightseeing, while the gentlemen went about their more important affairs. Joe was detailed for escort duty; and a fine time the poor lad had of it, trailing about with seven ladies by day and packing them into two cabs at night for the theatres and concerts they insisted on trying to enjoy in spite of heat and weariness.

Mrs. Homer and Jenny were soon tired of this "whirl of gayety," as they called it, and planned more quiet excursions with some hours each day for rest and the writing and reading which all wise tourists make a part of their duty and pleasure. Ethel rebelled, and much preferred the "rabble," as Joe irreverently called his troop of ladies, never losing her delight in Regent Street shops, the parks at the fashionable hour, and the evening shows in full blast everywhere during the season. She left the sober party whenever she could escape, and with Mrs. Sibley as chaperone, frolicked about with the gay girls to her heart's content. It troubled Jenny, and made her feel as if she were not doing her duty; but Mrs. Homer consoled her by the fact that a month was all they could give to London, and soon the parties would separate, for the Sibleys were bound for Paris, and the Professor for Switzerland and Germany, through August and September.

So little Jane gave herself up to the pleasures she loved, and with the new friends, whose kindness she tried to repay by every small service in her power, spent happy days among the famous haunts they knew so well, learning much and storing away all she saw and heard for future profit and pleasure. A few samples of the different ways in which our young travellers improved their opportunities will sufficiently illustrate this new version of the gay grasshopper and the thrifty ant.

When they visited Westminster Abbey, Ethel was soon tired of tombs and chapels, and declared that the startling tableau of the skeleton Death peeping out of the half-opened door of the tomb to throw his dart at Mrs. Nightingale, and the ludicrous has-relief of some great earl in full peer's robes and coronet being borne to heaven in the arms of fat cherubs puffing under their load, were the only things worth seeing.

Jenny sat spellbound in the Poets' Corner, listening while Mrs. Homer named the illustrious dead around them; followed the verger from chapel to chapel with intelligent interest as he told the story of each historical or royal tomb, and gave up Madam Tussaud's wax-work to spend several happy hours sketching the beautiful cloisters in the Abbey to add to her collection of water-colors, taken as she went from place to place, to serve as studies for her pupils at home.

At the Tower she grew much excited over the tragic spots she visited and the heroic tales she heard of the kings and queens, the noble hearts and wise heads, that pined and perished there. Ethel "hated horrors," she said, and cared only for the crown jewels, the faded effigies in the armor gallery, and the queer Highlanders skirling on the bagpipes in the courtyard.

At Kew Jenny revelled in the rare flowers, and was stricken with amazement at the Victoria Regia, the royal water-lily, so large that a child could sit on one of its vast leaves as on a green island. Her interest and delight so touched the heart of the crusty keeper that he gave her a nosegay of orchids, which excited the envy of Ethel and the Sibley girls, who were of the party, but had soon wearied of plants and gone off to order tea in Flora's Bower, - one of the little cottages where visitors repose and refresh themselves with weak tea and Bath buns in such tiny rooms that they have to put their wraps in the fireplace or out of the window while they feast.

At the few parties to which they went, - for the Homers' friends were of the grave, elderly sort, - Jenny sat in a corner taking notes of the gay scene, while Ethel yawned. But the Mouse got many a crumb of good conversation as she nestled close to Mrs. Homer, drinking in the wise and witty chat that went on between the friends who came to pay their respects to the Professor and his interesting wife. Each night Jenny had new and famous names to add to the list in her journal, and the artless pages were rich in anecdotes, descriptions, and comments on the day's adventures.

But the gem of her London collection of experiences was found in a most unexpected way, and not only gave her great pleasure, but made the young gadabouts regard her with sudden respect as one come to honor.

"Let me stay and wait upon you; I'd much rather than go to the Crystal Palace, for I shouldn't enjoy it at all with you lying here in pain and alone," said Jenny one lovely morning when the girls came down ready for the promised excursion, to find Mrs. Homer laid up with a nervous headache.

"No, dear, you can do nothing for me, thanks. Quiet is all I need, and my only worry is that I am not able to write up my husband's notes for him. I promised to have them ready last night, but was so tired I could not do it," answered Mrs. Homer, as Jenny leaned over her full of affectionate anxiety.

"Let me do them! I'd be so proud to help; and I can, for I did copy some one day, and he said it was well done. Please let me; I should enjoy a quiet morning here much better than the noisy party we shall have, since the Sibleys are to go."

With some reluctance the invalid consented; and when the rest were gone with hasty regrets, Jenny fell to work so briskly that in an hour or two the task was done. She was looking wistfully out of the window wondering where she could go alone, since Mrs. Homer was asleep and no one needed her, when the Professor came in to see how his wife was before he went to the British Museum to consult certain famous books and parchments.

He was much pleased to find his notes in order, and after a glance at the sleeping lady, told Jenny she was to come with him for a visit to a place which SHE would enjoy, though most young people thought it rather dull.

Away they went; and being given in charge to a pleasant old

Louisa May Alcott

man, Jenny roamed over the vast Museum where the wonders of the world are collected, enjoying every moment, till Mr. Homer called her away, as his day's work was done. It was late now, but she never thought of time, and came smiling up from the Egyptian Hall ready for the lunch the Professor proposed. They were just going out when a gentleman met them, and recognizing the American stopped to greet him cordially. Jenny's heart beat when she was presented to Mr. Gladstone, and she listened with all her ears to the silvery un-English voice, and stared with all her eyes at the weary yet wise and friendly face of the famous man.

"I'm so glad! I wanted to see him very much, and I feel so grand to think I've really had a bow and a smile all to myself from the Premier of England," said Jenny in a flutter of girlish delight when the brief interview was over.

"You shall go to the House of Commons with me and hear him speak some day; then your cup will be full, since you have already seen Browning, heard Irving, taken tea with Jean Ingelow, and caught a glimpse of the royal family," said the Professor, enjoying her keen interest in people and places.

"Oh, thanks! that will be splendid. I do love to see famous persons, because it gives me a true picture of them, and adds to my desire to know more of them, and admire their virtues or shun their faults."

"Yes, that sort of mental picture-gallery is a good thing to have, and we will add as many fine portraits as we can. Now you shall ride in a Hansom, and see how you like that."

Jenny was glad to do so, for ladies do not use these vehicles when alone, and Ethel had put on great airs after a spin in one with Joe. Jenny was girl enough to like to have her little adventures to boast of, and that day she was to have another which eclipsed all that her young companions ever knew.

A brisk drive, a cosy lunch at a famous chop-house where

Johnson had drunk oceans of tea, was followed by a stroll in the Park; for the Professor liked his young comrade, and was grateful for the well-written notes which helped on his work.

As they leaned against the railing to watch the splendid equipages roll by, one that seemed well known, though only conspicuous by its quiet elegance, stopped near them, and the elder of the two ladies in it bowed and beckoned to Professor Homer. He hastened forward to be kindly greeted and invited to drive along the Ladies' Mile. Jenny's breath was nearly taken away when she was presented to the Duchess of S - , and found herself sitting in a luxurious carriage opposite her Grace and her companion, with a white-wigged coachman perched aloft and two powdered footmen erect behind. Secretly rejoicing that she had made herself especially nice for her trip with the Professor, and remembering that young English girls are expected to efface themselves in the company of their elders, she sat mute and modest, stealing shy glances from under her hat-brim at the great lady, who was talking in the simplest way with her guest about his work, in which, as a member of one of the historical houses of England, she took much interest. A few gracious words fell to Jenny's share before they were set down at the door of the hotel, to the great admiration of the porter, who recognized the liveries and spread the news.

"This is a good sample of the way things go in Vanity Fair. We trudge away to our daily work afoot, we treat ourselves to a humble cab through the mud, pause in the park to watch the rich and great, get whisked into a ducal carriage, and come home in state, feeling rather exalted, don't we?" asked the Professor as they went upstairs, and he observed the new air of dignity which Jane unconsciously assumed as an obsequious waiter flew before to open the door.

"I think we do," answered honest Jane, laughing as she caught the twinkle of his eyes behind the spectacles. "I like splendor, and I AM rather set up to think I've spoken to a live duchess; but I think I like her beautiful old face and charming manners more than her fine coach or great name. Why, she was much more simply dressed than Mrs. Sibley, and talked as pleasantly as if she did not feel a bit above us. Yet one couldn't forget that she was noble, and lived in a very different world from ours."

"That is just it, my dear; she IS a noble woman in every sense of the word, and has a right to her title. Her ancestors were kingmakers, and she is Lady-in-waiting to the Queen; yet she leads the charities of London, and is the friend of all who help the world along. I'm glad you have met her, and seen so good a sample of a true aristocrat. We Americans affect to scorn titles, but too many of us hanker for them in secret, and bow before very poor imitations of the real thing. Don't fill your journal with fine names, as some much wiser folk do, but set down only the best, and remember, 'All that glitters is not gold.'"

"I will, sir." And Jenny put away the little sermon side by side with the little adventure, saying nothing of either till Mrs. Homer spoke of it, having heard the story from her husband.

"How I wish I'd been there, instead of fagging round that great palace full of rubbish! A real Duchess! Won't the Sibleys stare? We shall hear no more of Lady Watts Barclay after this, I guess, and you will be treated with great respect; see if you are not!" said Ethel, much impressed with her companion's good fortune and eager to tell it.

"If things of that sort affect them, their respect is not worth having," answered Jane, quietly accepting the arm Ethel offered her as they went to dinner, - a very unusual courtesy, the cause of which she understood and smiled at.

Ethel looked as if she felt the reproof, but said nothing, only set an example of greater civility to her companion, which the other girls involuntarily followed, after they had heard of Jenny's excursion with the Professor.

The change was very grateful to patient Jane, who had borne many small slights in proud silence; but it was soon over, for the parties separated, and our friends left the city far behind them, as they crossed the channel, and sailed up the Rhine to Schwalbach, where Mrs. Homer was to try the steel springs for her rheumatism while the Professor rested after his London labors.

A charming journey, and several very happy weeks followed as the girls roamed about the Little Brunnen, gay with people from all parts of Europe, come to try the famous mineral waters, and rest under the lindens.

Jenny found plenty to sketch here, and was busy all day booking picturesque groups as they sat in the Allee Saal, doing pretty woodland bits as they strolled among the hills, carefully copying the arches and statues in St. Elizabeth's Chapel, or the queer old houses in the Jews' Quarter of the town. Even the pigs went into the portfolio, with the little swineherd blowing his horn in the morning to summon each lazy porker from its sty to join the troop that trotted away to eat acorns in the oak wood on the hill till sunset called them home again

Ethel's chief amusement was buying trinkets at the booths near the Stahlbrunnen. A tempting display of pretty crystal, agate, and steel jewelry was there, with French bonbons, Swiss carvings, German embroidery and lace-work, and most delectable little portfolios of views of fine scenery or illustrations of famous books. Ethel spent much money here, and added so greatly to her store of souvenirs that a new trunk was needed to hold the brittle treasures she accumulated in spite of the advice given her to wait till she reached Paris, where all could be bought much cheaper and packed safely for transportation.

Jenny contented herself with a German book, Kaulbach's Goethe Gallery, and a set of ornaments for each sister; the purple, pink, and white crystals being cheap and pretty trinkets for young girls. She felt very rich with her generous salary to draw upon when she liked; but having made a list of proper gifts, she resisted temptation and saved her money, remembering how much every penny was needed at home.

Driving from the ruins of Hohenstein one lovely afternoon, the girls got out to walk up a long hill, and amused themselves gathering flowers by the way. When they took their places again, Ethel had a great bouquet of scarlet poppies, Jenny a nosegay of blue corn-flowers for Mrs. Homer, and a handful of green wheat for herself.

"You look as if you had been gleaning," said the Professor, as he watched the girls begin to trim their rough straw hats with the gay coquelicots and the bearded ears.

"I feel as if I were doing that every day, sir, and gathering in a great harvest of pleasure, if nothing else," answered Jenny, turning her bright eyes full of gratitude from one kind face to the other.

"My poppies are much prettier than that stiff stuff. Why didn't you get some?" asked Ethel, surveying her brilliant decoration with great satisfaction.

"They don't last; but my wheat will, and only grow prettier as it ripens in my hat," answered Jenny, contentedly settling the graceful spires in the straw cord that bound the pointed crown.

"Then the kernels will all drop out and leave the husks; that won't be nice, I'm sure," laughed Ethel.

"Well, some hungry bird will pick them up and be glad of them. The husks will last a long time and remind me of this happy day; your poppies are shedding their leaves already, and the odor is not pleasant. I like my honest breadmaking wheat better than your opium flowers," said Jenny, with her thoughtful smile, as she watched the scarlet petals float away leaving the green seed-vessels bare.

"Oh, I shall get some artificial ones at my little milliner's, and be fine as long as I like; so you are welcome to your useful, bristly old wheat," said Ethel, rather nettled by the look that passed between the elders.

Nothing more was said; but both girls remembered that little talk long afterward, for those two wayside nosegays served to point the moral of this little tale, if not to adorn it.

We have no space to tell all the pleasant wanderings of our travellers as they went from one interesting place to another, till they paused for a good rest at Geneva.

Here Ethel quite lost her head among the glittering display of jewelry, and had to be watched lest she rashly spend her last penny. They were obliged almost forcibly to carry her out of the enchanting shops; and no one felt safe till she was either on the lake, or driving to Chamouni, or asleep in her bed.

Jenny bought a watch, a very necessary thing for a teacher, and this was the best place to get a good one. It was chosen with care and much serious consultation with the Professor; and Mrs. Homer added a little chain and seal, finding Jenny about to content herself with a black cord.

"It is only a return for many daughterly services, my dear; and my husband wishes me to offer these with thanks to the patient secretary who has often helped him so willingly," she said, as she came to wake Jenny with a kiss on the morning of her twenty-first birthday.

A set of little volumes like those she had admired was the second gift, and Jenny was much touched to be so kindly remembered. Ethel gave her some thread lace which she had longed to buy for her mother at Brussels, but did not, finding it as costly as beautiful. It was a very happy day, though quietly spent sitting by the lake enjoying the well-chosen extracts from Shakspeare, Wordsworth, Byron, Burns, Scott, and other descriptive poets, and writing loving letters home, proudly stamped with the little seal.

After that, while Ethel haunted the brilliant shops, read novels in the hotel-garden, or listlessly followed the sight-seers, Jenny, with the help of her valuable little library, her industrious pencil, and her accomplished guides, laid up a store of precious souvenirs as they visited the celebrated spots that lie like a necklace of pearls around the lovely lake, with Mont Blanc as the splendid opal that fitly clasps the chain. Calvin and Geneva, Voltaire and Ferney, De Stael and Coppet, Gibbon's garden at Lausanne, Byron's Prisoner at Chillon, Rousseau's chestnut grove at Clarens, and all the legends, relics, and memories of Switzerland's heroes, romancers, poets, and philosophers, were carefully studied, recorded, and enjoyed; and when at last they steamed away toward Paris, Jenny felt as if her head and her heart and one little trunk held richer treasures than all the jewelry in Geneva.

At Lyons her second important purchase was made; for when they visited one of the great manufactories to execute several commissions given to Mrs. Homer, Jenny proudly bought a nice black silk for her mother. This, with the delicate lace, would make the dear woman presentable for many a day, and the good girl beamed with satisfaction as she pictured the delight of all at home when this splendid gift appeared to adorn the dear parent-bird, who never cared how shabby she was if her young were well feathered.

It was a trial to Jenny, when they reached Paris, to spend day after day shopping, talking to dressmakers, and driving in the Bois to watch the elegant world on parade, when she longed to be living through the French Revolution with Carlyle, copying the quaint relics at Hotel Cluny, or revelling in the treasures of the Louvre.

"Why DO you want to study and poke all the time?" asked Ethel, as they followed Mrs. Homer and a French acquaintance round the Palais Royal one day with its brilliant shops, cafes, and crowds.

"My dream is to be able to take a place as teacher of German and history in a girl's school next year. It is a fine chance, and I am promised it if I am fitted; so I must work when I can to be ready. That is why I like Versailles better than Rue de Rivoli, and enjoy talking with Professor Homer about French kings and queens more than I do buying mock diamonds and eating ices here," answered Jenny, looking very tired of the glitter, noise, and dust of the gay place when her heart was in the Conciergerie with poor Marie Antoinette, or the Invalides, where lay the great Napoleon still guarded by his faithful Frenchmen.

"What a dismal prospect! I should think you'd rather have a jolly time while you could, and trust to luck for a place by-and-by, if you must go on teaching," said Ethel, stopping to admire a window full of distracting bonnets.

"No; it is a charming prospect to me, for I love to teach, and I can't leave anything to luck. God helps those who help themselves, mother says, and I want to give the girls an easier time than I have had; so I shall get my tools ready, and fit myself to do good work when the job comes to me," answered Jenny, with such a decided air that the French lady glanced back at her, wondering if a quarrel was going on between the demoiselles.

"What do you mean by tools?" asked Ethel, turning from the gay bonnets to a ravishing display of bonbons in the next window.

"Professor Homer said one day that a well-stored mind was a tool-chest with which one could carve one's way. Now, my tools are knowledge, memory, taste, the power of imparting what I know, good manners, sense, and - patience," added Jenny, with a sigh, as she thought of the weary years spent in teaching little children the alphabet.

Ethel took the sigh to herself, well knowing that she had been a trial, especially of late, when she had insisted on Jane's company because her own French was so imperfect as to be nearly useless, though at home she had flattered herself that she knew a good deal. Her own ignorance of many things had been unpleasantly impressed upon her lately, for at Madame Dene's Pension there were several agreeable English and French ladies, and much interesting conversation went on at the table, which Jenny heartily enjoyed, though she modestly said very little. But Ethel, longing to distinguish herself before the quiet English girls, tried to talk and often made sad mistakes because her head was a jumble of new names and places, and her knowledge of all kinds very superficial. Only the day before she had said in a patronizing tone to a French lady, -

"Of course we remember our obligations to your Lamartine during our Revolution, and the other brave Frenchmen who helped us."

"You mean Lafayette, dear," whispered Jenny quickly, as the lady smiled and bowed bewildered by the queerly pronounced French, but catching the poet's name.

"I know what I mean; you needn't trouble yourself to correct and interrupt me when I'm talking," answered Ethel, in her pert way, annoyed by a smile on the face of the girl opposite, and Jenny's blush at her rudeness and ingratitude. She regretted both when Jane explained the matter afterward, and wished that she had at once corrected what would then have passed as a slip of the tongue. Now it was too late; but she kept quiet and gave Miss Cholmondeley no more chances to smile in that aggravatingly superior way, though it was very natural, as she was a highly educated girl.

Thinking of this, and many other mistakes of her own from which Jane tried to save her, Ethel felt a real remorse, and walked silently on, wondering how she could reward this kind creature who had served her so well and was so anxious to get on in her hard, humble way. The orders were all given now, the shopping nearly done, and Mademoiselle Campan, the elderly French lady who boarded at their Pension, was always ready to jaunt about and be useful; so why not give Jane a holiday, and let her grub and study for the little while left them in Paris? In a fortnight Uncle Sam was to pick up the girls and take them home, while the Homers went to Rome for the winter. It would be well to take Miss Bassett back in a good humor, so that her report would please Mamma, and appease Papa if he were angry at the amount of money spent by his extravagant little daughter. Ethel saw now, as one always does when it is too late to repair damages, many things left undone which she ought to have done, and regretted living for herself instead of putting more pleasure into the life of this good girl, whose future seemed so uninviting to our young lady with her first season very near.

It was a kind plan, and gratified Jenny very much when it was proposed and proved to her that no duty would be neglected if she went about with the Homers and left her charge to the excellent lady who enjoyed chiffons as much as Ethel did, and was glad to receive pretty gifts in return for her services.

But alas for Ethel's good resolutions and Jenny's well-earned holiday! Both came to nothing, for Ethel fell ill from too much pastry, and had a sharp bilious attack which laid her up till the uncle arrived.

Every one was very kind, and there was no danger; but the days were long, the invalid very fretful, and the nurse very tired, before the second week brought convalescence and a general cheering and clearing up took place. Uncle Sam was amusing himself very comfortably while he waited for his niece to be able to travel, and the girls were beginning to pack by degrees, for the accumulation of Ethel's purchases made her share a serious task.

"There! All are in now, and only the steamer trunk is left to pack at the last moment," said Jenny, folding her tired arms after a protracted struggle with half a dozen new gowns, and a perplexing medley of hats, boots, gloves, and perfumery. Two large trunks stood in the ante-room ready to go; the third was now done, and nothing remained but the small one and Jenny's shabby portmanteau.

"How nicely you have managed! I ought to have helped, only you wouldn't let me and I should have spoilt my wrapper. Come and rest and help me sort out this rubbish," said Ethel, who would have been dressed and out if the arrival of a new peignoir had not kept her in to enjoy the lovely pink and blue thing, all lace and ribbon and French taste.

"You will never get them into that box, dear," answered Jenny, gladly sitting down beside her on the sofa, which was strewn with trinkets of all sorts, more or less damaged by careless handling, and the vicissitudes of a wandering trunk.

"I don't believe they are worth fussing over. I'm tired of them, and they look very mean and silly after seeing real jewels here. I'd throw them away if I hadn't spent so much money on them," said Ethel, turning over the tarnished filigree, mock pearl, and imitation coral necklaces, bracelets, and brooches that were tumbling out of the frail boxes in which they came.

"They will look pretty to people at home who have not been seeing so many as we have. I'll sew up the broken cases, and rub up the silver, and string the beads, and make all as good as new, and you will find plenty of girls at home glad to get them, I am sure," answered Jenny, rapidly bringing order out of chaos with those skilful hands of hers.

Ethel leaned back and watched her silently for a few minutes. During this last week our young lady had been thinking a good deal, and was conscious of a strong desire to tell Jane Bassett how much she loved and thanked her for all her patient and faithful care during the six months now nearly over. But she was proud, and humility was hard to learn; self-will was sweet, and to own one's self in the wrong a most distasteful task. The penitent did not know how to begin, so waited for an opportunity, and presently it came.

"Shall you be glad to get home, Jenny?" she asked in her most caressing tone, as she hung her prettiest locket round her friend's neck; for during this illness all formality and coolness had melted away, and "Miss Bassett" was "Jenny dear" now.

"I shall be very, very glad to see my precious people again, and tell them all about my splendid holiday; but I can't help wishing that we were to stay till spring, now that we are here, and I have no teaching, and may never get such another chance. I'm afraid it seems ungrateful when I've had so much; but to go back without seeing Rome is a trial, I confess," answered honest Jane, rubbing away at a very dull paste bandeau.

"So it is; but I don't mind so much, because I shall come again by-and-by, and I mean to be better prepared to enjoy things properly than I am now. I'll really study this winter, and not be such a fool. Jenny, I've a plan in my head. I wonder if you'd like it? I should immensely, and I'm going to propose it to Mamma the minute I get home," said Ethel, glad to seize this opening.

"What is it, deary?"

"Would you like to be my governess and teach me all you know, quietly, at home this winter? I don't want to begin school again just for languages and a few finishing things, and I really think you would do more for me than any one else, because you know what I need, and are so patient with your bad, ungrateful, saucy girl. Could you? would you come?" and Ethel put her arms round Jenny's neck with a little sob and a kiss that was far more precious to Jane than the famous diamond necklace of Marie Antoinette, which she had been reading about.

"I could and I would with all my heart, if you want me, darling! I think we know and love each other now, and can be happy and helpful together, and I'll come so gladly if your mother asks me," answered Jenny, quick to understand what underlay this sudden tenderness, and glad to accept the atonement offered her for many trials which she would never have told even to her own mother.

Ethel was her best self now, and her friend felt well rewarded for the past by this promise of real love and mutual help in the future. So they talked over the new plan in great spirits till Mrs. Homer came to bring them their share of a packet of home letters just arrived. She saw that something unusual was going on, but only smiled, nodded, and went away saying, -

"I have good news in MY letters, and hope yours will make you equally happy, girls."

Silence reigned for a time, as they sat reading busily; then a sudden exclamation from Ethel seemed to produce a strange effect upon Jenny, for with a cry of joy she sprang up and danced all over the room, waving her letter wildly as she cried out, -

"I'm to go! I'm to go! I can't believe it - but here it is! How kind, how very kind, every one is to me!" and down she went upon her own little bed to hide her face and laugh and cry till Ethel ran to rejoice with her.

"Oh, Jenny, I'm so glad! You deserve it, and it's like Mrs. Homer to make all smooth before she said a word. Let me read what Mamma writes to you. Here's my letter; see how sweetly she speaks of you, and how grateful they are for all you've done for me."

The letters changed hands; and sitting side by side in an affectionate bunch, the girls read the happy news that granted the cherished wish of one and gave the other real unselfish pleasure in another's happiness.

Jane was to go to Rome with the Homers for the winter, and perhaps to Greece in the spring. A year of delight lay before her, offered in such a friendly way, and with such words of commendation, thanks, and welcome, that the girl's heart was full, and she felt that every small sacrifice of feeling, every lonely hour, and distasteful duty was richly repaid by this rare opportunity to enjoy still further draughts of the wisdom, beauty, and poetry of the wonderful world now open to her.

She flew off presently to try to thank her good friends, and came back dragging a light new trunk, in which she nearly buried her small self as she excitedly explained its appearance, while rattling out the trays and displaying its many conveniences.

"That dear woman says I'm to send my presents home in the old one by you, and take this to fill up in Rome. Think of it! A lovely new French trunk, and Rome full of pictures, statues, St. Peter's, and the Colosseum. It takes my breath away and makes my head spin."

"So I see. It's a capital box, but it won't hold even St. Peter's, dear; so you'd better calm down and pack your treasures. I'll help," cried Ethel, sweeping about in her gay gown, almost as wild as Jane, who was quite upset by this sudden delicious change in her prospects.

How happily she laid away in the old trunk the few gifts she had ventured to buy, and those given her, - the glossy silk, the dainty lace, the pretty crystals, the store of gloves, the flask of cologne, the pictures and books, and last of all the sketches which illustrated the journal kept so carefully for those at home.

"Now, when my letter is written and the check with all that is left of my salary put in, I am done. There's room for more, and I wish I'd got something else, now I feel so rich. But it is foolish to buy gowns to pay duties on, when I don't know what the girls need. I feel so rich now, I shall fly out and pick up some more little pretties for the dears. They have so few, anything will be charming to them," said Jenny, proudly surveying her box, and looking about for some foreign trifle with which to fill up the corners.

"Then let me put these in, and so be rid of them. I shall go to see your people and tell them all about you, and explain how you came to send so much rubbish."

As she spoke Ethel slipped in several Swiss carvings, the best of the trinkets, and a parcel of dainty Parisian ties and sashes which would gladden the hearts of the poor, pretty girls, just beginning to need such aids to their modest toilets. A big box of bonbons completed her contribution, and left but one empty corner.

"I'll tuck in my old hat to keep all steady; the girls will like it when they dress up, and I'm fond of it, because it recalls some of my happiest days," said Jenny, as she took up the well-worn hat and began to dust it. A shower of grain dropped into her hand, for the yellow wheat still kept its place and recalled the chat at Schwalbach. Ethel glanced at her own hat with its faded artificial flowers; and as her eye went from the small store of treasures so carefully and happily gathered to the strew of almost useless finery on her bed, she said soberly, -

"You were right, Jenny. My poppies are worthless, and my harvest a very poor one. Your wheat fell in good ground, and you will glean a whole stack before you go home. Well, I shall keep MY old hat to remind me of you: and when I come again, I hope I shall have a wiser head to put into a new one."

LITTLE BUTTON-ROSE

"If you please, I've come," said a small girl, as she walked into a large room where three ladies sat at work.

One of the ladies was very thin, one very stout, and the youngest very pretty. The eldest put on her glasses, the stout one dropped her sewing, and the pretty one exclaimed, -

"Why, it must be little Rosamond!"

"Yes, I've come; the man is taking my trunk upstairs, and I've got a letter for Cousin Penelope," said the child, with the sweet composure of one always sure of a welcome.

The stout lady held out her hand for the letter; but the little girl, after a keen look at the three faces, went to the old lady, who received her with a kiss, saying, -

"That's right; but how did you know, dear?"

"Oh, Papa said Cousin Penny is old, Cousin Henny fat, and Cousin Cicely rather pretty; so I knew in one minute," replied Rosamond, in a tone of innocent satisfaction at her own cleverness, and quite unconscious of the effect of her speech.

Miss Penelope hastily retired behind the letter. Miss Henrietta frowned so heavily that the gold-rimmed eye-glasses flew off her nose with a clash, and Cicely laughed outright, as she exclaimed, -

"I'm afraid we have got an enfant terrible among us, though I can't complain of my share of the compliments."

"I never expected to find Clara's child well mannered, and I see I was quite right. Take your hat off, Rosamond, and sit down. It tires Sister to lean on her in that way," said Miss Henny in a severe tone, with no offer of any warmer welcome.

Seeing that something was amiss, the child quietly obeyed, and perching herself in an ancient arm-chair crossed her short legs, folded her plump hands over the diminutive travelling-bag she carried, and sat looking about the room with a pair of very large blue eyes, quite unabashed, though rather pensive, as if the memory of some tender parting were still fresh in her little heart.

While Miss Penny slowly reads the letter, Miss Henny works daisies on a bit of canvas with pettish jerks of her silk, and Miss Cicely leans in the sofa-corner, staring at the newcomer, we will briefly introduce our small heroine. Her father was cousin to the elder ladies, and being called suddenly across the water on business, took his wife with him, leaving the little girl to the care of these relatives, thinking her too young for so long a journey. Cicely, an orphan niece who lived with the old ladies, was to have the care of Rosy; and a summer in the quiet country town would do her good, while change of scene would console her for this first separation from her mother. How she fared remains to be seen; and we need only add that the child had been well trained, made the companion of a sweet and tender woman, and was very anxious to please the parents whom she passionately loved, by keeping the promises she had made them, and being "as brave as Papa, as patient and kind as dear Mamma."

"Well, what do you think of it, Missy?" asked Cicely, as the blue eyes came back to her, after roving round the spacious, old-fashioned, and rather gloomy room.

"It's a pretty large, dark place for a little girl to be all alone in;"

and there was a suspicious quiver in the childish voice, as Rosy opened her bag to produce a very small handkerchief, evidently feeling that she might have sudden need of it if some one did not speak to her very soon.

"We keep it dark on account of Sister's eyes. When *I* was a little girl, it wasn't considered polite to say rude things about other people's houses, especially if they were very handsome ones," said Miss Henny, with a stern glance over the eye-glasses at the young offender, whose second remark was even more unfortunate than her first.

"I didn't mean to be rude, but I MUST tell the truth. Little girls like bright places. I'm sorry about Cousin Penny's eyes. I will read to her; I do to Mamma, and she says it is very well for a child only eight years old."

The gentle answer and the full eyes seemed to calm Miss Henny's wrath, for her size was her tender point, and the old house her especial pride; so she dropped the awe-inspiring glasses, and said more kindly, -

"There is a nice little room ready for you upstairs, and a garden to play in. Cicely will hear you read every day, and I will teach you to sew, for of course that MOST useful part of your education has been neglected."

"No, ma'am, I sew my four patches every day, and make little wee stitches, and I can hem Papa's hank'chifs, and I was learning to darn his socks with a big needle when - when they went away."

Rosy paused with a sudden choke; but too proud to break down, she only wiped two drops off her cheek with the long ends of her little gray silk glove, set her lips, and remained mistress of herself, privately planning to cry all she liked when she was safely in the "nice little room" promised her.

Cicely, though a lazy, selfish young lady, was touched by the child's pathetic face, and said in a friendly tone, as she patted the couch where she lay, -

"Come here, dear, and sit by me, and tell me what kind of a kitten you'd like best. I know of a sweet yellow one, and two grays. Our Tabby is too old to play with you; so you will want a kitty, I'm sure."

"Oh yes, if I may!" and Rosy skipped to the new seat with a smile which plainly proved that this sort of welcome was just what she liked.

"Now, Cicely, why will you put such an idea into Rosamond's head when you know we can't have kittens round the house for Sister to stumble over, not to mention the mischief the horrid things always do? Tabby is all the child needs, with her doll. Of course you have a doll?" and Miss Henny asked the question as solemnly as if she had said, "Have you a soul?"

"Oh yes, I have nine in my trunk, and two little ones in my bag, and Mamma is going to send me a big, big one from London, as soon as she gets there, to sleep with me and be my little comfort," cried Rosy, rapidly producing from her bag a tiny bride and groom, three seed-cakes, a smelling-bottle, and a purse out of which fell a shower of bright cents, also crumbs all over the immaculate carpet.

"Mercy on us, what a mess! Pick it all up, child, and don't unpack any more in the parlor. One doll is quite enough for me," said Miss Henny, with a sigh of resignation as if asking patience to bear this new calamity.

Rosy echoed the sigh as she crept about reclaiming her precious pennies, and eating the crumbs as the only way of disposing of them.

"Never mind, it's only her way; the heat makes her a little cross, you see," whispered Cicely, bending down to hold the bag, into which Rosy bundled her treasures in hot haste.

"I thought fat people were always pleasant. I'm glad YOU ain't fat," answered the little girl, in a tone which was perfectly audible.

What would have happened I tremble to think, if Miss Penny had not finished the letter at that moment and handed it to her sister, saying as she held out her arms to the child, -

"Now I know all about it, and you are to be my baby; so come and give me some sweet kisses, darling."

Down dropped the bag, and with a little sob of joy the child nestled close to the kind old heart that welcomed her so tenderly at last.

"Papa calls me his button-rose, 'cause I'm so small and pink and sweet, and thorny too sometimes," she said, looking up brightly, after a few moments of the fond and foolish cuddling all little creatures love and need so much when they leave the nest, and miss the brooding of motherly wings.

"We'll call you anything you like, darling; but Rosamond is a pretty old name, and I'm fond of it, for it was your grand-mamma's, and a sweeter woman never lived," said Miss Penny, stroking the fresh cheeks, where the tears shone like dew on pink rose-leaves.

"I shall call you Chicken Little, because we have Henny and Penny; and the girls and Tab downstairs can be Goosey-Loosey, Turkey-Lurkey, and Cocky-Locky. I'll be Ducky-Lucky, and I'm sure Foxy-Loxy lives next door," said Cicely, laughing at her own wit, while Miss Henny looked up, saying, with the first smile Rosy had seen, -

"That's true enough! and I hope Chicken Little will keep out of his way, no matter if the sky does fall."

"Who is it? A truly fox? I never saw one. Could I peep at him sometimes?" cried the child, much interested at once.

"No, dear; it's only a neighbor of ours who has treated us badly, at least we think so, and we don't speak, though we used to be good friends some years ago. It's sad to live so, but we don't quite see how to help it yet. We are ready to do our part; but Mr. Dover should take the first step, as he was in the wrong."

"Please tell about it. I have horrid quarrels with Mamie Parsons sometimes, but we always kiss and make up, and feel all happy again. Can't you, Cousin Penny?" asked the child, softly touching the little white curls under the lace cap.

"Well, no, dear; grown people cannot settle differences in that pretty way. We must wait till he apologizes, and then we shall gladly be friends again. You see Mr. Dover was a missionary in India for many years, and we were very intimate with his mother. Our gardens join, and a gate in our fence led across their field to the back street, and was most convenient when we wanted to walk by the river or send the maids on errands in a hurry. The old lady was very neighborly, and we were quite comfortable till Thomas came home and made trouble. He'd lost his wife and children, poor man, and his liver was out of order, and living among the heathen so long had made him melancholy and queer; so he tried to amuse himself with gardening and keeping hens."

"I'm glad! I love flowers and biddies," murmured Rosy, listening with deep interest to this delightful mixture of quarrels and heathen, sorrow, poultry, mysterious diseases, and gardens.

"He had no right to shut up our gate and forbid our crossing that little field, and no GENTLEMAN would have DARED to do it after all our kindness to his mother," exclaimed Miss Henny, so suddenly and violently that Rosamond nearly fell off the old lady's lap with the start she gave.

"No, sister, I don't agree there. Mr. Thomas had a perfect RIGHT to do as he liked with his own land; but I think we should have had no trouble if you had been willing to sell him the corner of our garden where the old summer-house is, for his hens," began Miss Penny in a mild tone.

"Sister! you know the tender memories connected with that bower, and how terrible it would have been to ME to see it torn down, and noisy fowls clucking and pecking where I and my poor Calvin once sat together," cried Miss Henny, trying to look sentimental, which was an impossible feat for a stout lady in a flowery muslin gown, and a fly-away cap full of blue ribbons, on a head once flaxen and now gray.

"We won't discuss the point, Henrietta," said the elder lady with dignity; whereupon the other returned to the letter, bridling and tossing her head in a way which caused Rosy to stare, and resolve to imitate it when she played be a proud princess with her dolls.

"Well, dear, that was the beginning of the trouble," continued Miss Penny; "and now we don't speak, and the old lady misses us, I'm sure, and I often long to run in and see her, and I'm so sorry you can't enjoy the wonders of that house, for it's full of beautiful and curious things, most instructive for children to observe. Mr. Thomas has been a great traveller, and has a tiger skin in the parlor so natural it's quite startling to behold; also spears, and bows and arrows, and necklaces of shark's teeth, from the Cannibal Islands, and the loveliest stuffed birds, my dear, all over the place, and pretty shells and baskets, and ivory toys, and odd dresses, and no end of wonderful treasures. Such a sad pity you can't see them!" and Miss Penny looked quite distressed at the child's loss.

"Oh, but I guess I will see 'em! Every one is good to me, and old gentlemen like little girls. Papa says so, and HE always does what I want when I say 'Please' with my wheedulin smile, as he calls it," said Rosy, giving them a sample of the most engaging sort.

"You funny little thing, do try it, and soften the heart of that tiresome man! He has the finest roses in town and the most delicious fruit, and we never get any, though he sends quantities everywhere else. Such a fuss over an old ear-wiggy arbor! It is perfectly provoking, when we might enjoy so much over there; and who knows what might happen!"

As Cicely spoke, she smoothed her brown curls and glanced at the mirror, quite conscious that a very pretty young lady of twenty was wasting her sweetness in the great gloomy house, with two elderly spinsters.

"I'll get some for you," answered Rosy, with a nod of such calm conviction of her own power, that Cicely laughed again, and proposed that she should go at once and view the battle-field.

"Could I RUN in the garden? I'd love to, after riding so long," asked Rosy, eager to be off; for her active legs ached for exercise, and the close, shady room oppressed her.

"Yes, dear; but don't get into mischief, or worry Tabby, or pick the flowers. Of course you wouldn't touch green fruit, or climb trees, or soil your little frock. I'll ring the bell for you to come in and be dressed for tea when it is time."

With these directions and a kiss, Miss Penny, as Cicely did not stir, let the child out at the back door of the long hall, and watched her walk demurely down the main path of the prim old garden, where no child had played for years, and even the toads and fat robins behaved in the most decorous manner.

"It's pretty dull, but it's better than the parlor with all the staring pictures," said Rosy to herself, after a voyage of discovery had shown her the few charms of the place. The sight of a large yellow cat reposing in the sun cheered her eyes at that moment, and she hastened to scrape acquaintance with the stately animal; for the snails were not social, and the toads stared even more fixedly at her than the painted eyes of her respected ancestors.

But Tabby disliked children as much as her mistress, and after submitting ungraciously to a few caresses from the eager little hands, she rose and retired majestically to a safer perch on the top of the high wall which enclosed the garden. Being too lazy to jump, she walked up the shelves of an old flower-stand moulding in a corner, and by so doing, gave Rosy a brilliant idea, which she at once put into action by following Tabby's example. Up this new sort of ladder she went, and peeped over the wall, delighted at this unexpected chance to behold the enemy's territory.

"Oh, what a pretty place!" she cried, clasping her grubby little hands with rapture, as the beauties of the forbidden land burst upon her view.

It was indeed a paradise to a child's eyes, - for flowers bloomed along the winding paths; ripening fruit lay rosy and tempting in the beds below; behind the wire walls that confined them clucked and strutted various sorts of poultry; cages of gay birds hung on the piazza; and through the open windows of the house one caught glimpses of curious curtains, bright weapons, and mysterious objects in the rooms beyond.

A gray-headed gentleman in a queer nankeen coat lay asleep on a bamboo lounge under the great cherry-tree, with a purple silk handkerchief half over his face.

"That's the missionary man, I s'pose. He doesn't look cross at all. If I could only get down there, I'd go and wake him with a softly kiss, as I do Papa, and ask to see his pretty things."

Being quite unconscious of fear, Rosy certainly would have carried out her daring plan, had it been possible; but no way of descending on the other side appeared, so she sighed and sat gazing wistfully, till Cousin Henny appeared for a breath of fresh air, and ordered her down at once.

"Come and see if my balsam-seeds have started yet. I keep planting them, but they WON'T come up," she said, pointing out a mound of earth newly dug and watered.

Rosy obediently scrambled up, and was trying to decide whether some green sprouts were chickweed or the dilatory balsams when a sudden uproar in the next garden made her stop to listen, while Miss Henny said in a tone of great satisfaction, as the cackle of hens arose, -

"Some trouble with those horrid fowls of his. I detest them, crowing in the night, and waking us at dawn with their noise. I wish some thief would steal every one of them. Nobody has a right to annoy their neighbors with troublesome pets."

Before Rosy could describe the beauties of the white bantams or the size of the big golden cock, a loud voice cried, -

"You rascal! I'll hang you if I catch you here again. Go home quicker than you came, and tell your mistress to teach you better manners, if she values your life."

"It's that man! Such language! I wonder who he's caught? That bad boy who steals our plums, perhaps."

The words were hardly out of Miss Henny's mouth when her question was answered in a sudden and dreadful way; for over the wall, hurled by a strong arm, flew Tabby, high in the air, to fall with a thump directly in the middle of the bed where they stood. Miss Henny uttered a shrill scream, caught up her stunned treasure, and rushed into the house as fast as her size and flounces permitted, leaving Rosy breathless with surprise and indignation.

Burning to resent this terrible outrage, she climbed quickly up the steps, and astonished the irate old gentleman on the other side by the sudden apparition of a golden head, a red childish face, and a dirty little finger pointed sternly at him, as this small avenging angel demanded, -

"Missionary man, how COULD you kill my cousin's cat?"

"Bless my soul! who are you?" said the old gentleman, staring at this unexpected actor on the field of battle.

"I'm Button-Rose, and I hate cruel people! Tabby's dead, and now there isn't any one to play with over here."

This sad prospect made the blue eyes fill with sudden tears; and the application of the dirty fingers added streaks of mud to the red cheeks, which much damaged the appearance of the angel, thought it added pathos to the child's reproach.

"Cats have nine lives, and Tabby's used to being chucked over the wall. I've done it several times, and it seems to agree with her, for she comes back to kill my chicks as bold as brass. See that!" and the old gentleman held up a downy dead chicken, as proof of Tabby's sin.

"Poor little chicky!" groaned Rosy, yearning to mourn over the dear departed and bury it with tender care. "It WAS very naughty of Tab; but, sir, you know cats are made to catch things, and they can't help it."

"They will have to help it, or I'll drown the lot. This is a rare breed, and I've but two left after all my trouble, thanks to that rascal of yours! What are you going to do about it?" demanded Mr. Dover, in a tone that made Rosy feel as if she had committed the murder herself.

"I'll talk to Tabby and try to make her good, and I'll shut her up in the old rabbit-house over here; then I hope she will be sorry and never do it any more," she said, in such a remorseful tone that the old gentleman relented at once, ashamed to afflict such a tender little soul.

"Try it," he said, with a smile that made his yellow face pleasant all at once. Then, as if ready to change the subject, he asked, looking curiously at the little figure perched on the wall, -

"Where did you come from? Never saw any children over there before. They don't allow 'em."

Rosy introduced herself in a few words, and seeing that her new acquaintance seemed interested, she added with the wheedling smile Papa found so engaging, -

"It's pretty lonely here, I guess; so p'r'aps you'll let me peep at your nice garden sometimes if it doesn't trouble you, sir?"

"Poor little soul! it must be desperately dull with those three tabbies," he said to himself, as he stroked the dead chicken in his hand, and watched the little face bent toward him.

"Peep as much as you like, child; or, better still, come over and run about. *I* like little girls," he added aloud, with a nod and a wave of welcome.

"I told 'em I was sure you did! I'd love to come, but they wouldn't let me, I know. I'm so sorry about the fight. Couldn't you make it up, and be pleasant again?" asked Rosy, clasping her hands with a beseeching gesture as her bright face grew sad and serious remembering the feud.

"So they've told you that nonsense already, have they? Nice neighbors THEY are," said the old gentleman, frowning as if ill pleased at the news.

"I'm glad I know; p'r'aps I can be a peace-maker. Mamma says they are good to have in families, and I'd like to be one if I could. Would you mind if I tried to peace-make a little, so I could come over? I do want to see the red birds and the tiger skin awfully, if you please."

"What do you know about 'em?" asked the old gentleman, sitting down on a garden chair, as if he didn't mind continuing the chat with this new neighbor.

Nearly tumbling off the wall in her earnestness, Rosy repeated all that Cousin Penny had said; and something in the reasonable words, the flattering description of his treasures, and the sincere regret of the old lady seemed to have a good effect upon Mr. Dover, for when Rosy paused out of breath, he said in such an altered tone that it was evident the peace-making had already begun, -

"Miss Carey is a gentlewoman! I always thought so. You tell her, with my compliments, that I'd be glad to see you any time if she has no objection. I'll put my step-ladder there, and you can come over instead of the cat. But mind you don't meddle, or I might give you a toss like Tabby."

"I'm not afraid," laughed Rosy. "I'll go and ask right away, and I won't touch a thing, and I know you'll like me for a friend. Papa says I'm a dear little one. Thank you very much, sir. Good-by till I come again;" and with a kiss of the hand, the yellow head sunk out of sight like the sun going down, leaving a sense of darkness behind when the beaming little face disappeared, though fresh stains of green mould from the wall made it rather like the tattooed countenances Mr. Dover used to see among his cannibal friends in Africa.

He sat musing with the dead chicken in his hand, forgetful of time, till a ring of his own door-bell called him in to receive a note from Miss Penelope, thanking him for his invitation to little Rosamond, but declining it in the most polite and formal words.

"I expected it! Bless the silly old souls! why can't they be reasonable, and accept the olive branch when I offer it? I'll be hanged if I do again! The fat one is at the bottom of this. Miss Pen would give in if that absurd Henrietta didn't hold her back. Well, I'm sorry for the child, but that's not my fault;" and throwing down the note, he went out to water his roses.

For a week or two, Button-Rose hardly dared glance toward the forbidden spot from her window, as she was ordered to play in the front garden, and sent to take sober walks with

Louisa May Alcott

Cicely, who loved to stop and gossip with her friends, while the poor child waited patiently till the long tales were told.

Nursing Tabby was her chief consolation; and so kind was she, that the heart of the old cat softened to her, and she actually purred her thanks at last, for all the saucers of cream, bits of chicken, soft pats, and tender words bestowed upon her by the little girl.

"Well, I declare! Tab won't do that even for me," said Miss Henny, one day when she came upon the child sitting alone in the hall with a picture-book and the cat comfortably asleep in her lap.

"Ammals always love me, if people don't," answered Button-Rose, soberly; for she had not yet forgiven the stout lady for denying her the delights offered by the "missionary man."

"That's because AN-I-MALS can't see how naughty you are sometimes," said Miss Henny tartly, not having recovered her temper even after many days.

"I shall make EVERY one love me before I go away. Mamma told me to, and I shall. I know how;" and Button smiled with a wise little nod that was pretty to see, as she proudly cuddled her first conquest.

"We shall see;" and Miss Henny ponderously departed, wondering what odd fancy the little thing would take into her head next.

It was soon evident; for when she came down from her long nap, later in the afternoon, Miss Henny found Rosamond reading aloud to her sister in the great dim parlor. They made a curious contrast, - the pale, white-haired, feeble old lady, with her prim dress, high cap, knitting, and shaded eyes; and the child, rosy and round, quaint and sweet, a pretty little ornament for the old-fashioned room, as she sat among the tea-poys and samplers, ancient china and furniture, with the portraits of great grandfathers and grandmothers simpering and staring at her, as if pleased and surprised to see such a charming little descendant among them.

"Bless the baby! what is she at now?" asked Miss Henny, feeling more amiable after her sleep.

"I'm reading to Cousin Penny, 'cause no one else does, and her poor eyes hurt her, and she likes stories, and so do I," answered Button, with one chubby finger on the place in her book, and eyes full of pride at the grown-up employment she had found for herself.

"So kind of the little dear! She found me alone and wanted to amuse me; so I proposed a story to suit us both, and she does very well with a little help now and then. I haven't read 'Simple Susan' for years, and really enjoy it. Maria Edgeworth was always a favorite of mine, and I still think her far superior to any modern writer for the young," said Miss Penny, looking quite animated and happy in the new entertainment provided for her.
"Go on, child; let me hear how well you can read;" and Miss Henny settled herself in the sofa-corner with her embroidery.

So Button started bravely on, and tried so hard that she was soon out of breath. As she paused, she said with a gasp, -

"Isn't Susan a dear girl? She gives ALL the best things to other people, and is kind to the old harper. She didn't send him away, as you did the music-man to-day, and tell him to be still."

"Organs are a nuisance, and I never allow them here. Go on, and don't criticise your elders, Rosamond."

"Mamma and I always talk over stories, and pick out the morals of 'em. SHE likes it;" with which remark, made sweetly not pertly, Button went on to the end, with an occasional lift over a long word; and the old ladies were interested, in spite of themselves, in the simple tale read in that childish voice.

"Thank you, dear, it is very nice, and we will have one every day. Now, what can I do for you?" asked Miss Penny, as the little girl pushed the curls off her forehead, with a sigh of mingled weariness and satisfaction.

"Let me go in the back garden and peep through the knot-hole at the pretty roses. I do long to see if the moss ones are out, and the cherries ripe," said Rosy, clasping her hands imploringly.

"It can do no harm, Henrietta. Yes, dear, run away and get some catnip for Tabby, and see if the balsams are up yet."

That last suggestion won Miss Henny's consent; and Button was off at once, skipping like a young colt all over the garden, which now seemed delightful to her.

At the back of the summer-house was a narrow space between it and the fence where certain plump toads lived; peeping in to watch them, Rosy had spied a large knot-hole in the old boards, and through it found she could get a fine view of several rose-bushes, a tree, and one window of the "missionary man's" house. She had longed for another peep since the flower-stand was gone, and climbing trees forbidden; now with joy she slipped into the damp nook, regardless of the speckled gentlemen who stared at her with dismay, and took a good look at the forbidden paradise beyond.

Yes, the "moss ones" were in bloom, the cherries quite red, and at the window was the gray head of Mr. Dover, as he sat reading in his queer yellow dressing-gown.

Button yearned to get in, and leaned so hard against the hateful fence that the rotten board cracked, a long bit fell out, and she nearly went after it, as it dropped upon the green bank below. Now the full splendor of the roses burst upon her, and a delightful gooseberry bush stood close by with purplish berries temptingly bobbing within reach. This obliging bush hid the hole, but left fine openings to see through; so the child popped her curly head out, and gazed delightedly at the chickens, the flowers, the fruit, and the unconscious old gentleman not far away.

"I'll have it for my secret; or maybe I'll tell Cousin Penny, and beg her to let me peep if I truly promise never to go in," thought Button, knowing well who her best friend was.

At bedtime, when the dear old lady came to give the good-night kiss, which the others forgot, Rosy, as Miss Penny called her, made her request; and it was granted, for Miss Penny had a feeling that the little peacemaker would sooner or later heal the breach with her pretty magic, and so she was very ready to lend a hand in a quiet way.

Next day at play-time, Button was hurrying down her last bit of gingerbread, which she was obliged to eat properly in the dining-room, instead of enjoying out-of-doors, when she heard a sudden flurry in the garden, and running to the window saw Roxy the maid chasing a chicken to and fro, while Miss Henny stood flapping her skirts on the steps, and crying, "Shoo!" till she was red in the face.

"It's the white banty, and it must have come in my hole! Oh dear, I hope they won't catch it! Cousin Henny said she'd wring the neck of the first one that flied over the wall."

Away went Rosy, to join in the hunt; for Miss Henny was too fat to run, and Roxy found the lively fowl too much for her. It was a long and hard chase; feathers flew, the maid lost her breath, Rosy tumbled down, and Miss Henny screamed and scolded till she was forced to sit down and watch in silence.

At last poor, hunted Banty ran into the arbor, for its clipped wings would not lift it over the wall. Button rushed after it, and dismal squalls plainly proclaimed that the naughty chicken was caught.

Miss Henny waddled down the path, declaring that she WOULD wring its neck; and Roxy went puffing after her, glad to rest. But the old summer-house was empty. No little girl, no ruffled bantam, appeared. Both had vanished like magic; and mistress and maid stared at each other in amazement, till they saw that the long-disused window was open, and a gleam of light came in from the narrow opening behind.

"My patience! if that child hasn't crept out there, and bolted through that hole in the fence! Did you ever, Miss?" exclaimed Roxy, trying not to look pleased at being spared the distasteful task of killing the poor chicken.

"Naughty girl!" began Miss Henny, when the sound of voices made both listen. "Slip in there, and see what is going on," said the mistress, well knowing that her stout person never could be squeezed into the small space between house and fence.

Roxy, being thin, easily obeyed, and in a whisper telephoned what went on beyond the hole, causing Miss Henny much vexation, surprise, and at last real pleasure, as the child performed her little part in the mission she had undertaken.

"Oh, please, it's all my fault! I kept the hole open, Mr. Thomas, and so Banty flied in. But it isn't hurt a bit, and I've brought it home all safe, 'cause I know you love your chickies, and Tabby ate lots of 'em," said the childish voice in its most conciliatory tone.

"Why didn't you fling it over the wall, as I did the cat?" asked Mr. Dover, smiling, as he shut up the truant fowl, and turned to look at the rosy, breathless child, whose pink frock bore the marks of many a tumble on grass and gravel.

"It would hurt Banty's feelings, and yours too, and not be polite. So I came myself, to make some pollygies, and say it was my fault. But, please, could I keep the hole to peep through, if I always put up a board when I go away? It is so dull in there, and SO sweet in here!"

"Don't you think a little gate would be nicer, - one just big enough for you, with a hook to fasten it? We'll call it a button-hole," laughed Mr. Dover. "Then you could peep; or perhaps the ladies will think better of it, and show that they pardon my ill treatment of Tabby by letting you come in and pick some cherries and roses now and then."

This charming proposal caused the little girl to clasp her hands and cry aloud, -

"That would be perfully sp'endid! I know Cousin Penny would like it, and let me. P'r'aps she'd come herself; she's so thin, she could, and she loves your mother and wants to see her. Only, Cousin Henny won't let us be nice and friendly. S'pose you send HER some cherries; she loves good things to eat, and maybe she will say yes, if you send lots."

Mr. Dover laughed at this artless proposal, and Miss Henny smiled at the prospect of a gift of the luscious black-heart cherries she had been longing for. Roxy wisely repeated only the agreeable parts of the conversation; so nothing ruffled the lady's temper. Now, whether Mr. Dover's sharp eye caught a glimpse of the face among the gooseberry bushes, and suspected eavesdroppers, or whether the child's earnest desire to make peace touched him, who shall say? Certain it is that his eyes twinkled like a boy's, as he said rather loudly, in his most affable tone, -

"I shall be most happy to send Miss Henrietta a basket of fruit. She used to be a charming young woman. It's a pity she shuts herself up so much; but that sad little romance of hers has darkened her life, I suppose. Ah, well, I can sympathize with her!"

Rosy stared at the sudden change in his manner, and was rather bewildered by his grown-up way of talking to her. But being intent on securing something nice to carry home, she stuck to the cherries, which she DID understand, and pointing to the piazza said with a business-like air, -

"There's a basket; so we might pick 'em right away. I love to go up in trees and throw 'em down; and I know Cousin Henny will like cherries ever so much, and not scold a bit when I take some to her."

"Then come on," cried Mr. Thomas, relapsing into the hearty manner she liked so much; and away he went, quite briskly, down the path, with his yellow skirts waving in the wind, and Button skipping after him in great glee.

"They actually ARE a-picking cherries, Miss, up in the tree like a couple of robins a-chirpin' and laughin' as gay as can be," reported Roxy, from her peep-hole.

"Rip off the rest of that board, then I can see," whispered Miss Henny, quivering with interest now; for she had heard Mr. Dover's words, and her wrath was appeased by that flattering allusion to herself.

Off came the rest of the board, and from the window, half hidden in woodbine, she could now see over the bushes into the next garden. The peep-hole commanded the tree, and she watched with eager eyes the filling of the basket to be sent her, planning the while a charming note of thanks.

"Do look, Miss; they are resting now, and she's on his knee. Ain't it a pretty picter?" whispered Roxy, unmindful of the earwigs, ants, and daddy-long-legs promenading over her as she crouched in her mouldy corner, intent on the view beyond.

"Very pretty! He lost several children in India and I suppose Rosy reminds him of them. Ah, poor man! I can sympathize with him, for *I* too have loved and lost," sighed Miss Henny, pensively surveying the group on the rustic seat.

They were playing cherry-bob; and the child's laughter made pleasant music in the usually quiet place, while the man's face lost its sad, stern look, and was both gay and tender, as he held the little creature close, and popped the ripe fruit into the red, laughing mouth.

As the last sweet morsel disappeared Rosy said, with a long breath of perfect content, -

"It's ALMOST as good as having Papa to play with. I do hope the cousins WILL let me come again! If they don't, I think my heart will break, 'cause I get so homesick over there, and have so many trials, and no one but Cousin Penny ever cuddles me."

"Bless her heart! We'll send her some flowers for that. You tell her that Mrs. Dover is poorly, and would like very much to see her; and so would Mr. Thomas, who enjoys her little niece immensely. Can you remember that?"

"Every word! SHE is very nice to me, and I love her, and I guess she will be glad to come. She likes MOSS-roses, and so do I," added the unblushing little beggar, as Mr. Dover took out his knife and began to make the bouquet which was to be Miss Penny's bribe. He could not bear to give up his little playmate, and was quite ready to try again, with this persistent and charming ally to help him heal the breach.

"Shall you send anything to Cis? You needn't mind about it, 'cause she can't keep me at home, but it might please her, and make her stop rapping my head with her thimble when I ask questions, and slapping my fingers when I touch any of her pretty things," suggested Button, as the flowers were added to the fruit, making a fine display.

"I never send presents to YOUNG ladies," said Mr. Thomas shortly, adding, with both hands out, and his most inviting smile, "But I ALWAYS kiss nice little girls if they will allow me?"

Louisa May Alcott

Button threw both arms about his neck and gave him a shower of grateful kisses, which were sweeter to the lonely old man than all the cherries that ever grew, or the finest flowers in his garden. Then Miss Rosamond proudly marched home, finding no trace of the watchers, for both had fled while the "cuddling" went on. Roxy was soberly setting the dinner-table, and Miss Henny in the parlor breathing hard behind a newspaper. Miss Penny and Cicely were spending the day out, so the roses had to wait; but the basket was most graciously received, also the carefully delivered message, and the child's heart was rejoiced by free permission to go and see "our kind neighbor now and then, if Sister does not object."

Rosy was in great spirits, and prattled away as they sat at dinner, emboldened by the lady's unusual amiability to ask all sorts of questions, some of which proved rather embarrassing to Miss Henny, and very amusing to Roxy, listening in the china-closet.

"I wish *I* had 'spepsia," was the abrupt remark of the small person as her plate of drum-sticks was removed and the pudding appeared, accompanied by the cherries.

"Why, dear?" asked Miss Henny, busily arranging the small dish of delicate tidbits, which left little but the skeleton of the roast fowl for the kitchen.

"Then I could have the nicest bits of chicken, and heaps of sauce on my pudding, and the butteryest slices of toast, and ALL the cream for my tea, as you do. It isn't a VERY bad pain, is it?" asked Rosy, in such perfect good faith that Miss Henny's sudden flush and Roxy's hasty dive into the closet never suggested to her that this innocent speech was bringing the old lady's besetting sin to light in the most open manner.

"Yes, child, it is VERY bad, and you may thank your stars that I try to keep you from it by feeding you on plain food. At my age, and suffering as I do, the best of everything is needed to keep up my strength," said Miss Henny, tartly. But the largest plate of pudding, with "heaps of sauce," went to the child this day, and when the fruit was served, an unusually small portion was put away for the invalid, who was obliged to sustain nature with frequent lunches through the day and evening.

"I'm s'prised that you suffer much, Cousin Henny. How brave you must be, not to cry about it, and go round in horrid pain, as you do, and dress so nicely, and see people, and work 'broidering, and make calls! I hope I shall be brave if I ever DO have 'spepsia; but I guess I shan't, you take such care to give me small pieces every time."

With which cheerful remark Rosy closed that part of the conversation and returned to the delights of her new friend's garden. But from that day, among other changes which began about this time, the child's cup and plate were well filled, and the dread of adding to her own sufferings seemed to curb the dyspeptic's voracious appetite. "A cheild was amang them takin' notes," and every one involuntarily dreaded those clear eyes and that frank tongue, so innocently observing and criticising all that went on. Cicely had already been reminded of a neglected duty by Rosy's reading to Miss Penny, and tried to be more faithful in that, as in other services which she owed the old lady. So the little missionary was evidently getting on, though quite unconscious of her work at home, so absorbed was she in her foreign mission; for, like many another missionary, the savage over the way was more interesting than the selfish, slothful, or neglected souls at home.

Miss Penny was charmed with her flowers and the friendly message sent her, and to Rosy's great delight went next day, in best bonnet and gown, to make a call upon the old lady "who was poorly," for that appeal could not be resisted. Rosy also, in honor of the great occasion, wore HER best hat, and a white frock so stiff that she looked like a little opera dancer as the long black legs skipped along the street; for it was far too grand a visit to be paid through a hole in the wall.

In the basket were certain delicacies for the old lady, and a card had been prepared, with the names of Miss Carey and Miss Rosamond Carey beautifully written on it by Cis, who was dying to go, but dared not after Rosy had told her Mr. Dover's remark about young ladies.

As the procession of two paused at the door, both the young and the old heart fluttered a little, for this was the first decided step toward reconciliation, and any check might spoil it all. The maid stared, but civilly led these unexpected guests in and departed with the card. Miss Penny settled herself in a large chair and looked about with pensive interest at the familiar room. But Rosy made a bee-line for the great tiger-skin, and regardless of her clean frock lay down on it to examine the head, which glared at her with yellow eyes, showing all its sharp teeth in the most delightfully natural manner.

Mr. Dover came in with a formal bow, but Miss Penny put out both hands, and said in her sweet old voice, -

"Let us be friends again for the sake of your mother."

That settled the matter at once, and Mr. Thomas was so eager to do his part that he not only shook the hands heartily, but kept them in his as he said like an honest man, -

"My dear neighbor, I beg your pardon! *I* was wrong, but I'm not too proud to own it and say I'm glad to let by-gones be by-gones for the sake of all. Now come and see my mother; she is longing for you."

What went on in the next room Rosy never knew or cared, for Mr. Thomas soon returned, and amused her so well, showing his treasures, that she forgot where she was till the maid came to say tea was ready.

"Are we going to stay?" cried the little girl, beaming from under a Feejee crown of feathers, which produced as comical an effect upon her curly head as did the collar of shark's teeth round her plump neck or the great Japanese war-fan in her hand.

"Yes, we have tea at five; come and turn it out. I've ordered the little cups especially for you," said her host, as he changed the small Amazon to a pretty child again and led her away to preside at the table, where the quaint china and silver, and the dainty cake and bread and butter proved much more attractive than the little old lady in a big cap who patted her head and smiled at her.

Never had Rosy enjoyed such a delicious meal; for the rapture of pouring real tea out of a pot shaped like a silver melon, into cups as thin as egg-shells, and putting in sugar with tongs like claws, not to mention much thick cream, also spicy, plummy cakes that melted in one's mouth, was too great for words.

The little maid was so absorbed in her new duties that she never minded what the elders talked about, till the plates were empty, the pot ran dry, and no one could be prevailed on to have any more tea. Then she leaned back in her chair and remarked with an air of calm satisfaction, as she looked from one to the other, and smiled that engaging smile of hers, -

"Isn't being friends a great deal nicer than fighting and throwing cats over walls and calling bad names?"

It was impossible not to laugh, and that cheerful sound seemed to tune every one to the sweetest harmony, while the little peacemaker was passed round as if a last course of kisses was absolutely necessary.

Then the party broke up, and Mr. Dover escorted his guests to their own gate, to the great amazement of the neighbors and the very visible pride of Miss Button-Rose, who went up the walk with her head as high as if the wreath of daisies on her little hat had been a conqueror's crown.

Now that the first step had been taken, all would have gone smoothly if Cicely, offended because Mr. Thomas took no notice of HER, had not put it into Miss Henny's head that as the original quarrel began between her and their neighbor, it would not be dignified to give in till Mr. Dover had come and begged pardon of HER as well as of Miss Penny. This suited the foolish old lady, who never could forget certain plain words spoken in the heat of battle, though the kindly ones lately heard had much softened her heart toward the offender.

"No, I shall not forget my dignity nor humble myself by going over there to apologize as Penelope has. SHE can do as she likes; and now that he has asked to be forgiven, there is perhaps no harm in HER seeing the old lady. But with me it is different. *I* was insulted, and till Thomas Dover conies here and solemnly asks my pardon I will NOT cross his threshold, no matter what bribes he sends," said Miss Henny, with an air of heroic firmness.

But it did cost her a pang when her sister went every now and then to take tea with the old lady and came home full of pleasant news; while Rosy prattled of the fine things she saw, the nice things she had to eat, and never failed to bring some gift to share, or to display to the exiles from Paradise. They ate the "bribes," however, as they called the fruit, admired the pretty trinkets and toys, and longed to share in the mild festivities of the pleasant house over the way, but stood firm in spite of all Rosy's wiles, till something unexpected happened to touch their hearts, conquer their foolish pride, and crown the little peacemaker's efforts with success.

One August afternoon Cicely was discontentedly looking over her small store of ornaments as she made ready for a party. She loved gayety, and went about a great deal, leaving many duties undone, or asking the little girl to attend to them for her, neglecting, however, to show any gratitude for these small services so cheerfully done.

As she sat tossing over her boxes, Button-Rose came in looking tired and listless, for it was a hot day, and she had been out twice to do errands for Cicely, besides trotting busily up and down to wait on the old ladies while the young one put fresh ribbons on her dress and curled her hair for the evening.

"Could I lie on your sofa, please, Cis? My head aches, and my legs are SO tired," said little Button, when her tap had been answered by a sharp "What do you want, child?"

"No, I'm going to lie there myself and have a nap as soon as I'm done here. It's cooler than the bed, and I must be fresh for to-night," said Cicely, too intent on her own affairs to see how used up Rosy looked.

"Then could I look at your pretty things if I don't touch 'em?" asked the child, longing to peep into the interesting boxes scattered on the table.

"No, you can't! I'm busy, and don't want you asking questions and meddling. Go away and let me alone."

Cicely spoke crossly, and waved her hand with a warning gesture, thereby upsetting the tray which held the beads of the necklace she had decided to wear for want of something better.

"There, now see what you've done! Pick up every one, and be quick, for I'm in a hurry."

"But I didn't touch 'em," began poor Button, as she crept about hunting for the black and white beads that looked like very ugly marbles.

"Don't talk; pick them up and then scamper; you are always in mischief!" scolded Cis, vexed with herself, and the heat, and the accident, and the whole world just then.

Rosy said no more, but several great tears dropped on the carpet as she groped in corners, under the bed, and behind the chairs for the run-aways; and when the last was found she put it in her tyrant's hand, saying, with a wistful look, -

"I'm very sorry I troubled you. Seems to me if *I* had a little cousin, I'd love to have her play with my things, and I wouldn't be cross to her. Now I'll go and try to AMOOSE myself with Bella; SHE is always good to me."

"Run along then. Thank goodness that doll came when it did, for I'm tired of 'amoosing' small girls as well as old ladies," said Cis, busy with her beads, yet sorry she had been so petulant with patient little Button, who seldom reproached her, being a cheery child, and blessed with a sweet temper.

Rosy felt too languid to play; so when she had told Bella, the London doll, her trials, and comforted herself with some kisses on the waxen cheeks, she roamed away to the summer-house, which was cool and quiet, longing for some one to caress her; for the little heart was homesick and the little head ached badly.

The "button-hole" had been made, the alley swept out, to the great dismay of the spiders, earwigs, and toads, who had fled to quieter quarters, and Rosy had leave to go and come when she liked if Mr. Dover did not object. He never did; and it was her greatest delight to walk in the pretty garden at her own sweet will, always with the hope of meeting its kindly owner, for now they were firm friends. She had been too busy for a run there that day; and now, as she peeped in, it looked so shady and inviting, and it seemed so natural to turn to her dear "missionary man" for entertainment, that she went straight up to his study window and peeped in.

He too seemed out of sorts that hot afternoon, for he sat leaning his head on both hands at the desk strewn with piles of old letters. Button-Rose's tender heart yearned over him at once, and stepping quietly in at the long open window she went to him, saying in her tenderest tone, -

"Does your head ache, sir? Let me soft it as I do Papa's; he says that always makes it more better. Please let me? I'd love to dearly."

"Ah, my darling, I wish you could. But the pain is in my heart, and nothing will ever cure it," sighed Mr. Thomas, as he drew her close and put his wrinkled yellow cheek to her soft one, which looked more like a damask rose than usual.

"You have trials too, I s'pose. Mine trouble me to-day, so I came over to see you. Shall I go away?" asked Rosy with a sigh and the wistful look again.

"No, stay, and we will comfort each other. Tell me your troubles, Button, and perhaps I can help them," the kind old gentleman said as he took her on his knee and stroked the curly head with a paternal touch.

So Rosy told her latest grief, and never saw the smile that crept about the lips that asked in a tone of deep interest, -

"Well, what do you mean to do to that unkind Cicely?"

"For a minute I wanted to slap her back when she tried to spat my hands. Then I 'membered that Mamma said a kiss for a blow was a good thing, so I picked up the beads and planned to do it; but Cis looked SO cross I couldn't. If I had a pretty necklace I'd go and give it to her, and then maybe she'd love me better."

"My dear little missionary, you SHALL have beads to win the heart of YOUR heathen, if that is all you need. See here; take anything you like, and give it with the kiss."

As he spoke, Mr. Dover pulled open a drawer in the desk and displayed a delightful collection of pretty, quaint, and curious trinkets picked up in foreign lands, and kept for keepsakes, since no little daughters of his own lived to wear them.

"How perf'ly dorgeous!" cried Rosy, who often fell into baby talk when excited; and plunging in her hands, she revelled for some minutes in sandal-wood cases, carved ivory fans, silver bangles, barbaric brooches, and necklaces of coral, shells, amber, and golden coins, that jingled musically.

"What SHALL I take for her?" cried the little maid, bewildered by such a mine of wealth. "You pick out one, Mr. Thomas, that will please her so much, 'cause you never send her anything, and she don't like it," said Rosy, fearing that her own taste was not to be trusted, as she liked the shells and shark's teeth ornaments best.

"No, I'll give YOU one, and you shall do as you like about giving it to her. This, now, is really valuable and pretty, and any young lady would like to wear it. It makes me think of you, my Button, for it is like sunshine, and the word cut on the little heart means peace."

Mr. Dover held up a string of amber beads with its carved amulet, and swung it to and fro where the light shone through it till each bead looked like a drop of golden wine.

"Yes, that is lovely, and it smells nice, too. She will be so s'prised and pleased; I'll go and take it to her right away," cried Rosy, forgetting to ask anything for herself, in her delight at this fine gift for Cis.

But as she lifted her head after he had fastened the clasp about her neck, something in his face recalled the look it wore when she first came in, and putting both hands upon his shoulders, she said in her sweet little way, -

"You've made my troubles go away, can't I make yours? You are SO kind to me, I'd love to help you if I could."

"You do, my child, more than you know; for when I get you in my arms it seems as if one of my poor babies had come back to me, and for a minute I forget the three little graves far away in India."

"Three!" cried Button, like a sad, soft echo; and she clung to the poor man as if trying to fill the empty arms with the love and pity that over-flowed the childish soul in her small body.

This was the comfort Mr. Thomas wanted, and for a few moments he just cradled her on his hungry heart, crooning a Hindostanee lullaby, while a few slow tears came dropping down upon the yellow head, so like those hidden for years under the Indian flowers. Presently he seemed to come back from the happy past to which the old letters had carried him. He wiped his eyes, and Rosy's also, with the big purple silk handkerchief, and pressing some very grateful kisses on the hot cheeks, said cheerfully again, -

"God bless you, child, that's done me good! But don't let it sadden you, dear; forget all about it, and tell no one what a sentimental old fool I am."

"I never truly will! Only when you feel sorry about the poor little babies, let me come and give you cuddlings. They always make people feel more better, and I love 'em, and don't get any now my dear people are away."

So the two made a tender little plan to comfort each other when hearts were heavy with longings for the absent, and parted at the small gate, both much cheered, and faster friends than ever.

Rosy hastened in with her peace-offering, forgetful now of headache or loneliness as she sat patiently in the wide entry window-seat listening till some sound in Cicely's room should show that she was awake. Before that happened, however, poor Button fell asleep herself, lulled by the quiet of the house, - for every one was napping, - and dreamed that Mr. Dover stood waving a rainbow over his head, while several Indian gods and three little girls were dancing round him, hand in hand, to the tune of "Ring around a rosy."

A loud yawn roused her, and there was Cis peeping out of her door to see what time it was by the old-fashioned clock on the landing. Up scrambled the child, feeling dizzy and heavy-eyed, but so eager to give pleasure that she lost no time in saying, as she swung the necklace in the sunshine, -

"See! this is for you, if you like it more better than the thunder-and-lightning marbles, as Cousin Penny calls the one you were going to wear."

"How lovely! Where DID you get it, child?" cried Cis, wide awake at once, as she ran to the glass to try the effect of the new ornament on her white neck.

"My dear Mr. Thomas gave it to me; but he said I could give it away if I liked, and I want you to have it, 'cause it's ever so much prettier than any you've got."

"That's very kind of you, Chicken, but why not keep it yourself? You like nice things as well as I do," said Cicely, much impressed by the value of the gift, for it was real amber, and the clasp of gold.

"Well, I've talked with Mr. Thomas about missionarying a great deal, and he told me how he made the savinges good by giving them beads, and things to eat, and being patient and kind to them. So I thought I'd play be a missionary, and call this house Africa, and try to make the people here behave more better," answered Rosy, with such engaging earnestness, as well as frankness, that Cis laughed, and exclaimed, -

"You impertinent monkey, to call us heathen and try to convert us! How do you expect to do it?"

"Oh, I'm getting on pretty well, only you don't CONVERT as quick as some of the savinges did. I'll tell you about it;" and Button went on eagerly. "Cousin Penny is the good old one, but rather fussy and slow, so I'm kind and patient, and now she loves me and lets me do things I like. She is my best one. Cousin Henny is my cannybel, 'cause she eats so much, and I please HER by bringing nice things and getting her cushions ready. You are my baddest one, who is cross to me, and fights, and raps my head, and slaps my hands; so I thought some beads would be nice for you, and I bringed these beauties. Mr. Thomas gave 'em to me when I told him my trials."

Cicely looked angry, amused, and ashamed, as she listened to the funny yet rather pathetic little play with which the lonely child had tried to cheer herself and win the hearts of those about her. She had the grace to blush, and offer back the necklace, saying in a self-reproachful tone, -

"Keep your beads, little missionary, I'll be converted without them, and try to be kinder to you. I AM a selfish wretch, but you shall play be my little sister, and not have to go to strangers for comfort in your trials any more. Come, kiss me, dear, and we'll begin now."

Rosy was in her arms at once, and clung there, saying with a face all smiles, -

"That's what I wanted! I thought I'd make a good savinge of you if I tried VERY hard. Please be kind to me just till Mamma comes back, and I'll be the best little sister that ever was."

"Why didn't you tell me all about it before?" asked Cicely, smoothing the tired head on her shoulder with a new gentleness; for this last innocent confession had touched her heart as well as her conscience.

"You never seemed to care about my plays, and always said, 'Don't chatter, child; run away and take care of yourself.' So I did; but it was pretty dull, with only Tabby to tell secrets to and Bella to kiss. Mr. Thomas said people over here didn't like children very well, and I found they didn't. HE does, dearly, so I went to him; but I like you now, you are so soft and kind to me."

"How hot your cheeks are! Come and let me cool them, and brush your hair for tea," said Cis, as she touched the child's feverish skin, and saw how heavy her eyes were.

"I'm all burning up, and my head is SO funny. I don't want any tea. I want to lie on your sofa and go to sleep again. Can I?" asked Rosy, with a dizzy look about the room, and a shiver at the idea of eating.

"Yes, dear, I'll put on your little wrapper, and make you all comfortable, and bring you some ice-water, for your lips are very dry."

As she spoke, Cicely bustled about the room, and soon had Rosy nicely settled with her best cologne-bottle and a fan; then she hastened down to report that something was wrong, with a fear in her own heart that if any harm did come to the child it would be her fault. Some days before Cicely had sent Button-Rose with a note to a friend's house where she knew some of the younger children were ill. Since then she had heard that it was scarlet fever; but though Rosy had waited some time for an answer to the note, and seen one of the invalids, Cis had never mentioned the fact, being ashamed to confess her carelessness, hoping no harm was done. Now she felt that it HAD come, and went to tell gentle Cousin Penny with tears of vain regret.

Great was the lamentation when the doctor, who was sent for in hot haste, pronounced it scarlet fever; and deep was the self-reproach of the two older women for their blindness in not before remarking the languid air and want of appetite in the child. But Cicely was full of remorse; for every quick word, every rap of the hateful thimble, every service accepted without thanks, weighed heavily on her conscience now, as such things have an inconvenient way of doing when it is too late to undo them. Every one was devoted to the child, even lazy Miss Henny gave up her naps to sit by her at all hours, Miss Penny hovered over the little bed like a grandmother, and Cicely refused to think of pleasure till the danger was over.

For soon Button-Rose was very ill, and the old house haunted by the dreadful fear that death would rob them of the little creature who grew so precious when the thought of losing her made their hearts stand still. How could they live without the sound of that sweet voice chirping about the house, the busy feet tripping up and down, the willing hands trying to help, the sunny face smiling at every one, and going away into corners to hide the tears that sometimes came to dim its brightness? What would comfort the absent mother for such a loss as this, and how could they answer to the father for the carelessness that risked the child's life for a girl's errand? No one dared to think, and all prayed heartily for Rosy's life, as they watched and waited by the little bed where she lay so patiently, till the fever grew high and she began to babble about many things. Her childish trials were all told, her longings for Mamma, whose place no one could fill, her quaint little criticisms upon those about her, and her plans for making peace. These innocent revelations caused many tears, and wrought some changes in those who heard; for Miss Penny quite forgot her infirmities to live in the sick-room as the most experienced nurse and tenderest watcher. Miss Henny cooked her daintiest gruel, brewed her coolest drinks, and lost many pounds in weight by her indefatigable trotting up and down to minister to the invalid's least caprice. Cicely was kept away for fear of infection, but HER penance was to wander about the great house, more silent than ever now, to answer the inquiries and listen to the sad forebodings of the neighbors, who came to offer help and sympathy; for all loved little Button-Rose, and grieved to think of any blight falling on the pretty blossom. To wile away the long hours, Cicely fell to dusting the empty rooms, setting closets and drawers to rights, and keeping all fresh and clean, to the great relief of the old cousins, who felt that everything would go to destruction in their absence. She read and sewed now, having no heart for jaunting about; and as she made the long neglected white pinafores, for Rosy, she thought much of the little girl who might never live to wear them.

Meantime the fever took its course, and came at last to the fateful day when a few hours would settle the question of life or death. The hot flush died out of the cheeks that had lost their soft roundness now, the lips were parched, the half-shut eyes looked like sick violets, and all the pretty curls were tangled on the pillow. Rosy no longer sung to Bella, talked of "three dear little girls" and Mr. Thomas, tigers and bangles, Cis and necklaces, hens and gates. She ceased to call for Mamma, asked no more why her "missionary man" never came, and took no notice of the anxious old faces bending over her. She lay in a stupor, and the doctor held the little wasted hand, and tried to see the face of his watch with dim eyes as he counted the faint pulse, whispering solemnly, -

"We can only hope and wait now. Sleep alone can save her."

As the sisters sat, one on either side the narrow bed that day, and Cicely walked restlessly up and down the long hall below, where both doors stood open to let in the cool evening air, as the sun went down, a quick but quiet step came up the steps, and Mr. Dover walked in without ringing. He had been away, and coming home an hour ago, heard the sad news. Losing not a moment, he hurried to ask about his little Button, and his face showed how great his love and fear were, as he said in a broken whisper, -

"Will she live? My mother never told me how serious it was, or I should have returned at once."

"We hope so, sir, but - " And there Cicely's voice failed, as she hid her face and sobbed.

"My dear girl, don't give way. Keep up your heart, hope, pray, will that the darling SHALL live, and that may do some good. We can't let her go! we won't let her go! Let me see her; I know much of fevers far worse than this, and might be able to suggest something," begged Mr. Dover, throwing down his hat, and waving an immense fan with such an air of resolution and cheery good-will that tired Cis felt comforted at once, and led the way upstairs entirely forgetting the great feud, as he did.

At the threshold of the door he paused, till the girl had whispered his name. Miss Penny, always a gentlewoman, rose at once and went to meet him, but Miss Henny did not even seem to see him, for just then, as if dimly feeling that her friend was near, Rosy stirred, and gave a long sigh.

Silently the three stood and looked at the beloved little creature lying there in the mysterious shadow of death, and they so helpless to keep her if the hour for departure had come.

"God help us!" sighed pious Miss Penny, folding her old hands, as if they did that often now.

"Drifting away, I fear;" and Miss Henny's plump face looked almost beautiful, with the tears on it, as she leaned nearer to listen to the faint breath at the child's lips.

"No; we will keep her, please the Lord! If we can make her sleep quietly for the next few hours she is safe. Let me try. Fan slowly with this, Miss Henrietta, and you, dear lady, pray that the precious little life may be given us."

As he spoke, Mr. Dover gave the great fan to Miss Henny, took the small cold hands in his, and sitting on the bedside held them close in his large warm ones, as if trying to pour life and strength into the frail body, as his eyes, fixed on the half-opened ones, seemed to call back the innocent soul hovering on the threshold of its prison, like the butterfly poised upon the chrysalis before it soars away.

Miss Penny knelt down near by, and laying her white head on the other pillow, again besought God to spare this treasure to the father and mother over the sea. How long they remained so none of them ever knew, silent and motionless but for the slow waving of the noiseless fan, which went to and fro like the wing of a great white bird, as if Miss Henny's stout arm could never tire. Miss Penny was so still she seemed to be asleep. Mr. Dover never stirred, but grew paler as the minutes passed; and Cicely, creeping now and then to look in and steal away, saw strange power in the black eyes that seemed to hold the fluttering spirit of the little child by the love and longing that made them both tender and commanding.

A level ray of sunlight stole through the curtain at last and turned the tangles of bright hair to pure gold. Miss Henny rose to shut it out, and as if her movement broke the spell, Rosy took a long full breath, turned on the pillow, and putting one hand under her cheek, seemed to fall asleep as naturally as she used to do when well. Miss Penny looked up, touched the child's forehead, and whispered, with a look of gratitude as bright as if the sunshine had touched her also, -

"It is moist! this is real sleep! Oh, my baby! oh, my baby!" And the old head went down again with a stifled sob, for her experienced eye told her that the danger was passing by and Rosy would live.

"The prayers of the righteous avail much," murmured Mr. Dover, turning to the other lady, who stood beside her sister looking down at the little figure now lying so restfully between them.

"How can we thank you?" she whispered, offering her hand, with the smile which had once made her pretty, and still touched the old face with something better than beauty.

Mr. Dover took the hand and answered, with an eloquent look at the child, -

"Let not the sun go down upon our wrath. Forgive me and be friends again, for her sake."

"I will!" And the plump hands gave the thin ones a hearty shake as the great feud ended forever over the bed of the little peacemaker whose childish play had turned to happy earnest.

MOUNTAIN-LAUREL AND MAIDEN-HAIR

Here's your breakfast, miss. I hope it's right. Your mother showed me how to fix it, and said I'd find a cup up here."

"Take that blue one. I have not much appetite, and can't eat if things are not nice and pretty. I like the flowers. I've been longing for some ever since I saw them last night."

The first speaker was a red-haired, freckle-faced girl, in a brown calico dress and white apron, with a tray in her hands and an air of timid hospitality in her manner; the second a pale, pretty creature, in a white wrapper and blue net, sitting in a large chair, looking about her with the languid interest of an invalid in a new place. Her eyes brightened as they fell upon a glass of rosy laurel and delicate maidenhair fern that stood among the toast and eggs, strawberries and cream, on the tray.

"Our laurel is jest in blow, and I'm real glad you come in time to see it. I'll bring you a lot, as soon's ever I get time to go for it."

As she spoke, the plain girl replaced the ugly crockery cup and saucer with the pretty china ones pointed out to her, arranged the dishes, and waited to see if anything else was needed.

"What is your name, please?" asked the pretty girl, refreshing herself with a draught of new milk.

"Rebecca. Mother thought I'd better wait on you; the little

Louisa May Alcott

girls are so noisy and apt to forget. Wouldn't you like a piller to your back? you look so kind of feeble seems as if you wanted to be propped up a mite."

There was so much compassion and good-will in the face and voice, that Emily accepted the offer, and let Rebecca arrange a cushion behind her; then, while the one ate daintily, and the other stirred about an inner room, the talk went on, - for two girls are seldom long silent when together.

"I think the air is going to suit me, for I slept all night and never woke till Mamma had been up ever so long and got things all nicely settled," said Emily, graciously, when the fresh strawberries had been enjoyed, and the bread and butter began to vanish.

"I'm real glad you like it; most folks do, if they don't mind it being plain and quiet up here. It's gayer down at the hotel, but the air ain't half so good, and delicate folks generally like our old place best," answered Becky, as she tossed over a mattress and shook out the sheet with a brisk, capable air pleasant to see.

"I wanted to go to the hotel, but the doctor said it would be too noisy for me, so Mamma was glad to find rooms here. I didn't think a farm-house COULD be so pleasant. That view is perfectly splendid!" and Emily sat up to gaze delightedly out of the window, below which spread the wide intervale, through which the river ran with hay-fields on either side, while along the green slopes of the hills lay farm-houses with garden plots, and big barns waiting for the harvest; and beyond, the rocky, wooded pastures dotted with cattle and musical with cow-bells, brooks, and birds.

A balmy wind kissed a little color into the pale cheeks, the listless eyes brightened as they looked, and the fretful lines vanished from lips that smiled involuntarily at the sweet welcome Nature gave the city child come to rest and play and grow gay and rosy in her green lap.

Becky watched her with interest, and was glad to see how soon the new-comer felt the charm of the place, for the girl loved her mountain home, and thought the old farm-house the loveliest spot in the world.

"When you get stronger I can show you lots of nice views round here. There's a woodsy place behind the house that's just lovely. Down by the laurel bushes is MY favorite spot, and among the rocks is a cave where I keep things handy when I get a resting-spell now and then, and want to be quiet. Can't get much at home, when there's boarders and five children round in vacation time."

Becky laughed as she spoke, and there was a sweet motherly look in her plain face, as she glanced at the three little red heads bobbing about the door-yard below, where hens cackled, a pet lamb fed, and the old white dog lay blinking in the sun.

"I like children; we have none at home, and Mamma makes such a baby of me I'm almost ashamed sometimes. I want her to have a good rest now, for she has taken care of me all winter and needs it. You shall be my nurse, if I need one; but I hope to be so well soon that I can see to myself. It's so tiresome to be ill!" and Emily sighed as she leaned back among her pillows, with a glance at the little glass which showed her a thin face and shorn head.

"It must be! I never was sick, but I have taken care of sick folks, and have a sight of sympathy for 'em. Mother says I make a pretty good nurse, being strong and quiet," answered Becky, plumping up pillows and folding towels with a gentle despatch which was very grateful to the invalid, who had dreaded a noisy, awkward serving-maid.

"Never ill! how nice that must be! I'm always having colds and headaches, and fusses of some kind. What do you do to keep well, Rebecca?" asked Emily, watching her with interest, as she came in to remove the tray.

Louisa May Alcott

"Nothing but work; I haven't time to be sick, and when I'm tuckered out, I go and rest over yonder. Then I'm all right, and buckle to again, as smart as ever;" and every freckle in Becky's rosy face seemed to shine with cheerful strength and courage.

"I'm 'tuckered out' doing nothing," said Emily, amused with the new expression, and eager to try a remedy which showed such fine results in this case. "I shall visit your pet places and do a little work as soon as I am able, and see if it won't set me up. Now I can only dawdle, doze, and read a little. Will you please put those books here on the table? I shall want them by-and-by."

Emily pointed to a pile of blue and gold volumes lying on a trunk, and Becky dusted her hands as she took them up with an air of reverence, for she read on the backs of the volumes names which made her eyes sparkle.

"Do you care for poetry?" asked Emily, surprised at the girl's look and manner.

"Guess I do! don't get much except the pieces I cut out of papers, but I love 'em, and stick 'em in an old ledger, and keep it down in my cubby among the rocks. I do love THAT man's pieces. They seem to go right to the spot somehow;" and Becky smiled at the name of Whittier as if the sweetest of our poets was a dear old friend of hers.

"I like Tennyson better. Do you know him?" asked Emily, with a superior air, for the idea of this farmer's daughter knowing anything about poetry amused her.

"Oh yes, I've got a number of his pieces in my book, and I'm fond of 'em. But this man makes things so kind of true and natural I feel at home with HIM. And this one I've longed to read, though I guess I can't understand much of it. His 'Bumble Bee' was just lovely; with the grass and columbines and the yellow breeches of the bee. I'm never tired of that;"

and Becky's face woke up into something like beauty as she glanced hungrily at the Emerson while she dusted the delicate cover that hid the treasures she coveted.

"I don't care much for him, but Mamma does. I like romantic poems, and ballads, and songs; don't like descriptions of clouds and fields, and bees, and farmers," said Emily, showing plainly that even Emerson's simplest poems were far above her comprehension as yet, because she loved sentiment more than Nature.

"I do, because I know 'em better than love and the romantic stuff most poetry tells about. But I don't pretend to judge, I'm glad of anything I can get. Now if you don't want me I'll pick up my dishes and go to work."

With that Becky went away, leaving Emily to rest and dream with her eyes on the landscape which was giving her better poetry than any her books held. She told her mother about the odd girl, and was sure she would be amusing if she did not forget her place and try to be friends.

"She is a good creature, my dear, her mother's main stay, and works beyond her strength, I am sure. Be kind to the poor girl, and put a little pleasure into her life if you can," answered Mrs. Spenser, as she moved about, settling comforts and luxuries for her invalid.

"I shall HAVE to talk to her, as there is no other person of my age in the house. How are the school marms? shall you get on with them, Mamma? It will be so lonely here for us both, if we don't make friends with some one."

"Most intelligent and amiable women all three, and we shall have pleasant times together, I am sure. You may safely cultivate Becky; Mrs. Taylor told me she was a remarkably bright girl, though she may not look it."

"Well, I'll see. But I do hate freckles and big red hands, and

Louisa May Alcott

round shoulders. She can't help it, I suppose, but ugly things fret me."

"Remember that she has no time to be pretty, and be glad she is so neat and willing. Shall we read, dear? I'm ready now."

Emily consented, and listened for an hour or two while the pleasant voice beside her conjured away all her vapors with some of Mrs. Ewing's charming tales.

"The grass is dry now, and I want to stroll on that green lawn before lunch. You rest, Mamma dear, and let me make discoveries all alone," proposed Emily, when the sun shone warmly, and the instinct of all young creatures for air and motion called her out.

So, with her hat and wrap, and book and parasol, she set forth to explore the new land in which she found herself.

Down the wide, creaking stairs and out upon the door-stone she went, pausing there for a moment to decide where first to go. The sound of some one singing in the rear of the house led her in that direction, and turning the corner she made her first pleasant discovery. A hill rose steeply behind the farm-house, and leaning from the bank was an old apple-tree, shading a spring that trickled out from the rocks and dropped into a mossy trough below. Up the tree had grown a wild grape-vine, making a green canopy over the great log which served as a seat, and some one had planted maidenhair ferns about both seat and spring to flourish beautifully in the damp, shady spot.

"Oh, how pretty! I'll go and sit there. It looks clean, and I can see what is going on in that big kitchen, and hear the singing. I suppose it's Becky's little sisters by the racket."

Emily established herself on the lichen-covered log with her feet upon a stone, and sat enjoying the musical tinkle of the water, with her eyes on the delicate ferns stirring in the wind, and the lively jingle of the multiplication-table chanted by childish voices in her ear.

Presently two little girls with a great pan of beans came to do their work on the back doorstep, a third was seen washing dishes at a window, and Becky's brown-spotted gown flew about the kitchen as if a very energetic girl wore it. A woman's voice was heard giving directions, as the speaker was evidently picking chickens somewhere out of sight.

A little of the talk reached Emily and both amused and annoyed her, for it proved that the country people were not as stupid as they looked.

"Oh, well, we mustn't mind if she IS notional and kind of wearing; she's been sick, and it will take time to get rid of her fretty ways. Jest be pleasant, and take no notice, and that nice mother of hers will make it all right," said the woman's voice.

"How anybody with every mortal thing to be happy with CAN be out-of-sorts passes me. She fussed about every piller, chair, trunk, and mite of food last night, and kept that poor tired lady trotting till I was provoked. She's right pleasant this morning though, and as pretty as a picture in her ruffled gown and that blue thing on her head," answered Becky from the pantry, as she rattled out the pie-board, little dreaming who sat hidden behind the grape-vine festoons that veiled the corner by the spring.

"Well, she's got redder hair 'n' we have, so she needn't be so grand and try to hide it with blue nets," added one little voice.

"Yes, and it's ever so much shorter 'n' ours, and curls all over her head like Daisy's wool. I should think such a big girl would feel real ashamed without no braids," said the other child, proudly surveying the tawny mane that hung over her shoulders, - for like most red-haired people all the children were blessed with luxuriant crops of every shade from golden auburn to regular carrots.

Louisa May Alcott

"I think it's lovely. Suppose it had to be cut off when she had the fever. Wish I could get rid of my mop, it's such a bother;" and Becky was seen tying a clean towel over the great knot that made her head look very like a copper kettle.

"Now fly round, deary, and get them pies ready. I'll have these fowls on in a minute, and then go to my butter. You run off and see if you can't find some wild strawberries for the poor girl, soon's ever you are through with them beans, children. We must kind of pamper her up for a spell till her appetite comes back," said the mother.

Here the chat ended, and soon the little girls were gone, leaving Becky alone rolling out pie-crust before the pantry window. As she worked her lips moved, and Emily, still peeping through the leaves, wondered what she was saying, for a low murmur rose and fell, emphasized now and then with a thump of the rolling-pin.

"I mean to go and find out. If I stand on that wash-bench I can look in and see her work. I'll show them all that *I*'m NOT 'fussy,' and can be 'right pleasant' if I like."

With this wise resolution Emily went down the little path, and after pausing to examine the churn set out to dry, and the row of pans shining on a neighboring shelf, made her way to the window, mounted the bench while Becky's back was turned, and pushing away the morning-glory vines and scarlet beans that ran up on either side peeped in with such a smiling face that the crossest cook could not have frowned on her as an intruder.

"May I see you work? I can't eat pies, but I like to watch people make them. Do you mind?"

"Not a bit. I'd ask you to come in, but it's dreadful hot here, and not much room," answered Becky, crimping round the pastry before she poured in the custard. "I'm going to make a nice little pudding for you; your mother said you liked 'em; or would you rather have whipped cream with a mite of jelly in it?" asked Becky, anxious to suit her new boarder.

"Whichever is easiest to make. I don't care what I eat. Do tell me what you were saying. It sounded like poetry," said Emily, leaning both elbows on the wide ledge with a pale pink morning-glory kissing her cheek, and a savory odor reaching her nose.

"Oh, I was mumbling some verses. I often do when I work, it sort of helps me along; but it must sound dreadfully silly," and Becky blushed as if caught in some serious fault.

"I do it, and it's a great comfort when I lie awake. I should think you WOULD want something to help you along, you work so hard. Do you like it, Becky?"

The familiar name, the kind tone, made the plain face brighten with pleasure as its owner said, while she carefully filled a pretty bowl with a golden mixture rich with fresh eggs and country milk -

"No, I don't, but I ought to. Mother isn't as strong as she used to be, and there's a sight to do, and the children to be brought up, and the mortgage to be paid off; so if I don't fly round, who will? We are doing real well now, for Mr. Walker manages the farm and gives us our share, so our living is all right; then boarders in summer and my school in winter helps a deal, and every year the boys can do more, so I'd be a real sinner to complain if I do have to step lively all day."

Becky smiled as she spoke, and straightened her bent shoulders as if settling her burden for another trudge along the path of duty.

"Do you keep school? Why, how old are you, Becky?" asked Emily, much impressed by this new discovery.

"I'm eighteen. I took the place of a teacher who got sick last

Louisa May Alcott

fall, and I kept school all winter. Folks seemed to like me, and I'm going to have the same place this year. I'm so glad, for I needn't go away and the pay is pretty good, as the school is large and the children do well. You can see the school-house down the valley, that red brick one where the roads meet;" and Becky pointed a floury finger, with an air of pride that was pleasant to see.

Emily glanced at the little red house where the sun shone hotly in summer, and all the winds of heaven must rage wildly in winter time, for it stood, as country schools usually do, in the barest, most uninviting spot for miles around.

"Isn't it awful down there in winter?" she asked, with a shiver at the idea of spending days shut up in that forlorn place, with a crowd of rough country children.

"Pretty cold, but we have plenty of wood, and we are used to snow and gales up here. We often coast down, the whole lot of us, and that is great fun. We take our dinners and have games noon-spells, and so we get on first rate; some of my boys are big fellows, older than I am; they clear the roads and make the fire and look after us, and we are real happy together."

Emily found it so impossible to imagine happiness under such circumstances that she changed the subject by asking in a tone which had unconsciously grown more respectful since this last revelation of Becky's abilities, -

"If you do so well here, why don't you try for a larger school in a better place?"

"Oh, I couldn't leave mother yet; I hope to some day, when the girls are older, and the boys able to get on alone. But I can't go now, for there's a sight of things to do, and mother is always laid up with rheumatism in cold weather. So much butter-making down cellar is bad for her; but she won't let me do that in summer, so I take care of her in winter. I can see to things night and morning, and through the day she's quiet, and sits piecing carpet-rags and resting up for next spring. We made and wove all the carpets in the house, except the parlor one. Mrs. Taylor gave us that, and the curtains, and the easy-chair. Mother takes a sight of comfort in that."

"Mrs. Taylor is the lady who first came to board here, and told us and others about it," said Emily.

"Yes, and she's the kindest lady in the world! I'll tell you all about her some day, it's real interesting; now I must see to my pies, and get the vegetables on," answered Becky, glancing at the gay clock in the kitchen with an anxious look.

"Then I won't waste any more of your precious time. May I sit in that pretty place; or is it your private bower?" asked Emily, as she dismounted from the wash-bench.

"Yes, indeed you may. That's mother's resting-place when work is done. Father made the spring long ago, and I put the ferns there. She can't go rambling round, and she likes pretty things, so we fixed it up for her, and she takes comfort there nights."

Becky bustled off to the oven with her pies, and Emily roamed away to the big barn to lie on the hay, enjoying the view down the valley, as she thought over what she had seen and heard, and very naturally contrasted her own luxurious and tenderly guarded life with this other girl's, so hard and dull and narrow. Working all summer and teaching all winter in that dismal little school-house, with no change but home cares and carpet-weaving! It looked horrible to pleasure-loving Emily, who led the happy, care-free life of girls of her class, with pleasures of all sorts, and a future of still greater luxury, variety, and happiness, opening brightly before her.

It worried her to think of any one being contented with such a meagre share of the good things of life, when she was unsatisfied in spite of the rich store showered upon her. She could not understand it, and fell asleep wishing every one could be comfortable, - it was so annoying to see them grubbing in kitchens, teaching in bleak school-houses among snow-drifts, and wearing ugly calico gowns.

A week or two of quiet, country fare and the bracing mountain air worked wonders for the invalid, and every one rejoiced to see the pale cheeks begin to grow round and rosy, the languid eyes to brighten, and the feeble girl who used to lie on her sofa half the day now go walking about with her alpenstock, eager to explore all the pretty nooks among the hills. Her mother blessed Mrs. Taylor for suggesting this wholesome place. The tired "school marms," as Emily called the three young women who were their fellow-boarders, congratulated her as well as themselves on the daily improvement in strength and spirits all felt; and Becky exulted in the marvellous effects of her native air, aided by mother's good cookery and the cheerful society of the children, whom the good girl considered the most remarkable and lovable youngsters in the world.

Emily felt like the queen of this little kingdom, and was regarded as such by every one, for with returning health she lost her fretful ways, and living with simple people, soon forgot her girlish airs and vanities, becoming very sweet and friendly with all about her. The children considered her a sort of good fairy who could grant wishes with magical skill, as various gifts plainly proved. The boys were her devoted servants, ready to run errands, "hitch up" and take her to drive at any hour, or listen in mute delight when she sang to her guitar in the summer twilight.

But to Becky she was a special godsend and comfort, for before the first month had gone they were good friends, and Emily had made a discovery which filled her head with brilliant plans for Becky's future, in spite of her mother's warnings, and the sensible girl's own reluctance to be dazzled by enthusiastic prophecies and dreams.

It came about in this way. Some three weeks after the two girls met, Emily went one evening to their favorite trysting-place, -

Becky's bower among the laurels. It was a pretty nook in the shadow of a great gray bowlder near the head of the green valley which ran down to spread into the wide intervale below. A brook went babbling among the stones and grass and sweet-ferns, while all the slope was rosy with laurel-flowers in their times, as the sturdy bushes grew thickly on the hill-side, down the valley, and among the woods that made a rich background for these pink and white bouquets arranged with Nature's own careless grace.

Emily liked this spot, and ever since she had been strong enough to reach it, loved to climb up and sit there with book and work, enjoying the lovely panorama before her. Floating mists often gave her a constant succession of pretty pictures; now a sunny glimpse of the distant lake, then the church spire peeping above the hill, or a flock of sheep feeding in the meadow, a gay procession of young pilgrims winding up the mountain, or a black cloud heavy with a coming storm, welcome because of the glorious rainbow and its shadow which would close the pageant.

Unconsciously the girl grew to feel not only the beauty but the value of these quiet hours, to find a new peace, refreshment, and happiness, bubbling up in her heart as naturally as the brook gushed out among the mossy rocks, and went singing away through hayfields and gardens, and by dusty roads, till it met the river and rolled on to the sea. Something dimly stirred in her, and the healing spirit that haunts such spots did its sweet ministering till the innocent soul began to see that life was not perfect without labor as well as love, duty as well as happiness, and that true contentment came from within, not from without.

On the evening we speak of, she went to wait for Becky, who would join her as soon as the after-supper chores were done. In the little cave which held a few books, a dipper, and a birch-bark basket for berries, Emily kept a sketching block and a box of pencils, and often amused herself by trying to catch some of the lovely scenes before her. These efforts usually ended in a

Louisa May Alcott

humbler attempt, and a good study of an oak-tree, a bit of rock, or a clump of ferns was the result. This evening the sunset was so beautiful she could not draw, and remembering that somewhere in Becky's scrap-book there was a fine description of such an hour by some poet, she pulled out the shabby old volume, and began to turn over the leaves.

She had never cared to look at it but once, having read all the best of its contents in more attractive volumes, so Becky kept it tucked away in the farther corner of her rustic closet, and evidently thought it a safe place to conceal a certain little secret which Emily now discovered. As she turned the stiff pages filled with all sorts of verses, good, bad, and indifferent, a sheet of paper appeared on which was scribbled these lines in school-girl handwriting: -

MOUNTAIN-LAUREL

My bonnie flower, with truest joy
Thy welcome face I see,
The world grows brighter to my eyes,
And summer comes with thee.
My solitude now finds a friend,
And after each hard day,
I in my mountain garden walk,
To rest, or sing, or pray.

All down the rocky slope is spread
Thy veil of rosy snow,
And in the valley by the brook,
Thy deeper blossoms grow.
The barren wilderness grows fair,
Such beauty dost thou give;
And human eyes and Nature's heart
Rejoice that thou dost live.

Each year I wait thy coming, dear,
Each year I love thee more,
For life grows hard, and much I need
Thy honey for my store.
So, like a hungry bee, I sip
Sweet lessons from thy cup,
And sitting at a flower's feet,
My soul learns to look up.

No laurels shall I ever win,

　　　　Louisa May Alcott

No splendid blossoms bear,
But gratefully receive and use
God's blessed sun and air;
And, blooming where my lot is cast,
Grow happy and content,
Making some barren spot more fair,
For a humble life well spent.

"She wrote it herself! I can't believe it!" said Emily, as she put down the paper, looking rather startled, for she DID believe it, and felt as if she had suddenly looked into a fellow-creature's heart. "I thought her just an ordinary girl, and here she is a poet, writing verses that make me want to cry! I don't suppose they ARE very good, but they seem to come right out of her heart, and touch me with the longing and the patience or the piety in them. Well, I AM surprised!" and Emily read the lines again, seeing the faults more plainly than before, but still feeling that the girl put herself into them, vainly trying to express what the wild flower was to her in the loneliness which comes to those who have a little spark of the divine fire burning in their souls.

"Shall I tell her I've found it out? I must! and see if I can't get her verses printed. Of course she has more tucked away somewhere. That is what she hums to herself when she's at work, and won't tell me about when I ask. Sly thing! to be so bashful and hide her gift. I'll tease her a bit and see what she says. Oh dear, I wish *I* could do it! Perhaps she'll be famous some day, and then I'll have the glory of discovering her."

With that consolation Emily turned over the pages of the ledger and found several more bits of verse, some very good for an untaught girl, others very faulty, but all having a certain strength of feeling and simplicity of language unusual in the effusions of young maidens at the sentimental age.

Emily had a girlish admiration for talent of any kind, and being fond of poetry, was especially pleased to find that her humble friend possessed the power of writing it. Of course she exaggerated Becky's talent, and as she waited for her, felt sure that she had discovered a feminine Burns among the New Hampshire hills, for all the verses were about natural and homely objects, touched into beauty by sweet words or tender sentiment. She had time to build a splendid castle in the air and settle Becky in it with a crown of glory on her head, before the quiet figure in a faded sunbonnet came slowly up the slope with the glow of sunset on a tired but tranquil face.

"Sit here and have a good rest, while I talk to you," said Emily, eager to act the somewhat dramatic scene she had planned. Becky sunk upon the red cushion prepared for her, and sat looking down at the animated speaker, as Emily, perched on a mossy stone before her, began the performance.

"Becky, did you ever hear of the Goodale children? They lived in the country and wrote poetry and grew to be famous."

"Oh yes, I've read their poems and like 'em very much. Do you know 'em?" and Becky looked interested at once.

"No, but I once met a girl who was something like them, only she didn't have such an easy time as they did, with a father to help, and a nice Sky-farm, and good luck generally. I've tried to write verses myself, but I always get into a muddle, and give it up. This makes me interested in other girls who CAN do it, and I want to help my friend. I'm SURE she has talent, and I'd so like to give her a lift in some way. Let me read you a piece of hers and see what you think of it."

"Do!" and Beck threw off the sunbonnet, folded her hands round her knees, and composed herself to listen with such perfect unconsciousness of what was coming that Emily both laughed at the joke and blushed at the liberty she felt she was taking with the poor girl's carefully hidden secret.

Becky was sure now that Emily was going to read something of her own after this artful introduction, and began to smile as the paper was produced and the first four lines read in a tone

Louisa May Alcott

that was half timid, half triumphant. Then with a cry she seized and crumpled up the paper, exclaiming almost fiercely, -

"It's mine! Where did you get it? How dar'st you touch it?"

Emily fell upon her knees with a face and voice so full of penitence, pleasure, sympathy, and satisfaction, that Becky's wrath was appeased before her friend's explanation ended with these soothing and delightful words, -

"That's all, dear, and I beg your pardon. But I'm sure you will be famous if you keep on, and I shall yet see a volume of poems by Rebecca Moore of Rocky Nook, New Hampshire."

Becky hid her face as if shame, surprise, wonder, and joy filled her heart too full and made a few happy tears drop on the hands so worn with hard work, when they ached to be holding a pen and trying to record the fancies that sung in her brain as ceaselessly as the soft sough of the pines or the ripple of the brook murmured in her ear when she sat here alone. She could not express the vague longings that stirred in her soul; she could only feel and dimly strive to understand and utter them, with no thought of fame or fortune, - for she was a humble creature, and never knew that the hardships of her life were pressing out the virtues of her nature as the tread of careless feet crush the sweet perfume from wild herbs.

Presently she looked up, deeply touched by Emily's words and caresses, and her blue eyes shone like stars as her face beamed with something finer than mere beauty, for the secrets of her innocent heart were known to this friend now, and it was very sweet to accept the first draught of confidence and praise.

"I don't mind much, but I was scared for a minute. No one knows but Mother, and she laughs at me, though she don't care if it makes me happy. I'm glad you like my scribbling, but really I never think or hope of being anybody. I couldn't, you know! but it's real nice to have you say I MIGHT and to make believe for a while."

"But why not, Becky? The Goodale girls did, and half the poets in the world were poor, ignorant people at first, you know. It only needs time and help, and the gift will grow, and people see it; and then the glory and the money will come," cried Emily, quite carried away by her own enthusiasm and good-will.

"Could I get any money by these things?" asked Becky, looking at the crumpled paper lying under a laurel-bush.

"Of course you could, dear! Let me have some of them, and I'll show you that I know good poetry when I see it. You will believe if some bank-bills come with the paper the verses appear in, I hope?"

Blind to any harm she might do by exciting vain hopes in her eagerness to cheer and help, Emily made this rash proposal in all good faith. meaning to pay for the verses herself if no editor was found to accept them.

Becky looked half bewildered by this brilliant prospect, and took a long breath, as if some hand had lifted a heavy burden a little way from her weary back, for stronger than ambition for herself was love for her family, and the thought of help for them was sweeter than any dream of fame.

"Yes, I would! oh, if I only COULD, I'd be the happiest girl in the world! But I can't believe it, Emily. I heard Mrs. Taylor say that only the VERY BEST poetry paid, and mine is poor stuff, I know well enough."

"Of course it needs polishing and practice and all that; but I'm sure it is oceans better than half the sentimental twaddle we see in the papers, and I KNOW that some of those pieces ARE paid for, because I have a friend who is in a newspaper office, and he told me so. Yours are quaint and simple and some very original. I'm sure that ballad of the old house is lovely, and I want to send it to Whittier. Mamma knows him; it's the sort he likes, and he is so kind to every one, he will criticise it, and be interested when she tells him about you. Do let me!"

"I never could in the world! It would be so bold, Mother would think I was crazy. I love Mr. Whittier, but I wouldn't dar'st to show him my nonsense, though reading his beautiful poetry helps me ever so much."

Becky looked and spoke as if her breath had been taken away by this audacious proposal; and yet a sudden delicious hope sprung up in her heart that there might, perhaps, be a spark of real virtue in the little fire which burned within her, warming and brightening her dull life.

"Let us ask Mamma; she will tell us what is best to do first, for she knows all sorts of literary people, and won't say any more than you want her to. I'm bent on having my way, Becky, and the more modest you are, the surer I am that you are a genius. Real geniuses always ARE shy; so you just make up your mind to give me the best of your pieces, and let me prove that I'm right."

It was impossible to resist such persuasive words, and Becky soon yielded to the little siren who was luring her out of her safe, small pool into the deeper water that looks so blue and smooth till the venturesome paper boats get into the swift eddies, or run aground upon the rocks and sandbars.

The greatest secrecy was to be preserved, and no one but Mrs. Spenser was to know what a momentous enterprise was afoot. The girls sat absorbed in their brilliant plans till it was nearly dark, then groped their way home hand in hand, leaving another secret for the laurels to keep and dream over through their long sleep, for blossom time was past, and the rosy faces turning pale in the July sun.

Neither of the girls forgot the talk they had that night in Emily's room, for she led her captive straight to her mother, and told her all their plans and aspirations without a moment's delay.

Mrs. Spenser much regretted her daughter's well-meant enthusiasm, but fearing harm might be done, very wisely tried to calm the innocent excitement of both by the quiet matter-of-fact way in which she listened to the explanation Emily gave her, read the verses timidly offered by Becky, and then said, kindly but firmly: -

"This is not poetry, my dear girls, though the lines run smoothly enough, and the sentiment is sweet. It would bring neither fame nor money, and Rebecca puts more real truth, beauty, and poetry into her dutiful daily life than in any lines she has written."

"We had such a lovely plan for Becky to come to town with me, and see the world, and write, and be famous. How can you spoil it all?"

"My foolish little daughter, I must prevent you from spoiling this good girl's life by your rash projects. Becky will see that I am wise, though you do not, and SHE will understand this verse from my favorite poet, and lay it to heart: -

"So near is grandeur to our Dust,
So nigh is God to man,
When Duty whispers low, 'Thou must!'
The youth replies, 'I can!'"

"I do! I will! please go on," and Becky's troubled eyes grew clear and steadfast as she took the words home to herself, resolving to live up to them.
"Oh, mother!" cried Emily, thinking her very cruel to nip their budding hopes in this way.

"I know you won't believe it now, nor be able to see all that I mean perhaps, but time will teach you both to own that I am right, and to value the substance more than the shadow," continued Mrs. Spenser. "Many girls write verses and think they are poets; but it is only a passing mood, and fortunately for the world, and for them also, it soon dies out in some more genuine work or passion. Very few have the real gift, and those to whom it IS given wait and work and slowly reach the height of their powers. Many delude themselves, and try to persuade the world that they can sing; but it is waste of time, and ends in disappointment, as the mass of sentimental rubbish we all see plainly proves. Write your little verses, my dear, when the spirit moves, - it is a harmless pleasure, a real comfort, and a good lesson for you; but do not neglect higher duties or deceive yourself with false hopes and vain dreams. 'First live, then write,' is a good motto for ambitious young people. A still better for us all is, 'Do the duty that lies nearest;' and the faithful performance of that, no matter how humble it is, will be the best help for whatever talent may lie hidden in us, ready to bloom when the time comes. Remember this, and do not let my enthusiastic girl's well-meant but unwise prophecies and plans unsettle you, and unfit you for the noble work you are doing."

"Thank you, ma'am! I WILL remember; I know you are right, and I won't be upset by foolish notions. I never imagined before that I COULD be a poet; but it sounded so sort of splendid, I thought maybe it MIGHT happen to me, by-and-by, as it does to other folks. I won't lot on it, but settle right down and do my work cheerful."

As she listened, Becky's face had grown pale and serious, even a little sad; but as she answered, her eyes shone, her lips were firm, and her plain face almost beautiful with the courage and confidence that sprung up within her. She saw the wisdom of her friend's advice, felt the kindness of showing her the mistake frankly, and was grateful for it, - conscious in her own strong, loving heart that it was better to live and work for others than to dream and strive for herself alone.

Mrs. Spenser was both surprised and touched by the girl's look, words, and manner, and her respect much increased by the courage and good temper with which she saw her lovely castle in the air vanish like smoke, leaving the hard reality looking harder than ever, after this little flight into the fairy regions of romance.

She talked long with the girls, and gave them the counsel all eager young people need, yet are very slow to accept till experience teaches them its worth. As the friend of many successful literary people, Mrs. Spenser was constantly receiving the confidences of unfledged scribblers, each of whom was sure that he or she had something valuable to add to the world's literature. Her advice was always the same, "Work and wait;" and only now and then was a young poet or author found enough in earnest to do both, and thereby prove to themselves and others that either they DID possess power, or did not, and so settle the question forever. "First live, then write," proved a quietus for many, and "Do the duty that lies nearest" satisfied the more sincere that they could be happy without fame. So, thanks to this wise and kindly woman, a large number of worthy youths and maidens ceased dreaming and fell to work, and the world was spared reams of feeble verse and third-rate romances.

After that night Becky spent fewer spare hours in her nest, and more in reading with Emily, who lent her books and helped her to understand them, - both much assisted by Mrs. Spenser, who marked passages, suggested authors, and explained whatever puzzled them. Very happy bits of time were these, and very precious to both, as Emily learned to see and appreciate the humbler, harder side of life, and Becky got delightful glimpses into the beautiful world of art, poetry, and truth, which gave her better food for heart and brain than sentimental musings or blind efforts to satisfy the hunger of her nature with verse-writing.

Their favorite places were in the big barn, on the front porch, or by the spring. This last was Emily's schoolroom, and she both taught and learned many useful lessons there.

One day as Becky came to rest a few minutes and shell peas, Emily put down her book to help; and as the pods flew, she said, nodding toward the delicate ferns that grew thickly all about the trough, the rock, and the grassy bank, -

"We have these in our greenhouse, but I never saw them growing wild before, and I don't find them anywhere up here. How did you get such beauties, and make them do so well?"

"Oh, they grow in nooks on the mountain hidden under the taller ferns, and in sly corners. But they don't grow like these, and die soon unless transplanted and taken good care of. They always make me think of you, - so graceful and delicate, and just fit to live with tea-roses in a hot-house, and go to balls in beautiful ladies' bokays," answered Becky, smiling at her new friend, always so dainty, and still so delicate in spite of the summer's rustication.

"Thank you! I suppose I shall never be very strong or able to do much; so I AM rather like a fern, and do live in a conservatory all winter, as I can't go out a great deal. An idle thing, Becky!" and Emily sighed, for she was born frail, and even her tenderly guarded life could not give her the vigor of other girls. But the sigh changed to a smile as she added, -

"If I am like the fern, you are like your own laurel, - strong, rosy, and able to grow anywhere. I want to carry a few roots home, and see if they won't grow in my garden. Then you will have me, and I you. I only hope YOUR plant will do as well as mine does here."

"It won't! ever so many folks have taken roots away, but they never thrive in gardens as they do on the hills where they belong. So I tell 'em to leave the dear bushes alone, and come up here and enjoy 'em in their own place. You might keep a plant of it in your hot-house, and it would blow I dare say; but it would never be half so lovely as my acres of them, and I guess it would only make you sad, seeing it so far from home, and pale and pining," answered Becky, with her eyes on the green slopes where the mountain-laurel braved the wintry snow, and came out fresh and early in the spring.

"Then I'll let it alone till I come next summer. But don't you take any of the fern into the house in the cold weather? I should think it would grow in your sunny windows," said Emily, pleased by the fancy that it resembled herself.

"I tried it, but it needs a damp place, and our cold nights kill it. No, it won't grow in our old house; but I cover it with leaves, and the little green sprouts come up as hearty as can be out here. The shade, the spring, the shelter of the rock, keep it alive, you see, so it's no use trying to move it."

Both sat silent for a few minutes, as their hands moved briskly and they thought of their different lots. An inquisitive ray of sunshine peeped in at them, touching Becky's hair till it shone like red gold. The same ray dazzled Emily's eyes; she put up her hand to pull her hat-brim lower, and touched the little curls on her forehead. This recalled her pet grievance, and made her say impatiently, as she pushed the thick short locks under her net, -

"My hair is SUCH a plague! I don't know what I am to do when I go into society by-and-by. This crop is so unbecoming, and I can't match my hair anywhere, it is such a peculiar shade of golden-auburn."

"It's a pretty color, and I think the curls much nicer than a boughten switch," said Becky, quite unconscious that her own luxuriant locks were of the true Titian red, and would be much admired by artistic eyes.

"I don't! I shall send to Paris to match it, and then wear a braid round my head as you do sometimes. I suppose it will cost a fortune, but I WON'T have a strong-minded crop. A friend of mine got a lovely golden switch for fifty dollars."

"My patience! do folks pay like that for false hair?" asked Becky, amazed.

"Yes, indeed. White hair costs a hundred, I believe, if it is long.

Why, you could get ever so much for yours if you ever wanted to sell it. I'll take part of it, for in a little while mine will be as dark, and I'd like to wear your hair, Becky."

"Don't believe Mother would let me. She is very proud of our red heads. If I ever do cut it, you shall have some. I may be hard up and glad to sell it perhaps. My sakes! I smell the cake burning!" and off flew Becky to forget the chat in her work.

Emily did not forget it, and hoped Becky would be tempted, for she really coveted one of the fine braids, but felt shy about asking the poor girl for even a part of her one beauty.

So July and August passed pleasantly and profitably to both girls, and in September they were to part. No more was said about poetry; and Emily soon became so interested in the busy, practical life about her that her own high-flown dreams were quite forgotten, and she learned to enjoy the sweet prose of daily labor.

One breezy afternoon as she and her mother sat resting from a stroll on the way-side bank among the golden-rod and asters, they saw Becky coming up the long hill with a basket on her arm. She walked slowly, as if lost in thought, yet never missed pushing aside with a decided gesture of her foot every stone that lay in her way. There were many in that rocky path, but Becky left it smoother as she climbed, and paused now and then to send some especially sharp or large one spinning into the grassy ditch beside the road.

"Isn't she a curious girl, Mamma? so tired after her long walk to town, yet so anxious not to leave a stone in the way," said Emily, as they watched her slow approach.

"A very interesting one to me, dear, because under that humble exterior lies a fine, strong character. It is like Becky to clear her way, even up a dusty hill where the first rain will wash out many more stones. Let us ask her why she does it. I've observed the habit before, and always meant to ask," replied

Mrs. Spenser.

"Here we are! Come and rest a minute, Becky, and tell us if you mend roads as well as ever so many other things;" called Emily, beckoning with a smile, as the girl looked up and saw them.

"Oh, it's a trick of mine; I caught it of Father when I was a little thing, and do it without knowing it half the time," said Becky, sinking down upon a mossy rock, as if rest were welcome.

"Why did he do it?" asked Emily, who knew that her friend loved to talk of her father.

"Well, it's a family failing I guess, for his father did the same, only HE began with his farm and let the roads alone. The land used to be pretty much all rocks up here, you know, and farmers had to clear the ground if they wanted crops. It was a hard fight, and took a sight of time and patience to grub out roots and blast rocks and pick up stones that seemed to grow faster than anything else. But they kept on, and now see!"

As she spoke, Becky pointed proudly to the wide, smooth fields lying before them, newly shorn of grass or grain, waving with corn, or rich in garden crops ripening for winter stores. Here and there were rocky strips unreclaimed, as if to show what had been done; and massive stone walls surrounded pasture, field, and garden.

"A good lesson in patience and perseverance, my dear, and does great honor to the men who made the wilderness blossom like the rose," said Mrs. Spenser.

"Then you can't wonder that they loved it and we want to keep it. I guess it would break Mother's heart to sell this place, and we are all working as hard as ever we can to pay off the mortgage. Then we'll be just the happiest family in New Hampshire," said Becky, fondly surveying the old farm-house, the rocky hill, and the precious fields won from the forest.

"You never need fear to lose it; we will see to that if you will let us," began Mrs. Spenser, who was both a rich and a generous woman.

"Oh, thank you! but we won't need help I guess; and if we should, Mrs. Taylor made us promise to come to her," cried Becky. "She found us just in our hardest time, and wanted to fix things then; but we are proud in our way, and Mother said she'd rather work it off if she could. Then what did that dear lady do but talk to the folks round here, and show 'em how a branch railroad down to Peeksville would increase the value of the land, and how good this valley would be for strawberries and asparagus and garden truck if we could only get it to market. Some of the rich men took up the plan, and we hope it will be done this fall. It will be the making of us, for our land is first-rate for small crops, and the children can help at that, and with a deepot close by it would be such easy work. That's what I call helping folks to help themselves. Won't it be grand?"

Becky looked so enthusiastic that Emily could not remain uninterested , though market-gardening did not sound very romantic.

"I hope it will come, and next year we shall see you all hard at it. What a good woman Mrs. Taylor is!"

"Ain't she? and the sad part of it is, she can't do and enjoy all she wants to, because her health is so poor. She was a country girl, you know, and went to work in the city as waiter in a boarding-house. A rich man fell in love with her and married her, and she took care of him for years, and he left her all his money. She was quite broken down, but she wanted to make his name loved and honored after his death, as he hadn't done any good while he lived; so she gives away heaps, and is never tired of helping poor folks and doing all sorts of grand things to make the world better. I call that splendid!"

"So do I, yet it is only what you are doing in a small way, Becky," said Mrs. Spenser, as the girl paused out of breath. "Mrs. Taylor clears the stones out of people's paths, making their road easier to climb than hers has been, and leaving behind her fruitful fields for others to reap. This is a better work than making verses, for it is the real poetry of life, and brings to those who give themselves to it, no matter in what humble ways, something sweeter than fame and more enduring than fortune."

"So it does! I see that now, and know why we love Father as we do, and want to keep what he worked so hard to give us. He used to say every stone cleared away was just so much help to the boys; and he used to tell me his plans as I trotted after him round the farm, helping all I could, being the oldest, and like him, he said."

Becky paused with full eyes, for not even to these good friends could she ever tell the shifts and struggles in which she had bravely borne her part during the long hard years that had wrested the little homestead from the stony-hearted hills.

The musical chime of a distant clock reminded her that supper time was near, and she sprang up as if much refreshed by this pleasant rest by the way-side. As she pulled out her handkerchief, a little roll of pale blue ribbon fell from her pocket, and Emily caught it up, exclaiming mischievously, "Are you going to make yourself fine next Sunday, when Moses Pennel calls, Becky?"

The girl laughed and blushed as she said, carefully folding up the ribbon, -

"I'm going to do something with it that I like a sight better than that. Poor Moses won't come any more, I guess. I'm not going to leave Mother till the girls can take my place, and only then to teach, if I can get a good school somewhere near."

"We shall see!" and Emily nodded wisely.

Louisa May Alcott

"We shall!" and Becky nodded decidedly, as she trudged on up the steep hill beside Mrs. Spenser, while Emily walked slowly behind, poking every stone she saw into the grass, unmindful of the detriment to her delicate shoes, being absorbed in a new and charming idea of trying to follow Mrs. Taylor's example in a small way.

A week later the last night came, and just as they were parting for bed, in rushed one of the boys with the exciting news that the railroad surveyors were in town, the folks talking about the grand enterprise, and the fortune of the place made forever.

Great was the rejoicing in the old farm-house; the boys cheered, the little girls danced, the two mothers dropped a happy tear as they shook each other's hands, and Emily embraced Becky, tenderly exclaiming, - "There, you dear thing, is a great stone shoved out of YOUR way, and a clear road to fortune at last; for I shall tell all my friends to buy your butter and eggs, and fruit and pigs, and everything you send to market on that blessed railroad."

"A keg of our best winter butter is going by stage express to-morrow anyway; and when our apples come, we shan't need a railroad to get 'em to you, my darling dear," answered Becky, holding the delicate girl in her arms with a look and gesture half sisterly, half motherly, wholly fond and grateful.

When Emily got to her room, she found that butter and apples were not all the humble souvenirs offered in return for many comfortable gifts to the whole family.

On the table, in a pretty birch-bark cover, lay several of Becky's best poems neatly copied, as Emily had expressed a wish to keep them; and round the rustic volume, like a ring of red gold, lay a great braid of Becky's hair, tied with the pale blue ribbon she had walked four miles to buy, that her present might look its best.

Of course there were more embraces and kisses, and thanks

and loving words, before Emily at last lulled herself to sleep planning a Christmas box, which should supply every wish and want of the entire family if she could find them out.

Next morning they parted; but these were not mere summer friends, and they did not lose sight of one another, though their ways lay far apart. Emily had found a new luxury to bring more pleasure into life, a new medicine to strengthen soul and body; and in helping others, she helped herself wonderfully.

Becky went steadily on her dutiful way, till the homestead was free, the lads able to work the farm alone, the girls old enough to fill her place, and the good mother willing to rest at last among her children. Then Becky gave herself to teaching, - a noble task, for which she was well fitted, and in which she found both profit and pleasure, as she led her flock along the paths from which she removed the stumbling-blocks for their feet, as well as for her own. She put her poetry into her life, and made of it "a grand sweet song" in which beauty and duty rhymed so well that the country girl became a more useful, beloved, and honored woman than if she had tried to sing for fame which never satisfies.

So each symbolical plant stood in its own place, and lived its appointed life. The delicate fern grew in the conservatory among tea-roses and camelias, adding grace to every bouquet of which it formed a part, whether it faded in a ball-room, or was carefully cherished by some poor invalid's bed-side, - a frail thing, yet with tenacious roots and strong stem, nourished by memories of the rocky nook where it had learned its lesson so well. The mountain-laurel clung to the bleak hillside, careless of wintry wind and snow, as its sturdy branches spread year by year, with its evergreen leaves for Christmas cheer, its rosy flowers for spring-time, its fresh beauty free to all as it clothed the wild valley with a charm that made a little poem of the lovely spot where the pines whispered, woodbirds sang, and the hidden brook told the sweet message it brought from the mountain-top where it was born.

Louisa May Alcott

THE END. fern grew in the conservatory among tea-roses and camelias, adding grace to every bouquet of which it formed a part, whether it faded in a ball-room, or was carefully cherished by some poor invalid's bed-side, - a frail thing, yet with tenacious roots and strong stem, nourished by memories of the rocky nook where it had learned its lesson so well. The mountain-laurel clung to the bleak hillside, careless of wintry wind and snow, as its sturdy branches spread year by year, with its evergreen leaves for Christmas cheer, its rosy flowers for spring-time, its fresh beauty free to all as it clothed the wild valley with a charm that made a little poem of the lovely spot where the pines whispered, woodbirds sang, and the hidden brook told the sweet message it brought from the mountain-top where it was born.

Choose from Thousands of 1stWorldLibrary Classics By

Adolphus WilliamWard
Aesop
Agatha Christie
Alexander Aaronsohn
Alexander Kielland
Alexandre Dumas
Alfred Gatty
Alfred Ollivant
Alice Duer Miller
Alice Turner Curtis
Alice Dunbar
Ambrose Bierce
Amelia E. Barr
Andrew Lang
Andrew McFarland Davis
Anna Sewell
Annie Besant
Annie Hamilton Donnell
Annie Payson Call
Anton Chekhov
Arnold Bennett
Arthur Conan Doyle
Arthur Ransome
Atticus
B. M. Bower
Basil King
Bayard Taylor
Ben Macomber
Booth Tarkington
Bram Stoker
C. Collodi
C. E. Orr
C. M. Ingleby
Carolyn Wells
Catherine Parr Traill
Charles A. Eastman
Charles Dickens
Charles Dudley Warner
Charles Farrar Browne
Charles Ives
Charles Kingsley
Charles Lathrop Pack
Charles Whibley
Charles Willing Beale
Charlotte M. Braeme
Charlotte M.Yonge
Clair W. Hayes
Clarence Day Jr.
Clarence E. Mulford

Clemence Housman
Confucius
Cornelis DeWitt Wilcox
Cyril Burleigh
D. H. Lawrence
Daniel Defoe
David Garnett
Don Carlos Janes
Donald Keyhole
Dorothy Kilner
Dougan Clark
E. Nesbit
E.P.Roe
E. Phillips Oppenheim
Edgar Allan Poe
Edgar Rice Burroughs
Edith Wharton
Edward J. O'Biren
John Cournos
Edwin L. Arnold
Eleanor Atkins
Elizabeth Cleghorn
Gaskell
Elizabeth Von Arnim
Ellem Key
Emily Dickinson
Erasmus W. Jones
Ernie Howard Pie
Ethel Turner
Ethel Watts Mumford
Eugenie Foa
Eugene Wood
Evelyn Everett-Green
Everard Cotes
F. J. Cross
Federick Austin Ogg
Ferdinand Ossendowski
Francis Bacon
Francis Darwin
Frances Hodgson Burnett
Frank Gee Patchin
Frank Harris
Frank Jewett Mather
Frank L. Packard
Frederick Trevor Hill
Frederick Winslow Taylor
Friedrich Kerst
Friedrich Nietzsche
Fyodor Dostoyevsky

Gabrielle E. Jackson
Garrett P. Serviss
Gaston Leroux
George Ade
Geroge Bernard Shaw
George Ebers
George Eliot
George MacDonald
George Orwell
George Tucker
George W. Cable
George Wharton James
Gertrude Atherton
Grace E. King
Grant Allen
Guillermo A. Sherwell
Gulielma Zollinger
Gustav Flaubert
H. A. Cody
H. B. Irving
H. G. Wells
H. H. Munro
H. Irving Hancock
H. Rider Haggard
H. W. C. Davis
Hamilton Wright Mabie
Hans Christian Andersen
Harold Avery
Harold McGrath
Harriet Beecher Stowe
Harry Houidini
Helent Hunt Jackson
Helen Nicolay
Hendy David Thoreau
Henrik Ibsen
Henry Adams
Henry Ford
Henry Frost
Henry James
Henry Jones Ford
Henry Seton Merriman
Henry Wadsworth
Longfellow
Henry W Longfellow
Herbert A. Giles
Herbert N. Casson
Herman Hesse
Homer
Honore De Balzac

Horace Walpole
Horatio Alger, Jr.
Howard Pyle
Howard R. Garis
Hugh Lofting
Hugh Walpole
Humphry Ward
Ian Maclaren
Israel Abrahams
J.G.Austin
J. Henri Fabre
J. M. Barrie
J. Macdonald Oxley
J. S. Knowles
J. Storer Clouston
Jack London
Jacob Abbott
James Allen
James Lane Allen
James Andrews
James Baldwin
James DeMille
James Joyce
James Oliver Curwood
James Oppenheim
James Otis
Jane Austen
Jens Peter Jacobsen
Jerome K. Jerome
John Burroughs
John F. Kennedy
John Gay
John Glasworthy
John Habberton
John Joy Bell
John Milton
John Philip Sousa
Jonathan Swift
Joseph Carey
Joseph Conrad
Joseph Jacobs
Julian Hawthrone
Julies Vernes
Justin Huntly McCarthy
Kakuzo Okakura
Kenneth Grahame
Kate Langley Bosher
L. A. Abbot
L. T. Meade
L. Frank Baum
Laura Lee Hope

Laurence Housman
Leo Tolstoy
Leonid Andreyev
Lewis Carroll
Lilian Bell
Lloyd Osbourne
Louis Tracy
Louisa May Alcott
Lucy Fitch Perkins
Lucy Maud Montgomery
Lydia Miller Middleton
Lyndon Orr
M. H. Adams
Margaret E. Sangster
Margaret Vandercook
Maria Edgeworth
Maria Thompson Daviess
Mariano Azuela
Marion Polk Angellotti
Mark Overton
Mark Twain
Mary Austin
Mary Cole
Mary Rowlandson
Mary Wollstonecraft
Shelley
Max Beerbohm
Myra Kelly
Nathaniel Hawthrone
O. F. Walton
Oscar Wilde
Owen Johnson
P.G.Wodehouse
Paul and Mable Thorn
Paul G. Tomlinson
Paul Severing
Peter B. Kyne
Plato
R. Derby Holmes
R. L. Stevenson
Rabindranath Tagore
Rahul Alvares
Ralph Waldo Emmerson
Rene Descartes
Rex E. Beach
Richard Harding Davis
Richard Jefferies
Robert Barr
Robert Frost
Robert Gordon Anderson
Robert L. Drake

Robert Lansing
Robert Michael Ballantyne
Robert W. Chambers
Rosa Nouchette Carey
Ross Kay
Rudyard Kipling
Samuel B. Allison
Samuel Hopkins Adams
Sarah Bernhardt
Selma Lagerlof
Sherwood Anderson
Sigmund Freud
Standish O'Grady
Stanley Weyman
Stella Benson
Stephen Crane
Stewart Edward White
Stijn Streuvels
Swami Abhedananda
Swami Parmananda
T. S. Ackland
The Princess Der Ling
Thomas A. Janvier
Thomas A Kempis
Thomas Anderton
Thomas Bailey Aldrich
Thomas Bulfinch
Thomas De Quincey
Thomas H. Huxley
Thomas Hardy
Thomas More
Thornton W. Burgess
U. S. Grant
Valentine Williams
Victor Appleton
Virginia Woolf
Walter Scott
Washington Irving
Wilbur Lawton
Wilkie Collins
Willa Cather
Willard F. Baker
William Makepeace
Thackeray
William W. Walter
Winston Churchill
Yei Theodora Ozaki
Young E. Allison
Zane Grey